I0541276

No
Other
Option

No
Other
Option

Rochelle Padzensky

HERO
PUBLISHING

No Other Option
Published by HERO Publishing LLC
Denver, Colorado

Copyright ©2018 ROCHELLE PADZENSKY. All rights reserved.

No part of this book may be reproduced in any form or by any
mechanical means, including information storage and retrieval
systems without permission in writing from the publisher/author,
except by a reviewer who may quote passages in a review.

All images, logos, quotes, and trademarks included in this book are
subject to use according to trademark and copyright laws of the
United States of America.

Library of Congress Control Number: 2018906212
PADZENSKY, ROCHELLE, Author
NO OTHER OPTION
ROCHELLE PADZENSKY

ISBN: 978-0-9985034-3-1

FICTION / Women
FAMILY & RELATIONSHIPS / Adoption & Fostering
SOCIAL SCIENCE / Abortion & Birth Control

QUANTITY PURCHASES: Schools, companies, professional groups,
clubs, and other organizations may qualify for special terms when
ordering quantities of this title. For information, email heropadz@q.com.

All rights reserved by Rochelle Padzensky
and HERO Publishing LLC.
This book is printed in the United States of America.

HERO
PUBLISHING

To all women who faced this most difficult of decisions
and were courageous enough to make
the decision that was right for them.

PART ONE

ONE

POST-PARTUM DEPRESSION.

Is that what this black hole is in the pit of my stomach? The anguish in my heart? The pain in my head? Is this what Dr. Burke told me I might experience?

Ellen Gordon reflected upon recent events as she sat on the train speeding away from Denver, the only home she had ever known, toward her new home in San Diego. She focused on those few moments spent with her newborn son on July 10, 1954. Four days earlier, an eternity ago. She recalled each detail with perfect clarity, and intuitively she knew the heart wrenching experience would be branded into her brain, where those images would remain forever.

She remembered gazing down at her baby as he opened his eyes. He seemed incredibly solemn. They looked at each other for a few moments, and it suddenly became clear to Ellen that his name should be Daniel, because he was going to have to be very brave. He would have to face the lions alone. Tears trickled from her eyes.

"I'm so sorry, Danny. I want to keep you, but I know I can't. I just can't. I'm only seventeen. Too young to take care of a baby. The adoption agency will find you a good home. I know they will, and you'll have two parents to love and take good care of you, which is how it should be."

Her baby boy's deep blue eyes shone when she spoke to him. "It's going to be all right, isn't it?"

She got the feeling he agreed. Yes, it would be all right.

From a box beside her, Ellen removed the quilt she had so painstakingly made over the months of confinement. She spread it out on the hospital bed. Lifting Danny ever so carefully, she swaddled him in it. He was so precious it made her cry all the more. *This is not how I want my baby to remember me.* She dabbed her eyes and blew her nose with a tissue. She stroked him and caressed his tiny head.

～

TOO PAINFUL. THE MEMORIES were still too fresh. She willed herself back to the present, viewing her mother, Pearl, as she slept beside Ellen, her mother's purse tucked protectively under her arm.

Protecting her purse. Just like she's always tried to protect Pop and me. I wish she could have protected me from getting pregnant.

It was at this moment that the resentment she had suppressed during these last few months rose up in her throat. Yes, she knew her parents had done what they thought best for her. But sending her away and making her give away her baby didn't feel like what was best. But, what would have been best? She just didn't know. The anger swirled in the void where her heart and stomach used to be, until it made her ache all over. Ellen stared out the window. She felt as black as the night outside. *Will it always be this way? Will I ever be able to forgive ... and forget?*

Pearl woke up with a snort. It took her a few seconds to orient herself. She studied Ellen's reflection in the glass and felt the familiar hurt in her heart.

My poor baby. She used to have such beautiful raven hair. Look at it now, like a rag on her head. Her green eyes, "kitten eyes," her dad called them, now glazed and lifeless. No more glow, no more fun in them. She used to smile and laugh all the time. Now her mouth is set in a grim line. Why, she's as flat as day-old champagne. Oh, God, please help Nate and me make her whole again.

"Ellen."

Startled out of her reverie, Ellen faced her mother. "Yes, Mom."

"I think it's time to go to the dining car and have a little dinner. Ready?"

"Sure, Mom."

Perhaps during dinner I can get her to talk. I'll tell her more about San Diego and the house. "I'll just give my hair a little comb and we'll go." Pearl took a comb out of her purse and fluffed out her hair. She freshened her lipstick, stood, and gestured for Ellen to follow.

Pearl tried to make conversation as they walked toward the dining car. "Why is it that food on the train always tastes so wonderful? I had some delicious meals on my way to Denver."

Ellen shrugged. Pearl noticed her apathy, once again hoping she could get her engaged in conversation during their meal. They made their way through several other passenger cars, the club car—which was hot, noisy, and smoky—and the observation car. At last they reached their destination.

It was true. Magic pervaded the dining car with its fresh, snowy white linens, gleaming silver, shiny glassware, and starched napkins standing at attention. Small lamps glowed, and the bud vase on each table with its single flower completed the picture.

The waiter, in his immaculate starched white jacket, approached them. "Table for two, madam?"

"Yes, thank you," Pearl replied.

The waiter seated them and handed them each a menu. "The specials tonight are the roast beef dinner and the trout almondine. I recommend the trout. It's fresh today from the mountains outside Denver."

"Thank you," Pearl responded.

She and Ellen perused their menus. They both decided to have the trout dinner. Pearl ordered for the two of them when the waiter returned.

"Wait till you see the new house, Ellen. And your room. It's on the second floor, and you can see the ocean from your window. And we're close to Balboa Park. Walking distance, actually."

"Sounds great, Mom."

Does it? Or are you just trying to make me happy? "Oh, and the shop. Pop's done an incredible job. Open just a few weeks and already the darling of the San Diego matrons."

"I thought when Pop sold Gordon's after his heart attack, he planned to retire. What made him open another store?" Ellen inquired.

"You know I always said, 'You can take the man out of retail, but you can't take the retail out of the man.' He became so energized after we moved that he soon began to prowl the beach towns. You know how Pop always likes to explore every bit of any place we go. Besides, it gave him something to do and a way to meet new people. It wasn't long before he became buddies with several of the shop owners on Mission Beach. He *kibbitzed* with them almost every day. When his buddy, Jack, decided to go out of business, he hatched his plan. Zippity do dah, one, two, three, he's got a store. I'll let him tell you all about it. Since you have a little time before you start your senior year, he wants you to work there until school starts." Pearl paused, hoping for a response.

"Sounds great, Mom. I'm looking forward to seeing the store. But where did he get that name, Titillations?"

Pearl grinned. "When you see the store, you'll understand."

She seems to be genuinely interested, but is she really? Pearl couldn't help but notice how Ellen picked at her dinner. She made a mental note to make some of Ellen's favorite foods when they got home.

Having finished dinner, Pearl paid the bill, and they made their way back to their compartment. The porter already had their beds made up, so they prepared to get some rest.

~

AS ELLEN LAY IN the darkness, she recalled the last time she had seen her dad. It was during winter break, when Mom and Pop drove her to Colorado Springs to stay with their good friends, Tom and Ginny, during the rest of her pregnancy. Ginny had prepared a lovely lunch, and both she and Tom had done their best to make it a pleasant day. The only thing Ellen remembered was feeling cold and numb and praying that Mom and Pop wouldn't really abandon her. After they left, she went to the room Ginny had fixed up for her and wept silently, hating everything and everyone.

A couple of weeks later, right after the holidays, they had received the call from Mom. Pop had had a heart attack, and his recovery at the time seemed uncertain. Ellen remembered how she had bawled. It was all her fault. She knew it had to be her fault. How much she had wanted to see him, to touch him.

Pop was strong, and luckily he had gotten better. As soon as he recovered, he made the decision to sell Gordon's—the department store he had founded more than twenty years before—and move to San Diego. This surprised Ellen. Denver had always been their home as a family, and he had loved that store. She recalled how he would stand on the balcony and listen. If the hum from below sounded calm and smooth, all was well. If the air was charged with friction, it was not, and he knew he needed to get into the action. The store was his life.

Her parents sold the business and their home and moved in a matter of just a few weeks, without ever coming to say goodbye to her. She did not see either Mom or Pop even once after they moved. That's when the anger really set in.

When Mom called her to let her know about the move, she promised Ellen she would be back in time for the delivery. But Ellen hadn't talked to Pop, not once since the day he had abandoned her in Colorado Springs. *Will he be glad to see me? Does he still love me? Am I still his princess? And how will I feel when I see him? Will he still be the same loving Pop he was before?*

Eventually, overcome by fatigue, Ellen fell into a troubled sleep.

~

NATE ARRIVED MORE THAN an hour early at the station. It was small compared to the cavern that was Union Station in Denver. Due to the early hour, there were few people around.

Nervous, he paced, checked his watch for the third time in five minutes, and continued pacing. He had flowers for Pearl and chocolates for Ellen. He realized he hadn't seen his daughter since they had taken her to Tom and Ginny.

On the one hand he felt guilty, but on the other, he was relieved he hadn't seen her. As long as he lived, he would never forget that terrible night when they found out Ellen was pregnant. He relived how he had covered her up in a blanket and rocked her until she fell asleep. He had never in his life heard such a keening sound from a human being. All he could think about was who had done this terrible thing to his princess. Nate was so enraged, he probably would have harmed the boy. Actually, he probably could have killed him.

Nate wondered how Ellen felt about him now. *Will I still be her "lovable Pop"? Or has she hardened her heart against me for neglecting her?* He continued to measure time by his footsteps. *Will that train never come?*

~~~

THE TRAIN PULLED INTO the station five minutes early. Perspiration trickled from Pearl's armpits and into the waistband of her girdle. Butterflies jitterbugged in her stomach. *Will the relationship between Nate and Ellen still be the same?*

As they waited to get off of the train, Pearl and Ellen saw Pop standing on the platform. The tension that hung in the air evaporated immediately when Nate opened his arms to Ellen and she flew into them. Pearl realized she had been holding her breath. She exhaled and breathed a sigh of relief when she saw that Nate's love for Ellen had not changed, and neither had hers for him.

Nate kept his arm draped around Ellen as his eyes met his wife's. "These flowers are for you, darling. I missed you so much. And these chocolates are for my princess."

After Nate picked up their luggage, he told Pearl, "Now it's time to take Ellen to her new home and her new life."

They departed the station as a family, but with a cloud hanging over each of them. For Ellen, it was the shame of having had an illegitimate baby. For Nate and Pearl, it was the knowledge that somewhere out there they had a grandson they would never know.

TWO

ELLEN STEPPED OUTSIDE THE station into the radiant sunshine and found herself captivated. The light shimmering on the water, the palm trees, the explosion of flowers in front of the station with their riot of color all brought a hint of a smile to her face. She breathed in the wonderful fragrance, and for one brief moment her heart lightened.

On the way home, Nate pointed out various landmarks and points of interest. In just minutes, they reached their new home on Third and Nutmeg, a charming two-story house.

Pearl pointed to the room on the second floor. "That's it, Ellen. Your new room. I hope you like it."

"I'm sure it's beautiful, Mom. Ellen shaded her eyes and squinted up at the room.

Ellen felt strange walking into a home she didn't know, but as she wandered into the living room, she recognized several pieces of furniture and favorite objects from her home in Denver. On the coffee table were the repoussé cigarette holder, matchbox, and ashtrays. And there, on the pie table, was the emerald green glass candy dish with its ruffled edge. The wing chair was still there, too, but it had been reupholstered in a beige fabric with pink petit point flowers. Ellen thought it looked nice. It was also a relief to see that the new house was enough like their old home to feel, well ... comfortable.

Pearl called to her, "Come upstairs, I'm anxious for you to see your room."

Ellen advanced hesitantly, afraid of seeing something unfamiliar. Her friends in Denver used to tease her about her room being *the princess suite*. As the owner of Gordon's Department Store, Nate had access to a myriad of furniture and accessory wholesalers and the ability to purchase items not readily available in the Denver area.

She found her new bedroom the same, yet different. The furniture and many of her favorite things were still there, but Pearl had endeavored to give the room a sunnier, more California appearance, using buttercup yellows and lilac in the drapes and bedspread.

As Ellen looked at her furniture, she remembered all the happy times she and her best friend, Bev, had spent in her room, painting their toenails weird colors and making yucky green beauty masques. Some days they did all kinds of make-up and then giggled hysterically at the results. *If I had known I would probably never see Bev again, I would have spent more time with her during those last days.* She felt her insides heave with sadness.

"So, what do you think, Ellen?"

I hate it. It's not my room. It certainly isn't who I am anymore. "As usual, Mom, you've done a fantastic job." *It's not Mom's fault. She did her best.*

In that instant, she realized nothing would ever be the same because *she* wasn't the same. *I'm not an innocent child. I'm not even a girl anymore. I'm a woman who has had a baby. I will never be able to go back to those days.*

"Come, look out the window. Such a gorgeous view. You couldn't want any better."

Ellen walked to the window. Mom was right. It was a gorgeous view, but it didn't ease the distress in her heart.

After lunch, they spent the rest of the afternoon going through Ellen's clothes. When they finished, Pearl said, "Looks to me like we need to do some shopping. If you feel up to it, we'll go out tomorrow."

Will new clothes hide this ugly body? Will new clothes hide my shame and conceal this overwhelming pain? Humiliation and grief welled up in Ellen as she nodded her head yes.

The three of them spent a quiet evening, and Ellen went to bed early. Every muscle in her body screamed and left her feeling exhausted from the effort of trying to be pleasant.

AFTER BREAKFAST, ELLEN SAT down to write a letter to Mrs. O'Connor, the teacher Nate had hired in Colorado Springs to tutor her during her pregnancy. Mrs. O'Connor had been Ellen's teacher, mentor, and good friend during that time. After the school year ended, she made Ellen promise to write to let her know when the baby was born and to fill her in on all the details.

July 15, 1954
Dear Mrs. O'Connor,

I arrived in San Diego yesterday. My son was born on July 10th. I was only able to see him briefly before the lady from the agency took him away.

He looked so beautiful to me. It was so hard for me to

give him up, but I knew I had to. I know I'm too young to accept the responsibility of being a parent. I know he needs two parents to love him and take care of him.

Ellen paused and thought for a second about her emotions. *I hated giving him up. I tried to think of some way I could keep him, but I couldn't.*

I wrapped him in the quilt Ginny helped me make. He looked so precious that I couldn't help but cry. I decided to name him Daniel, and that is who he will always be to me. I pray I have made the right decision.

Once again, she put her pen down, overcome with grief. Her stomach poured acid into her veins. She knew it wasn't the right decision; it felt like a betrayal. But, then, what other option was there? She picked up her pen to finish the letter.

Thank you for all you did for me. I will always treasure the time you spent with me. Please keep in touch.
     With love,
     Ellen Gordon

Ellen sealed the envelope and put it on her dresser to mail later.

The following Monday at dinner, Nate told Ellen he thought it was time for her to come to work at the store. A knot formed in her stomach. *Can't I just stay home in my cocoon and not go out?* She assented in spite of her reservations. Pop seemed pleased.

THREE

SAN DIEGO WAS A Navy town, and during his wanderings Nate became acquainted with several of the Navy wives. Since their husbands spent most of their time at sea, the wives were at liberty to take classes, learn new skills, and develop their talents. They enjoyed sharing their projects with Nate. As a retailer, he was a great *shmoozer*, and he appreciated their work. He saw they needed a showcase for their various enterprises.

Nate had considered this could be the start of a new venture. He could provide the space, the marketing know-how, and the merchandising. The wives could provide the goods on consignment. He'd take a percentage and everyone would be happy. Nate realized he'd been stagnant for too long. He was too young to be retired and was anxious to start anew.

A GRIN BROKE OUT on Nate's face as he shared this information with Ellen on their drive to Titillations the next day. When they arrived at the store, the first thing Nate did was give Ellen the VIP tour. To begin, he stopped at the section devoted to beachwear and beach toys for the young set.

"Sue Ann designs these beach outfits for children. She calls them Beachfits. And Dorrie, another artist, designs the sand forms the children use to build sand sculptures," Nate said as he pointed out the area.

Ellen examined the adorable outfits with their cheery appliqués and felt a lump in her throat. *Would Danny look cute in one of these outfits? And would he spend all day happily playing with those wonderful sand toys? Stop. Get a grip. Pop is talking, pay attention.*

"This is the adult section," Pop continued. "Mikki designs these cover-ups. I think they're positively gorgeous, don't you? I know they'll walk right out the door."

They certainly wouldn't cover up my disgrace. They wouldn't hide my humiliation. "Most definitely, Pop."

Next to the cover-ups, Nate pointed out the colorful hand-painted beach towels. "I thought when I first saw these towels that I'd like to frame one, not dry my body with it."

Now that's a good cover-up. Bright on the outside, cover the rotten inside. Ellen murmured yes.

Nate led her through the other sections of the store. Ellen was especially fascinated by Nadine's shell art. Living in a land-locked area all her life, she had never experienced shell art and found it quite beautiful and interesting.

As they strolled through the area Nate referred to as the Ladies Luncheon Group section, Ellen remarked, "I bet this is Mom's favorite section. You know how she's always searching for this kind of stuff … luncheon sets, scorecards, hostess gifts, and everything matching. I bet she has a ball here."

"You're right about that. She's one of my best customers."

Finally they reached the front counter, which housed the piece de resistance. Handmade jewelry by Irene. Irene had worked as a welder during the war, and after the war she used her welding skills and turned to jewelry making. She cut and polished rocks and semi-precious stones and then set them into unusual designs welded from brass or silver.

"These pieces are the most precious items in the store. Each piece is one of a kind. I know they'll make Irene famous. What do you think?"

"I think so, Pop. Unique. So different than anything I've ever seen."

Nate waved his hand with a flourish. "Finished. So, how do you like the store?"

"Wow Pop. You've taken a dinky storefront and turned it into a real gem. A Fabergé egg. Like Mom always says, 'You're the king of retail.'"

"Thank you. Of course your mom has always been my best cheerleader. Now it's time to get to work." Nate assigned Ellen the job of setting up the counter displays for the day. From her years of working at Gordon's, Nate knew she would be relaxed doing that kind of job.

Once Ellen was settled, he headed outside to open up the children's area in front. After a couple of disastrous days of children roaming around the store when he first opened, Nate decided he needed a place where kids could have fun. So he'd designed a portable craft and snack center for kids outside, near the front of the store. He hired two teenage girls to serve the children lemonade and cookies, do craft projects, and play simple games with them while their moms shopped. To his delight, this was an enormous success.

After Ellen finished setting up the displays, Nate dispatched her to the back room to unpack the new merchandise that had been picked up from his artists.

When she completed this job, Nate commented, "You've done a good job this morning, Ellen. It's time for you to take a break now. Two doors down, my friend Max runs a coffee shop. Here's some money. Go. Have yourself a little snack."

"Thanks, Pop. I could use a Coke."

As she sauntered out the front door of the store, Ellen experienced the full impact of the children's area. Moms with toddlers hanging on their legs and diaper bags on one shoulder and a baby on the other made her think of Danny.

Oh God. Has Danny been adopted yet? Does he look like any of these babies? Is he sleeping peacefully on his mom's shoulder? Ellen's stomach turned queasy, and a chill crept over her body, even though the sun warmed the bright summer day. She stumbled down the sidewalk to the coffee shop, slid through the door, and sat down at an empty table, her heart still as frozen as a frosty winter day.

Ellen didn't even see the man who came to the table until he said, "Good morning, young lady. You, I don't know, so I'm guessing you're Nate's daughter. He told me you were going to start working today."

A kindly older gentleman, whose wavy silver hair and eyebrows reminded Ellen of soft, feathery angel wings, held an order pad in his hand. His gray-blue eyes twinkled with humor, and his animated face exuded warmth and friendliness.

"Yes, I'm Nate's daughter, Ellen. You must be Max." Ellen liked this man at once.

"I am. So, what can I get you, young lady?"

"A Coke, please." Ellen's natural reticence kept her from saying more.

Max guffawed. "No, no. It's almost lunchtime. A good lunch is what you need. Leave it to me."

Ellen could see that protesting would serve no purpose, so

she set her face in a pleasant, she hoped, expression and sat back to observe the busy diner.

In a few minutes, Max returned with a cup of tomato soup and a golden grilled cheese sandwich. The aroma of the tomato soup was unusual, and Ellen sniffed, trying to recognize the smell.

Max grinned. "My secret seasoning. Taste, you'll love it. And a cheese sandwich like this, you never had. It'll melt in your mouth."

Max was right. She was hungry after all, and the lunch did taste delicious.

"You enjoyed?" he questioned when he came to pick up the dishes.

"It was wonderful. Thanks so much."

"Next time you'll come in later, after the lunch rush, and we'll get acquainted. Right now I have to get ready for the lunch crowd. Say hello to your father for me." Max waved and strode back to the kitchen.

When Ellen went to pay the bill, she found out Max had already taken care of it. *What a nice man he is.*

The warmth in her body dissipated as soon as she went back through the outdoor craft area to the store. The sound of children's laughter and crows of delight made her heart ache anew.

FOUR

THE FOLLOWING NIGHT, NEEDING a break from her parents, Ellen decided to walk to Balboa Park. When she arrived, she found a nice place to sit and remembered her first day of high school.

SHE'D ANTICIPATED WITH EXCITEMENT attending East High School in the fall of 1952 as a sophomore. Not only did the elite, smartest kids go there, but it would also give her a chance to spend more time with her friends from synagogue.

She would never forget the first time she met Kenny Johnson that fall. Of course, she already knew who he was. As a junior, who didn't know Kenny Johnson? Was he not, after all, Mr. East High School, captain of the football team, Homecoming King, winner of several trophies for debate, and a member of the dramatic society? And, of course, on top of all this, he was gorgeous, with his sunny blonde hair, sapphire blue eyes, broad shoulders, small waist, and great butt, a look that appealed to all the nice Jewish girls because it was so All-American. While his handsome features made her heart beat wildly, she actually liked Kenny, because she found him to be intelligent, kind, and not the animal that typified high school jocks.

When Ellen had the opportunity to sign up for clubs, she joined the debating club. She enjoyed debate and was good at it. With a father like Pop, Mr. Retail-Smooth-Talker himself, it was no big surprise. Besides, wouldn't that be a way to get to know Kenny better?

IT WAS LATE OCTOBER and they were on their way back from a competition Ellen had won. Kenny happened to sit next to her on the bus.

"Congratulations on the win, Ellen. Nice job. I hope you don't mind if I make a suggestion to you, though." Kenny's eyes lit with thoughtfulness.

Wow, he thought I was okay. What can I answer that'll sound clever and smart? "That would be great." *Oh, damn, how dumb can you get?*

"Okay." He looked directly into her eyes. "When you're making an important point, it's effective to pause, look at the audience, and place the emphasis in your voice on what you think is important."

"Good idea. Thanks, I'll remember that." *Some talker I am. Swift, really swift, Ellen.*

From then on, Kenny always stopped to talk to Ellen whenever he saw her in the halls, and he continued to offer help with her debating style.

Her sophomore year ended on that friendly note. She saw Kenny a couple of times during the summer at Elitch Gardens at the Trocadero, where all the kids went to dance to the big bands. He was with his date, and she was with hers. They had genial conversation, and that was all. Then the summer ended.

September came and with it a new school year. Ellen went to the debate table to sign up for the 1953 fall semester. As she turned to leave, she felt a tap on her shoulder.

"Hey, Ellen, I'm glad to see you signing up. I was hoping you'd be in the club again."

A tingle ran down her back. "Thanks, Kenny, I wouldn't miss it."

Ellen stared into those sapphire blue eyes, and suddenly she felt hot all over.

With a gleam in his eyes, he remarked, "There's something different about you, Ellen Gordon."

Now, at sixteen, Ellen had blossomed into an attractive young girl, and he definitely noticed.

"I hope that's a compliment."

He chuckled. The bell signaling first class rang.

Ellen fluttered her eyelashes. "I guess that bell tolls for me. I have a class, see ya around."

She waved and hurried down the hall. *Oh god, he gave me a compliment. Why the heck wasn't I more sparkly?*

After school, Kenny stopped at her locker and asked her if she wanted to get a Coke with him.

Surprised, her throat suddenly became dry. "Sure, I'd love to." *That was a witty reply.* "I need to let Bev know, and then I'll be ready."

It was a mild afternoon. As they strolled along the Esplanade, Ellen wondered why Kenny had invited her for a Coke. She'd heard he was involved with Gwennie Hanson, who was the kind of girl you'd expect someone like Kenny Johnson to want. The typical blonde blue-eyed cheerleader. The kind of girl generally referred to as a dumb blonde. Perhaps he wanted to make Gwennie jealous. Or maybe he just wanted to talk to a friend. She'd just have to wait and see.

As they drank their Cokes, Ellen listened to Kenny talk about his plans for the year and how he was working hard so he could get into the University of Chicago. Then she noticed the time. "Uh oh, Mom's gonna kill me. I didn't realize how late it's gotten."

"Uh, sorry. I don't wanna get you in trouble. C'mon, I'll drive you home." They hustled to his car, and as they drove, Kenny asked Ellen if she would like to go to the mixer at school with him on Friday night.

Would I like to go with him? What kind of question is that? I'd kill to go with him. "Sure, Kenny I'd like to, but I'll have to meet you at school."

"Is there a problem?"

Yes, but you don't need to know about it. Going out with a shegetz *is a no-no with Mom. Like mixing oil with water.* "Oh, no, it's just that we visit relatives on Friday nights."

"Cool. The mixer starts at eight. Can ya make it by then?"

"No problem." *I hope. Gonna take some fancy doing.* "I'll meet you at the front door of the gym."

When they arrived at her house, she jumped out of the car.

"Thanks for the ride, see ya tomorrow."

"Who was that boy who brought you home, Ellen?" inquired Mom as soon as she walked in the front door.

"Oh, just a friend from debate." Mom had eyes like a hawk and a memory like a steel trap.

"Well, it was nice of him to bring you home so you didn't have to *shlep* on the bus during rush hour. Debate club, you didn't tell me you had club today."

"Talk to you in a minute, Mom, I have to go to the bathroom."

Her heart racing, she ran up the stairs, taking them two at a time in hopes of escaping Mom's inquest, at least for the time being. Mom would have a cow if she knew he wasn't Jewish.

When she went back downstairs, Mom was busy making dinner.

"So come and help me, Ellen. You'll set the table and make salad."

"Sure, Mom."

"So tell me, that boy didn't look Jewish to me. Who is he?"

Here goes. "His name is Kenny Johnson, and he isn't Jewish. We're in debate club together. He's the one who helped me. Remember I told you about him."

Ellen hoped her mom wouldn't notice her nervousness.

"Um, yes, I remember." She gave Ellen the *mother look*. "Just you remember not to get involved. Need I remind you that mixed marriages don't work? There's still plenty of anti-Semitism here. Besides, it's important for us, as Jews, not to dilute our culture."

THE NEXT DAY, SHE told Mom about the dance at school on Friday. Mom was always happy when she participated in school activities. Better safe at school than out on the streets.

Ellen called her best friend. She knew she could always count on Bev. They had been friends since pre-school.

"It's me. So far, so good. I told Mom about the mixer. I said I was going with you. You will pick me up, won't you?"

Bev giggled, as usual. She had an infectious laugh and was always bubbly. "Am I your best friend? Of course I'll pick you up."

She's more excited than I am that I'm going with Kenny Johnson. Frankly, I'm just plain scared to death.

Friday night, Ellen went upstairs to get ready. She must have changed her clothes seven times. Frustrated, she called Bev. "I don't know what to wear. Help!" Bev suggested the navy blue skirt and red sweater.

"Can't wear that. The sweater has a spot on it."

Bev made several other suggestions, all of which Ellen found something wrong with. Finally, Bev announced in her best Molly Goldberg accent, "Dollink, whatever you wear will be perfect."

Ellen ended up wearing a red-and-green-plaid skirt with fringe at the bottom and a gold safety pin down the side. She paired it with a matching forest green sweater set. She thought the outfit went well with her dark hair and green eyes, making her eyes seem almost as green as her sweater.

When Ellen went downstairs, Pop wanted to make sure she had a ride. She assured him she did. As if to confirm she was telling the truth, they heard the horn honk at that precise moment.

"Bye, Mom, bye, Pop."

"See ya later, alligator." Pop always tried to keep up with the latest slang.

"After a while, crocodile." She always knew her lines too.

THEY HAD A BLAST at the dance. Kenny placed his arms around her, and she put her head on his shoulder. He placed his hand on the small of her back, and they glided effortlessly across the floor. Kenny was an excellent dancer and easy to follow. She could feel the soft purr of his heart. *Can he feel mine too?*

"Hey, you're a great dancer, Ellen."

When he told her that, it made her heart flutter. She felt ecstatic.

As they left the dance, she noticed how bright the moon seemed and how the stars twinkled down on them. Kenny let his arm fall around her shoulders, and she thought she would die of happiness. The goose bumps rose on her arms and neck where his arm touched her. When Kenny parked in front of her house, he kissed her lightly on the cheek.

"I had a super time," he whispered in her ear. "Would you like to go to the movies with me tomorrow night?"

Ellen had to think fast. She told him yes, but explained she would be at Bev's house working on their history project, so he could call and pick her up there. He promised to call, whispered goodnight, and drove off.

Ellen floated into the house and up the stairs to her room, feeling exhilarated and lighthearted. She kissed Kenny all night long in her dreams. God, how she hated to wake up.

The following morning, Ellen went downstairs as Pop finished breakfast, getting ready for a busy Saturday at the store. He asked Ellen about her plans for the day.

"I'm going to Bev's to work on our history project, and then we'll probably catch a flick tonight."

"Good, I hope you didn't forget that Mom and I are going to the Klines' party at Green Gables Country Club tonight."

"Which means," Mom commented, "we probably won't be home until around two. You know the Klines, they always have to serve breakfast at the end of the party. God forbid you should go home without being stuffed to the gills."

"Not a problem, Mom."

"So, okay, you'll let me know if your plans change. I don't want to worry." Her mom then headed upstairs to get ready for the beauty shop.

The Saturday morning ritual included Pearl going to get her hair and nails done. Because of the big party tonight, she would probably get a facial and an eyebrow tweeze as well. This meant Ellen had a couple of hours to fool around.

Then it dawned on her. What luck. Mom and Pop would leave by six thirty or so, which meant she could have Kenny pick her up at home, since he wouldn't plan to be at her house until sometime after seven. Perfect.

Ellen called Bev, and as soon as Bev heard Ellen's voice, she wanted to know about the previous night. Ellen tried her best to describe what a wonderful night it had been, but it wasn't enough for her best friend. She wanted lurid details.

"It was a fabulous evening." Ellen sighed as she closed her eyes, reliving the date. "We danced like Fred Astaire and Ginger Rogers. I can't remember ever having such a fantastic time. I just felt so comfortable with him. We talked as though we had known each other all our lives. When he brought me home, he kissed me on the cheek. I thought I'd just die. And then ... he asked me to go to the movies tonight, and I said yes." Ellen then told Bev she'd be over after lunch.

Bev squealed with pleasure. "I'm so excited for you."

Ellen knew she meant it, because that's the kind of friend Bev was. She hung up and went upstairs to wash her hair and do her nails. After all, it was important to maintain the Saturday ritual.

Afterwards she put on her jeans, her dad's white shirt, and her penny loafers with bobby sox. She was ready to begin the day.

Ellen had just gathered her things together to go to Bev's when Mom came home from the beauty shop. "So Mom, you're looking gorgeous."

"And you look lovely too."

Ellen wore her hair short this year, as this was one of the new styles, and she knew Mom thought it was a good style for her. Mom said it suited her small face and delicate features and made her eyes appear larger.

"Like mother, like daughter," Ellen quipped. Then she told her mother she was going to Bev's.

"So, I'll see you before we leave for the party?"

"Would I miss seeing you in your new dress? What time will that be?"

"Cocktails are called for six thirty. So that means we'll leave at six thirty to be there at seven Jewish Standard Time"

Perfect, just like I thought. It's going to work out great.

AS SHE STROLLED TO Bev's house, Ellen realized how good she felt. Light. Like there were bubbles in her chest wanting to burst. Like champagne, maybe. When she reached Bev's house, she found her standing at the door. They went into the den where Bev had a couple of card tables set up for their work.

"Okay, before we get started, tell me how you plan to meet Kenny tonight."

"Mom and Pop are going to a party at Green Gables. They'll be gone before Kenny gets there. It's a cinch."

"Ah, as Charlie Chan says, 'Clever girl figure it out.'"

It was time to work on their civil war history project. After two hours, they decided they needed a break. Bev grabbed some Cokes, and they went out on the patio with the phone that had the twenty-five foot cord.

Bev tittered. "We wouldn't want to miss any phone calls, would we?" Then she licked her lips. "I'm starving. Do you want some candy, or cookies, or something?"

Bev was a bit on the pudgy side—not really fat, but certainly not skinny—so as a good friend, Ellen said, "I think we should just stick with the Cokes, don't you?"

Bev didn't like it, but she consented.

They had just sat down in the swing when the phone rang. Bev answered in her most friendly voice, listened, and said, "Yes, Kenny, Ellen's here. I'll get her." She made bump-and-grind gestures as Ellen got up to answer the phone.

"Stop it," Ellen whispered to Bev, "before I start giggling."

"Hi Ellen, just checking to see if we're still on for tonight."

Shivers ran through Ellen. *Boy, is his voice sexy.* "Things are going well. As a matter of fact, you can pick me up at home."

"Good, I'll be there around seven thirty. I'll let you get back to your project now. See ya tonight."

"Bye now," she said, still feeling tingly from the sound of his voice when she hung up the phone.

Later, as she prepared to go home, Ellen reminded Bev that they were supposed to be going to the movies together tonight, in case she happened to talk to Ellen's mom.

"Okay, okay. I'll remember. Listen, have a really super time tonight, but be careful. I don't want you to get hurt, just in case he makes up with Gwennie and drops you.

Ellen squeezed her. "Don't be silly, we're just going to a movie."

By the time Ellen got home, it was almost five thirty. Mom had just gotten out of the tub and was getting ready to put on her make-up.

"Glad to see you made it home. How did your day go?"

"It went well. I'm going to have some soup and chicken and then I'm going to the movies around seven thirty." She hadn't lied yet. She hoped she wouldn't have to.

"Do you have a ride?" Mom asked.

"I do. Don't worry, just have a fabulous time at the party. Shouldn't Pop be home soon?" Ellen asked to divert Mom away from probing any further about her evening plans.

"He should be here any minute."

Just then they heard Nate's car in the driveway. "Speak of the devil, and here he comes."

Ellen hurried to the kitchen to greet Nate. "Hi-Pop-hope-you-had-a-good-day-at-work," all came out as one word.

"Saturdays are always great," he hummed. "I love Saturdays, the hustle, the bustle, the bell ringing on the cash register, the excitement of people buying new things. It was a fantastic Saturday, one of the best we've ever had."

Pop, exhilarated, was in such a pleasant mood, she knew her parents would have a marvelous time. It would also be a late night. *Perfect. Just perfect.*

Ellen made herself some dinner, and just as she finished, Mom and Dad came into the kitchen. "Oh, Mom, you look like a queen. I love the dress. You're handsome too, Pop."

Nate took Pearl's hand and kissed it. "When I saw the dress, I knew it was made for my darling Pearl. For some reason, it reminded me of the first time I saw her in the alterations room of the store. She looked regal, even then, bent over her sewing machine."

"Oh, Nate, please." Pearl blushed a rosy pink.

"This is not the time to reminisce. Time for you two to be on your way." Ellen kissed them both and saw them to the door.

⁓

NOW IT WAS TIME for her to get ready. She leaned back, relishing the quiet warmth of the tub and the delicate feel of the bubbles on her skin, when her eye suddenly caught the clock on the vanity.

Oy vey. *It's getting late. I better move it.* She got out of the tub, dried herself off quickly, and went to the closet to make the final decision about what to wear.

Tonight, the navy blue skirt with the lime green jacket appealed to her. She decided to wear the pearls too. Mom always said a girl couldn't go wrong with pearls—they go with any outfit, and simple is always good.

Hurry, she chastised herself. *You have to be ready when the doorbell rings.* She put on her make-up, dressed, finished her hair, and took one last glance in the mirror.

Thank God, no pimples tonight. I think most of my baby fat is gone too. Now remember what Miss Morgan at Charm School says. "Tuck under, stomach in, chest out." I even look a trifle sexy. Not bad.

Just as she glided down the stairs, the doorbell rang.

"Hi Kenny, come on in." Dressed in a powder blue V-neck sweater with a white shirt underneath and navy blue pants, he looked so cool.

"Hi," he said, as he glanced around the room, apparently expecting to meet Mom and Dad.

"Mom and Pop are at a party. That's why they're not here."

"Oh, okay. I thought we'd see *Island in the Sky* tonight, the new John Wayne movie, if that's okay with you." He gazed at her. "You look really pretty tonight, Ellen."

She blushed and felt warm all over as she thanked him for the compliment.

There was a long line at the movies, as usual on a Saturday night. They saw several friends, and Ellen didn't miss the envious glances she received from many of the girls she knew. *How lucky I am to be with Kenny. Just look at those girls staring at me. I know they wonder what I'm doing with Kenny Johnson.*

Ellen's stomach heaved as she noticed various Jewish boys also staring at her, obviously realizing she was with Kenny. *Oh, God, I hope this doesn't get back to Mom. She'll kill me if she finds out.* Although the gawking made her stomach queasy, she decided to ignore both her gut and the stares.

Kenny took her hand in his when the movie started. The hair on the back of Ellen's neck stood up, and a shiver ran down her arm. She was so conscious of the warmth and the delicious feelings racing through her body that she had no idea what the movie was about, only what she was feeling and thinking.

Kenny and Ellen sauntered out of the movies into one of those perfect Denver evenings that flaunted a cool breeze. Kenny held her hand as they walked back to the car.

"Good movie, I thought. I'm used to seeing John Wayne as a cowboy, not a pilot, though. I thought he did a cool job. What do you think?"

Ellen babbled. "Um, yes, I think he's a fantastic actor." She had been so busy fantasizing about Kenny kissing her that she really hadn't paid any attention to the movie.

They decided to get pizza, and by the time they finished, it was getting late. Kenny asked Ellen what time she had to be home.

"Mom usually likes me home between twelve and twelve thirty."

"Cool, we have plenty of time then." He draped his arm around her. When they arrived at her house, Kenny parked the car in front and shut off the motor. As they talked, Kenny moved closer to her.

"You know, Ellen, I really enjoy being with you. You're smart and funny and beautiful, and God, you smell good."

Ellen quivered, her heart beating fast. Kenny could feel it and held her closer. He kissed her softly as he ran his fingers down her neck and back. She knew she should stop. Then he kissed her more passionately and she responded, kissing him back as though she was thirsty and his lips were the water she needed and craved. She became liquid fire. It felt so good. That's when she knew it was definitely time to stop.

"Kenny, Kenny, stop. Please. It wouldn't be right for my folks to come home and find us out here like this."

Kenny breathed hard. "You're right, Ellen. It's time for me to go."

As he walked her up to the house, he pulled her close to him and gave her a hug. "Thanks for a super evening. I'll see ya."

"I had a fabulous time, thanks for asking me. See you Monday."

Ellen went into the house and watched him as he sprinted back to his car and drove away. She floated to her room and checked the mirror to see if she had changed. She definitely had. Her eyes were shiny, and her cheeks were flushed. She put on her PJs and jumped into bed, wanting to fall asleep right away, so she could relive the whole evening in her dreams.

SUNDAY MORNING CAME TOO soon. At breakfast, Ellen heard all about the party.

"Your mother was the most beautiful woman there. I'm some lucky man to have such a wonderful wife." Nate beamed with pride.

"And your father was the life of the party, as usual." Pearl tousled Nate's gray curls as she picked up the dishes. "And your evening, Ellen, how was it?"

"Good. We saw the John Wayne movie." Then she told Mom she would be going to Bev's to finish their project. That was fine with Pearl. She just wanted to rest and recover.

As Ellen dressed to go to Bev's, she realized Kenny hadn't asked her for another date. She hoped this didn't mean anything. She would just die if he were already dumping her. Ellen stopped in the kitchen on the way out and told Mom she would be back sometime after lunch.

Bev pounced on her as soon as Ellen got to her house. She

hustled Ellen into the den. "So, give."

"We went to see *Island in the Sky*. Kenny held my hand, and it made me so crazy that I had no idea what was going on in the movie. Then we went for pizza, and when we got to my house, we parked and he kissed me. I thought I'd faint. Oh, Bev, it was so wonderful. I'm just nuts about him. But then I made him stop. It was getting too heavy." Ellen sighed. "Do you think he's mad because I made him stop?"

Bev didn't think so. "Kenny doesn't seem like the kind of guy who'd be like that. Don't worry about it. I'm sure he respects you, that's all."

"I hope you're right. I'm really scared, though. I don't know what to think or how to act."

"I know I'm right," Bev answered. "Trust your best friend. Now, let's get this project finished."

They went to work and finished at about two thirty. When Ellen got home, Mom and Pop were in the den. Pop was cutting out the Sunday ads and pasting them on a board. On Monday mornings, Pop had a company meeting with all the employees, where they discussed the ads and sales promotions and planned sales strategies for the week.

Mom was working on the Sunday crossword puzzle, just like she did every Sunday. She asked if Ellen and Bev had finished their project.

"Yes, all done. I'm going to read before I finish my homework."

The rest of the day passed uneventfully, as Sundays usually did, which unnerved her because she had been praying that Kenny would call. Perhaps he was just trying to make Gwennie jealous after all.

A SLIGHT CHANGE IN the breeze reminded Ellen it was getting late and she needed to leave the park and head for home. As the memories subsided, she wept. Tears of bitterness, rather than tears of healing, spilled uncontrollably until she had no tears left. As she dried her eyes, her depression deepened.

FIVE

ELLEN'S FIRST THOUGHTS WHEN she woke up each morning were of Danny. *Has he been adopted yet? Does he have loving parents? Is he happy? What does he look like?*

It was hard to imagine how he looked, since she had only seen him for a few brief moments after his birth. She constantly viewed the children at Titillations and compared them to how Danny might behave and look. *Like that adorable nine-month-old infant with his curly black hair and black eyes? Or would he turn out to be a tubby little toddler, like the one sleeping on his mom's shoulder?*

The summer seemed to pass slowly. She enjoyed working in the shop, because it kept her from dwelling on Danny and the past. It was the daily encounters with the children that were painful and left her feeling heavy-hearted.

Ellen found lunchtime with Max to be the best time of each day. Max, the philosopher and storyteller, amused her and unknowingly urged her to think about things other than Danny.

Almost every evening, she walked to Balboa Park and sat in the darkness. Night was her friend. It had no face and offered quiet and peace. On this particular night, she once again recalled the early days of her relationship with Kenny.

———

SHE WAS ON HER way to her first class Monday morning, when Kenny tapped her on the shoulder from behind. "Ellen, how about having lunch with me today?"

Ellen frowned. "I'm really sorry, Kenny, but I promised to have lunch with my friends today."

"That's okay. I understand. How about meeting me under the clock after school and we'll have a Coke or something?"

"I'll be there." *Damn. I'd rather have lunch with you.*

The bell rang, and Kenny waved as they both hurried off to class.

Since it was a warm autumn day, the gang met in its favorite spot on the grass in front of the school. When Ellen joined the group, she found them gossiping about Elaine's outfit.

"Really, guys, what's to talk about? It's no different than the clothes most of us wear," Ellen commented. She sat down next to Bev, and they talked quietly while they ate their lunch.

"Well, I'm ready to hit the pavement, how about you?" Bev asked Ellen as she finished her lunch.

"Yeah, I'm ready." Ellen picked up her bag, tossed her leftover orange into it, and smoothed out her skirt. "Let's see what's happening at the bell."

The *bell* was a replica of the Liberty Bell mounted on a pedestal and was a favorite meeting spot of all the kids. They used it as a platform to talk about issues, make announcements, or issue challenges. Ellen and Bev came around the corner just in time to hear Gil, Kenny's best friend, challenge Kenny to recite the Gettysburg Address from the top of the bell. There was a hush as the kids waited to hear Kenny's answer.

"You're on, buddy." Kenny leaped up on the bell. "Four score and seven years ago ..."

When he finished, the crowd applauded loudly, and one of the guys shouted, "Kenny, Kenny."

He's so smart and handsome. I just love him so much. She could feel the heat simmer in her veins as she thought about how much she liked when Kenny kissed and touched her. The school bell rang, signaling the end of lunch period. She would have to delay telling Kenny how amazing she thought he was until later.

When the final bell sounded at the end of the day, she grabbed her books and hurried to the clock, where Kenny stood waiting for her. As she approached, he gave her a big smile, which caused shivers to run down her spine.

As they drove to the drugstore, she told him, "I heard you recite the Gettysburg Address today. Pretty impressive. I think Mr. Lincoln would've approved." She tried to be serious, but she busted up laughing, and so did Kenny.

"I didn't see you there. Actually, it was a real kick. I don't think Gil thought I'd be dumb enough to act like a fool and jump up on the bell."

As they drank their Cokes, Kenny asked, "Will you come to the football game on Saturday? We can grab a bite afterwards. I'm sorry I won't have time to see you before then, what with football practice, homework, and everything."

She agreed. Her life was hectic as well.

"Meet me at the players' exit after the game," Kenny added, obviously pleased.

At her house, Ellen slid out of the car quickly and said goodbye. She didn't want to take the chance of Kenny kissing her in broad daylight in front of her house.

AT LAST IT WAS Saturday, and Pearl was getting ready to go to the beauty shop. "So, Ellen, what are you doing tonight?"

Ellen told her she'd be going to the football game and afterward out to get something to eat.

"Football, shmootball. I don't know what you kids see in that game. I don't understand it at all. All those boys chasing each other and knocking each other down just to get a little ball. It makes no sense to me."

Ellen knew any explanation would be in vain, so she said, "Oh, Mom, it's what we kids do."

The game turned out to be exciting at the end. It was during the last two minutes, when East, losing by a field goal, had the ball. Instead of throwing a pass, Kenny handed the ball off to Lee.

"What a play," the announcer screamed. "He's going, going, going to make a touchdown. And East wins! What a game, folks. What a play by quarterback Kenny Johnson."

Still shrieking herself, Ellen made her way toward the players' exit. In the crush, she couldn't find Kenny. Then he grabbed her around the waist and spun her around. Still riding high from the win, he squeezed Ellen so hard she could barely breathe. He realized what he was doing and let her go.

"Are you okay, Ellen? Gosh, I almost crushed you to death."

"I'll live I think." *Oh, hell, I loved it. You didn't have to stop.* She straightened up. "So what's the plan?"

"We're meeting at the Chat 'n Chew, where there's plenty of big tables in the back."

On the way to the restaurant they talked about the game. Ellen wanted to show off her newfound knowledge. She had spent several hours during the past week with Bev's brother learning about the game. After all, what does a nice Jewish girl know about football? Nothing, that's what. But now she knew a smidgen, and she was anxious to impress Kenny.

"So, why did you hand off to Lee instead of throwing a pass?"

Kenny, surprised, replied, "Coach knew they expected the pass, so he opted for the run. I didn't realize you knew anything about football, Miss Gordon."

"I guess there are a lot of things you don't know about me, Mr. Johnson."

She felt smug, but not too smug. They arrived at the Chat and hurried to get in line with the rest of the kids.

When they finished eating, Kenny excused them from the group, so he could spend some time with Ellen alone. Kenny parked by a neighbor's house when they reached her block. He fiddled with the radio until he found a station that played some of their favorites. Pulling her close, he murmured, "I missed you so much all week, I could hardly concentrate."

"Me, too," she whispered.

They kissed, and it didn't take long for the kissing to become passionate. Ellen's heart pounded, and she could feel the heat build. Kenny's tongue explored the inside of her mouth. She thought she would faint. *I shouldn't be doing this, but I can't stop.*

The kisses became deeper, and she got hot, so hot. He reached under her sweater and swiftly unhooked her bra. His hand cupped her breast. She shivered at the electric shocks it sent through her body.

It seemed as though her mind had ceased to function, and her body had taken over in a way she never knew it could. Soon, he was lying on top of her and touching her body all over. So hot, so hot. She became liquid all over. Suddenly his hand was inside her pants. She collided again with reality.

"It's okay, Ellen," he said, as he kept touching and kissing her.

Her mind yelled stop, but her body countered, "Don't stop!" *Oh God, it feels so wonderful.* And then suddenly, he was inside her, and a searing pain ripped through her. She screamed.

Kenny kept stroking her, murmuring, "I love you so, Ellen, it's okay."

And then she was on fire and melting. Suddenly, it was over.

Afterwards she sobbed. "We shouldn't have Kenny. It's wrong. We shouldn't have."

Kenny apologized. "I just wanted you so badly, I couldn't stop. I wanted you to be mine. I'm so sorry, Ellen."

She had to forgive him. Ellen also had to admit to herself that she had wanted him too. She tried to get herself together, but she was trembling, knowing she couldn't go in the house looking like this. If her parents happened to be awake, they would know immediately.

"Let's go to a gas station, so I can wash my face and comb my hair."

They went to a station near her house. As Ellen washed her face and stared into the mirror, it amazed her to find she really didn't appear that much different.

Kenny, silent on the drive home, held her close. "I hope you know how special you are to me and how much tonight meant to me."

Ellen was still too choked up and upset to talk. As they walked up to her door, Kenny asked if he could call her the next day. "Yes," she managed to get out. He gave her a sweet kiss and sprinted back to his car.

Thankfully, Mom and Pop were asleep. She lay in bed and wondered if she really loved him, and she worried about what had happened earlier. Exhausted, she fell asleep.

When she woke the next morning, it hit her. She was no longer a virgin. *Oh, God, what have I done? But how could it be bad, when it felt so right and so good? And I do love him. He's so sweet and wonderful.* Her gut burned. The bile rose in her throat. *No matter how wonderful it was, no one can find out. I could never live down the shame.*

Her thoughts were interrupted by Pop's Sunday morning question. "Pancakes or French toast?"

Trying to act as normal as possible, Ellen hollered down to him, "French toast," and then dragged herself to the kitchen.

Mom glanced up from the paper and asked, "So how was your evening?"

Ellen's throat felt so dry she could hardly speak. "The game was exciting," she croaked. "We won on the last play."

At that moment, the phone rang, startling Ellen and making her a little nervous. It turned out to be Bev wanting to know about the evening.

"You don't even give a person time to eat breakfast," Ellen complained as she walked into the living room with the phone.

"What's more important, breakfast or telling your best friend the latest scoop on your romance?"

As Ellen gave Bev the details of the date, she wondered what Bev would think if she knew the rest of what had happened.

"So did you kiss and stuff?" Bev wanted to know everything.

"We did. Oh, Bev, I'm crazy about him. I just love him so much." It was true, and Ellen couldn't wait to talk to him. "I just pray that he feels the same way about me."

Kenny called late in the afternoon. They talked for at least an hour and discovered that neither of them had been able to concentrate on their homework thus far.

"Will you meet me under the clock after school tomorrow?"

She smiled to herself. *He has no idea how happy that makes me. I'm so thankful he isn't dumping me after last night.* "I'll be there."

He blew her a kiss over the phone as he said goodbye. Even though Ellen still felt pangs of guilt over what she had done, she thought she had died and gone to heaven.

~

DURING THE NEXT FEW weeks, Kenny and Ellen became inseparable. They saw each other as often as possible. After debate club, at basketball games from which they sneaked away early, and after their other school clubs. They had places in City Park where they went to make love.

Ellen decided she must be lovesick, because her energy seemed low and she started feeling puny. Then she missed her period. She was always so regular. *Oh, God, what's wrong?* She knew in her heart what was wrong, but she didn't want to admit it, even to herself. After a few more days, Ellen got frantic. *How could this have happened? We've tried to be so careful. Kenny has always used a rubber. What will I do? God is punishing me. I know it. I've got to tell Kenny.*

The following day, they met under the clock after school. Ellen could see that Kenny sensed something was wrong. She choked.

"Let's go somewhere quiet. We need to talk."

They went to his car. Once they were settled, he took her hand, gently kissed it, and waited.

Ellen cried. "Oh, God, Kenny, I missed my period. I think I'm pregnant."

Kenny seemed stunned. After what felt like an hour, he spoke.

"Are you sure, Ellen? Could it be something else? We've been careful."

"What else could it be? I'm always right on the dot, and now

I'm overdue. Oh, God, Kenny, what are we going to do?"

He bit his nail. "Don't worry, Ellen, we'll figure it out. Just give me some time to think it over."

She sniffled. "I've got to get home. Can you take me?"

They were quiet as they drove to her house. He told Ellen to meet him under the clock the following day and made her promise not to worry as she got out of the car and ran up the sidewalk.

~

THE NEXT DAY, AS planned, she met Kenny under the clock.

"C'mon, let's go to Pencol and have a soda."

They sat down in a booth, and Kenny ordered a black-and-white sundae, and she ordered a cherry Coke.

As he gently stroked Ellen's hand, he told her, "I made some calls last night, and I think I found the perfect doctor to solve our problem."

Ellen withdrew her hand. "What are you talking about? You found the perfect doctor to do what? I don't understand how a doctor's going to solve our problem."

"To ... you know. To get rid of ... you know ..."

"An abortion? You want me to have an abortion?" Near hysteria, she got up and ran for the door.

"Ellen, where are you going? Wait, Ellen." Kenny threw some money on the table and sprinted after her.

Feeling a sense of revulsion, she pushed him away. "How could you even think about doing that? Are you crazy? I could die or go to jail."

Without a backward glance, she ran to the bus stop and got there just in time to catch the next bus. She felt a sense of deep horror as she sat down. *How could Kenny even suggest such a thing? How could he do that if he really loves me?* Her stomach heaved as she realized the obvious. *He doesn't really love me. It was just sex.* She didn't even realize tears were running down her face.

⁓

THE SOUND OF A dog barking brought her back to the present and reminded her she needed to get home before her parents started to worry. Once again, she cried until she had no more tears. This time, she recognized her tears of bitterness. Would they ever become tears of healing?

SIX

AT LAST, SUMMER WAS over and it was time to start school. In many ways, going to a new school was harder than working at Titillations. In Ellen's view, all the girls were true California girls, with their blonde hair, blue eyes, and perfect tans. All they did was giggle and talk about boys, hanging out at the beach, and their latest swimsuits. The boys were the same, with their bleached blonde hair, blue eyes, perfect tans, and bulging muscles. All they talked about were girls and surfing.

Of course, this wasn't really true. It just seemed that way to Ellen. Several people made friendly overtures to her, but after they were rebuffed, they finally left her alone, which is what she really wanted. *I don't fit in with these girls, and besides, I'm unfit to be anyone's friend anyway. I'm imperfect, damaged goods.* It was no better for her at the synagogue. She didn't want to make friends. Many people tried, but when she didn't respond, eventually they gave up. She knew all the kids thought she was stuck up, but it didn't matter.

All she did was study to make sure her grades were perfect, every paper she wrote was perfect, and every book report she gave was perfect. That was who she was in their eyes ... Miss Perfect Ellen Gordon, and she had no desire to change their minds.

On the evenings when she finished her homework early, Ellen made her usual pilgrimage to Balboa Park. On this particular night, she remembered when she had told her parents.

~

THE HOUSE WAS QUIET when she got home. She went into her room, undressed, and crawled into bed. She was so cold. Kenny's words burned in her memory. *No matter what, I won't have an abortion. But what will I do? I'm going to have to tell Mom. Oh, God, I don't want to tell her, but I have to.* She wrestled with those thoughts, torturing herself until she heard Mom let herself into the house.

"Yoo hoo, Ellen, are you home?"

"I'm in my room, Mom."

Finding Ellen in bed, Pearl observed, "What's wrong? You look like death warmed over."

Ellen began to cry. She sobbed so hard, her whole body trembled. Alarmed, Pearl took her in her arms and rocked her.

"Honey, whatever it is, it'll be okay. Tell me what's wrong."

Trembling uncontrollably, her nose running, Ellen cried even harder.

"No matter what it is, it's okay, Ellen. Tell me what's wrong."

Eventually, her sobbing subsided. Ellen blew her nose and cuddled back into Pearl's arms.

"It's awful, I'm so sorry, Mom. It's awful. I can't tell you."

She wailed again. Pearl held her close until she calmed. Pearl took Ellen's face in her hands. "There isn't anything so awful we can't face it together."

With that, Ellen blurted out, "I'm pregnant."

Pearl froze as she pushed Ellen away. Then she screamed, "You're having sex with a boy like some *nafka,* a streetwalker? My daughter! You're sixteen. What's the matter with you, are you crazy?"

Ellen cringed. This was not the response she'd been hoping for.

Pearl raised her hand. "How could you do this to me? I can't believe my daughter would do such a thing." Then, just as suddenly, Pearl deflated like a balloon. Her face turned white and withered. Shuddering, she gasped, "How ... do you know ... you're pregnant?"

"I'm three ... weeks ... late. And I'm nauseated."

Visibly upset, Pearl tried to calm herself. "We need to take a moment to compose ourselves and then we can take things one at a time." Together, they sat silently for a few moments. Then Pearl continued, "We'll see a doctor to make sure, then we'll make a plan. What about the boy? Are you going to tell me who it is? Does he know?"

By the time Pearl finished, her voice was hysterical again. This scared Ellen, who wept some more. *Will my parents disown me or throw me out? If so, what will I do?*

Quietly Pearl finally said, "Let's stay calm now. Rest while I make some soup for your dinner."

"Thanks, Mom, but I don't want anything." *God, she's doing the Jewish Mother thing. Like making soup will make this go away.*

~

AS PEARL DEPARTED ELLEN'S room, she thought about what

Ellen had just told her. *Some mother I am. I didn't even know she had a boyfriend.* Suddenly it dawned on her. It had to be that *shegetz*, that boy in her debate club. No wonder she hadn't known. Ellen had hidden her relationship with him because he wasn't Jewish.

My poor girl, what could she know about being pregnant? Don't kid yourself, Pearl. Girls today know everything, not like when you were a girl and nobody even discussed sex.

As she entered the kitchen, she experienced such a terrible pain she could hardly breathe. She knew this was her heart breaking for her daughter. Surely, there's nothing worse for a parent than a tragedy that befalls their child. The tears welled up, and she stopped for a minute to gain control. *That SOB! That nogoodnik! How could he do this to my daughter? I'll kill him. Oh, how will I ever tell Nate? Ellen is his baby, his shining star, and his life. How will he take it? Whatever he and I feel, we must stand by Ellen.*

She opened the refrigerator and was glad to see there was still some split pea soup on the shelf. As it heated, she haphazardly took food out for dinner. *Get control Pearl, pay attention. Get dinner together.*

She glanced at the clock. *Almost time for Nate to get home. Better wash my face and make myself presentable.* She held a cool washcloth to her eyes in an effort to get the red out. Then she put on some make-up and her favorite Lilac Champagne lipstick. She heard the garage door. Nate was home. She pasted on a smile and prepared to greet her husband.

"I'm home, honey."

She met him in the hall. "I'm just finishing up. Dinner will be ready in a few minutes." She avoided him as she hurried back to the kitchen.

"What, no kiss, no hello, no how are you?" Pearl had already disappeared into the kitchen as he meandered toward the bathroom to wash up.

Pearl made a tray and went upstairs. She knocked on the door. When Ellen didn't answer, she opened it. Ellen lay there with her arm covering her face and her eyes.

"I brought you some nice split pea soup. Please try to eat it. I know you don't feel like it, but try. I'll just leave it here." She put the tray on the nightstand and went to join Nate downstairs.

Nate was sitting at the table when Pearl came into the kitchen. "*Nu*, where's Ellen? Is something the matter?"

"Ellen isn't feeling well. I took a tray to her." Pearl busied herself at the stove and then served dinner.

"What's the matter with Ellen? Nothing serious I hope. I've noticed she's been somewhat droopy lately."

"Eat your dinner, dear. We'll talk about it later. So, how was business?"

Nate discussed his day. Pearl hardly paid any attention as she desperately tried to figure out how she was going to tell Nate about Ellen. At last dinner was over.

"You hardly ate a bite of food, and you certainly didn't hear a word I said. Please tell me what's going on," Nate said in a low voice. "Just tell me what it is, Pearl."

Pearl gazed at Nate. *My love, how can I tell him?* She took his hand.

"I have something upsetting to tell you, Nate. Please try to be calm." Pearl plunged in. "Ellen is pregnant. She just told me today. We need to help her, Nate. We've got to figure out what to do."

Pearl could see that Nate was stunned as he tried to digest the news. Then he banged on the table and yelled, "You're telling me my daughter is pregnant, like some slut."

His face, beet red, caused Pearl to fear he'd have a stroke. Then the questions came.

"What do we know? Who is the boy? Are you sure she's pregnant?"

"Ellen told me she missed her period, and she's having morning sickness. Tomorrow, I'll make an appointment with the doctor to make sure. She won't say anything about the boy, but I have my suspicions."

Pearl knew that Nate was attempting to gain control of his anger as he tried to comfort her. "Ellen is my daughter. I won't let anything happen to her. Should I go to her? What should I say to her?"

"I'm not sure. But I do think she needs to know that you know and that we'll take care of her."

NATE STOOD OUTSIDE ELLEN'S door for several minutes until he gained control of his emotions. No sound came from within. Finally, he put his shoulders back and knocked on the door. "Ellen, it's Pop. Can I come in?"

No response. Quietly, he opened the door a crack. Ellen faced the wall. She lay noticeably still and had several blankets piled up on top of her, even though the room was warm. He approached her bed and sat down on the edge. "I'm so sorry, baby."

Ellen began to howl. Nate had never heard such a thing in his entire life. There was so much pain in the sound she made that he could feel his own heart aching again. He wrapped her in his arms and rocked her as he had done when she was a baby. He didn't know how long they sat like that. Finally, Ellen fell asleep. He laid her down solicitously and realized he had been crying. Rapidly, he got up and left so his sobbing wouldn't wake her.

Nate was like a boiler ready to explode, the fire in his belly burning and consuming him. He was filled with rage at the boy. At the same time, he felt furious with Ellen. *How could she do this to Pearl and me? How could this have happened?* He felt the urge to put his fist through the face of the boy, and at the same time he experienced helplessness. Ellen was his baby. *Who could have hurt my baby this way?* He would find a way to help her. He *must* help her.

Two hours later, after Nate had looked in on Ellen, he went to bed. The night seemed interminable. Neither he nor Pearl slept. Mostly they held each other.

~

THE NEXT MORNING, THEY were both emotionally drained.

"I have some business to take care of this morning, but I'll be able to get away by lunchtime." Nate checked his date book. "I'll call later, and if you get an appointment with Dr. Kramer for today, I'll drive you down to the Springs. Best if I get an early start," Nate added. "I'm not going to bother Ellen this morning. Tell her I love her." He put his coffee cup in the sink and kissed Pearl on the cheek.

Pearl promised to call and let him know if she got an immediate appointment. Clinging to him, she said, "I love you, Nate."

That was all she could get out. She went back into the kitchen and poured herself a second cup of coffee, turned off the percolator, and sat down. When she felt in control again, Pearl found a Colorado Springs directory. She debated, but after a few minutes decided to call Dr. Kramer at home. It had been several years since she had seen or spoken to him, and she hoped he would remember her. He had taken care of her when she lived in Colorado Springs, and they had developed a special relationship. The maid answered the phone. Pearl explained who she was and waited, with nerves on end, for him to pick up.

"Well, it's about time you called me, Pearl Gordon. I was beginning to think you'd forgotten about old Doc Kramer."

Pearl immediately felt better. His voice, as comforting as ever, felt like having her favorite quilt wrapped around her shoulders. She quickly explained the situation and expressed her hope that he would be able to see Ellen later that day.

"I'm sorry, Pearl. I don't practice anymore, but I'm sure the young fellow who took over my practice will do whatever he can." He promised to call Dr. Burke and get back to Pearl right away. She thanked him and breathed a sigh of relief.

Thank God for that blessed man. With his help we'll get through this. As she hung up, she noticed it was almost nine thirty. *Better make sure Ellen is awake. It's going to be a long day.*

~~~

ELLEN WOKE UP WHEN the sun streamed through her window. *Why is the sun shining when I turned to stone overnight? It's too late to warm me now.* A penetrating cold ran through her body. *My heart has already become a block of ice, and my body is numb.*

She debated whether she could ever get out of bed again, but finally she had no choice. She definitely had to go to the bathroom.

She groaned when she eyed herself in the mirror. Her face was swollen, her eyes mere slits, and her nose was one big red bulbous mess. Her head felt like it was splitting open, and she felt nauseated. *It would be best if I just died now*, she thought. Then she threw up.

Mom knocked as she opened the door and saw Ellen on her knees, her head hanging over the toilet bowl. She wet a washcloth with warm water, put it on Ellen's forehead, and gave her a drink of water.

"You're okay. I'll run you a warm bath, we'll put in some bubble bath, and you'll feel like a new woman."

Ellen didn't miss the fact that Mom said woman, not girl. *God, I wish I were still a girl.* She hung her head. Time to face facts. She glanced at her mom. "What did Pop say when you told him?"

Mom told her that Pop would do everything in his power to help. "In the meantime, I called my old doctor in Colorado Springs."

Puzzled, Ellen questioned, "Colorado Springs, why?"

"Well, we wouldn't want to run into anybody we know, would we?"

The blood rushed to Ellen's face. *Of course. I'm an embarrassment now. We'll have to hide Ellen, won't we?* Humiliation and shame rocked her to the core.

The phone rang, and Pearl went to answer it. When she came back, she confirmed they had an appointment for that afternoon.

"Okay, Mom, I think I'll go back to bed now."

"First you'll have some breakfast, young lady. You need to eat. Then you'll spend some time on your schoolwork. Just because you didn't go to school today doesn't mean this is a day off."

Ellen managed to get dressed and ready to go. She spent the rest of the morning trying unsuccessfully to concentrate on doing her homework.

Before lunch, as Pearl prepared a casserole for dinner, she pondered the situation. *How do you tell your daughter how you feel? Do you say you're devastated, that you blame yourself, that you're brokenhearted? Do you say you want to kill the boy who did this, that you're saddened to the very core of your being? Or that you somehow wish you could take the tragedy onto yourself? Do you say you would do anything in the world to make it better, to make it go away? No. You try to be normal.*

Pearl heard the garage door open. "Ellen, Pop is home. It's time to go."

"Coming, Mom." *I don't want to go. Do I have to do this? Oh, God, I can't.* With those thoughts running through her head, she put down her books, grabbed her coat, and headed down the stairs.

～

AS THE EVENING TURNED dark, Ellen knew it was time to go home. She readied herself to leave the park, but was once again overcome with tears as she remembered that terrible, fateful day. And once again, her tears were filled with bitterness and pain.

SEVEN

IT WAS THE SPRING of 1955 in San Diego and nearing time for graduation. Ellen wasn't voted the winner of any popularity contests, but her grades made her the class valedictorian. The seniors were indignant, as Tony, one of her classmates, voiced his displeasure for the whole class.

"God, anyone but Miss Perfect, Ellen Gordon."

Ellen had mixed feelings about being valedictorian. She didn't feel she deserved this honor, believing someone else more involved should have been given this acknowledgment. *After all, I'm nothing but a fraud. But how can I refuse? I know Mom and Pop will be pleased.* She decided to surprise them at dinner with the news.

"Mom, Pop, I've been named valedictorian of the senior class."

"That's wonderful news, Ellen," both Nate and Pearl said together. Pop hugged Ellen and Pearl gave her a squeeze.

"We are so proud of you," Mom said as a tear escaped her eye. "I think I'll just sit and kvell for a bit."

Ellen felt like she wanted to heave, so she excused herself and went to her room to contemplate how to handle this honor, knowing how much her classmates didn't want her to have it.

~

FOR PEARL, IT DIDN'T feel like the school year was coming to an end. In other ways, it felt like Ellen's senior year had dragged on forever. She had been concerned, because Ellen seemed so remote and distant all year. Ellen hadn't made any friends and didn't attend any school or synagogue events. Yet, Pearl felt proud of her daughter's accomplishments. *Has it been almost two years since that awful night? That night we found out our beloved daughter was pregnant?* As she sat on the sofa, Pearl recalled the events and her emotions that day. The tears fell from her eyes as she remembered her heart breaking for Ellen.

When Nate heard that Ellen had been selected to be the class valedictorian at her new school, he felt gratified with her success and proud of her accomplishments. Still, he felt sad that Ellen hadn't enjoyed her senior year and seemed to have been unavailable and uninvolved socially the entire year.

As they sat together in their living room in San Diego, both Pearl and Nate still felt disturbed and upset about Ellen as they reflected upon the events of the past. While Ellen had worked extremely hard at making her life appear normal, they knew things were far from normal. She may have been chosen class valedictorian, but that was only an indication of her innate abilities and the result of her constant studying. Unfortunately, they had no idea what to do.

Nate consoled Pearl. "It's just going to take more time than we thought. I know Ellen … she'll be okay. Don't worry, honey, it'll work out."

Pearl, her shoulders slumping, lamented. "I hope so, I certainly hope so. I hope we did the right thing. It's so hard to know." Pearl felt depressed herself.

EIGHT

AFTER GRADUATION, NATE EXPECTED Ellen to work at Titillations. Ellen dreaded the thought because it meant being reminded of Danny constantly, but she knew she had no choice. She summoned up all her inner resources and prepared to go back to work.

At first, the same feelings stirred within her as she watched the children come and go. However, as the days passed, it started to become easier. She could observe the adorable toddlers and not think and agonize over her child. The sameness of the routine each day had begun to numb her senses. All she had to do was get up, go to work, go to lunch, go home, repeat.

Every day at one thirty, she went to the coffee shop for lunch and her daily conversation with Max. Max had been widowed for five years, and since both of his daughters were married and lived with their families in the east, Ellen became like a daughter to him. She sensed how much he looked forward to their daily visits and knew it gave him something to think about during the lonely nights.

He wiped his hands on a towel, went to her table, and sank his weary bones into the chair.

"So, nu, what's new?" he greeted Ellen with a huge smile.

"Same old, same old."

Now that the preliminaries were over, they could have their usual lunchtime discussion. Ellen was fond of Max and discovered that his advice was well-given and worthy of consideration. During the last few days, they had been discussing college. Ellen was uncertain about what she wanted to major in, and they had been chatting about her various considerations.

"I think, Ellen, that life has many pathways. I believe we should explore as many of them as possible. Take your time deciding on a major, but should it turn out to be the wrong one, don't worry. Everything you learn is of value and will stand you in good stead. In the long term of your life, a couple of years one way or the other won't matter."

"But won't it be a mistake to waste my college education and end up with a degree I'm not going to use?"

"Education is never wasted. You will learn many useful life lessons as well."

She agreed, thanked him for his advice, and headed back to work. "See ya tomorrow."

That night after dinner, Nate asked Ellen if she had made any decisions yet.

"I think I'll just spend the first year as an arts and science major and see where that leads me."

"So are you telling me you don't have any ideas about what you'd like to do?"

"I guess. I just want to spend some time exploring my options."

"That makes sense. Just don't waste too much valuable time making a decision. Begin to start making decisions as soon as you get a feel for your options. Well then, let's get the paperwork completed this weekend. I don't want you to miss out because you didn't get your forms in on time."

With her grades, Ellen could have chosen any school in the country, but she wasn't yet ready to face the world. So she had chosen to attend the University of California at San Diego. She had been offered a full scholarship that included tuition, room and board, and books. She had already accepted and needed only to return the forms.

Ellen's sentiments about going to college were mixed. She wasn't sure she was ready to leave the security of home. She knew she definitely wasn't ready to make new friends yet. The thought of dating a boy repulsed her, and the thought of having a roommate made her shudder. She kept all these thoughts to herself, however. Mom and Pop expected her to go to college, and short of getting married, it was her only choice. She had caused them enough grief. Now she needed to do what was expected.

That night, as she sat in the park pondering the distress that going to college caused her, her mind once again slipped back into the past and the trip to Colorado Springs.

～

THE THREE OF THEM were silent during the ride to Colorado Springs, each lost in his or her own thoughts. It had been an unusually long and stunning autumn, and on this Thursday morning an Indian summer day painted the landscape with exotic colors. The air smelled fresh and cool, the scrub oak along the road blazed in shades of red, orange, and yellow. In the distance, the mountains paraded several hues of exquisite purple. On any other day this would have been a ride to savor, to experience the glorious mood, but not today.

They reached the Springs in good time. As they pulled up to Dr. Burke's office on Bijou Street, Nate questioned Pearl and

Ellen. "Do you want me to go with you or pick you up later?"

"Later," Ellen responded.

Ellen saw the relief on Pop's face. "Fine, I'll just go into one of the coffee shops, read my paper, and have a cup. How long do you think you'll be?"

"About an hour and a half," Pearl replied. "The wait is usually about fifteen minutes and the usual doctor visit is about forty-five minutes, give or take."

After Pop drove off, they entered the office building. Pearl didn't even have to check the directory. She remembered the office number and simply pushed the elevator button. The office was empty when they entered. Pearl went to the desk and spoke with the nurse, who told her the doctor would be with them in just a few minutes.

Ellen huddled in a chair in the corner with her head down. Pearl sat down next to her and placed her hand on top of Ellen's. Just as the warmth of Mom's hand seeped into her veins and eased her distress somewhat, the nurse appeared and asked that they follow her into a small office crowded with bookshelves, a desk stacked with files, a worn chair behind it, and two chairs in front of it.

Dr. Burke entered the room. "Good afternoon, Ellen. I'm Dr. Burke. I spoke with Dr. Kramer this morning. He said you think you're pregnant. Can you please tell why you think so?"

"I've been tired and nauseated, and I missed my period." *God, I wish I were somewhere else right now. Maybe on a tropical island.*

Dr. Burke listened and took notes. "I want to examine you to see if you're actually pregnant or if something else could be the cause of these symptoms. I'll have my nurse, Miss Morris, take you to an examination room, and I'll get some additional information from your mother."

Miss Morris regaled Ellen with jokes about Dr. Burke as they strolled to the exam room. "Ellen, please undress and put on the gown that's on the table. I need a urine sample. You'll find the cup in the bathroom. When you're finished, holler, and then I'll weigh and measure you. Any questions?"

Ellen bit her lip as she tried to hold back a hysterical chuckle. Miss Morris recognized this emotion and knew she meant no. Ellen gaped at the examination table with its stirrups on either side, and she thought she would faint.

Oh, God, I can't do this. Don't think about it. Just do as you're told.

As Ellen closed the door to the bathroom, she pretended she was about to embark on a journey to Europe. When she finished, she went back into the exam room and plopped down on the examination table.

"Miss Morris, I'm ready."

The nurse came back with a label stuck to her finger. "We'll label your specimen and get it to the lab and then we'll get you weighed and measured."

Ellen stepped on the scale and allowed Miss Morris to take her blood pressure and prick her finger for a blood sample.

So far, it was just like going to see Dr. Abelman, her pediatrician. They went into the exam room, and as Miss Morris was leaving, she told Ellen, "I'll just take this to the lab. Dr. Burke will be here soon, so just relax."

Ellen sat on the edge of the table. *Relax. What kind of joke is that?* She wiped the sweat from her palms onto the gown and closed her eyes. In no time, Dr. Burke knocked on the door.

He entered the room, followed by Miss Morris, who handed him Ellen's chart and reported the results of the urine and blood tests. He thanked her and faced Ellen.

"Now, Ellen, if I can have you lie on the table and push

yourself down toward the edge, until you can put your feet into the stirrups here on either side."

Ellen felt excessively hot and yet cold and shaky at the same time. *Oh, God, please let me die.* She willed her mind to blankness during the examination. As Dr. Burke talked, Miss Morris wrote in the chart.

At last, the ordeal ended. Dr. Burke held out his hand and helped Ellen sit up. He told her to meet him back in his office after she got dressed. She dressed and plodded back down the hall to the office where Mom sat. "Okay, Ellen?"

"Okay." She sat in the second chair, closed her eyes, and put her head down.

Dr. Burke came in and sat down. "Ellen, the examination indicates that you are pregnant. I'm going to give you some vitamins, and I want to see you again in a month. I'm sure you have a lot of questions, and I'll be happy to answer them. I suspect you'll want to think about things and talk later. Call me whenever you're ready."

He asked Pearl if she had any questions. He gave them an approximate due date of July first.

Questions? Yes, I have questions. Why did this happen to me? Are you sure I'm pregnant? Oh, God, what am I going to do? Still feeling paralyzed, Ellen arose as she saw Pearl stand. Somewhere in the haze, she heard her mom thank Dr. Burke. Somehow she managed to choke out a goodbye and a thank you as well.

Dr. Burke took her hand, squeezed it, and said, "Everything is going to be all right, Ellen."

Without a word, Pearl and Ellen walked to the elevator. Pop pulled up just as they stepped outside. He peered at both of them. There was no need to ask. Mom sniffed.

"Just take us home, please."

During the ride home, Ellen agonized over the fact that she was pregnant, her mind and body numb.

"I have a nice casserole in the fridge," Mom stated with forced enthusiasm. "I just have to heat it up."

"I'm not hungry. I just want to go to bed."

After they pulled into the garage, Pop took charge. He announced he had made some plans earlier in the day that he wanted to discuss.

"I'm really tired. I'd rather go to bed."

"I'm sorry, Ellen, but this is important. Besides, it's also important for you to eat. Starving yourself is not good for you or the baby."

Pearl heated up the casserole and called them to dinner. When they were all seated around the table, Pop told them about the arrangements he had made. While Pearl and Ellen had been in the doctor's office, Pop had gone to see Tom and Ginny. Tom was a former employee and friend. He and Ginny had moved to Colorado Springs after the war because of the injuries Tom had sustained, which put him in a wheelchair. The two couples had remained friends through the years. Ellen would stay with them until after she had the baby.

"I think this can work. What do you think?"

Ellen glared at him as though he belonged on another planet. She was dumbfounded. Her father was throwing her out of the house? Her head swam with emotion. *Doesn't Pop love me anymore? I didn't mean to do anything bad.*

She wailed. "I'm sorry, Pop, I didn't mean for this to happen. Please don't send me away."

"I'm not throwing you out. I'm just trying to protect you. It is impossible for you to stay home. Your life would be ruined if everyone knew you were having a baby."

Mom swallowed. "I'm stunned but amazed that you thought

of all this just today and got it done. How did you do it?"

"I spent all night trying to come up with a plan. This is the best I could do. I'm sorry."

Ellen was exhausted. She felt rejected and abandoned. *Throw Ellen away. She's an embarrassment. Hide her as far away as possible.*

Mom took Ellen's hand, led her up to her room, and helped her undress and get into bed. "Just remember, darling, we love you. We're only trying to do what's best."

She kissed Ellen, turned off the light, and shut the door.

FRIDAY AND SATURDAY WERE depressing. Pop went to work as usual. Mom and Ellen moped separately. Sunday finally came. They sat at the breakfast table when Pop spoke. "We need to talk. We can't go on like this. We have to get on with living our lives. First you, Ellen. Tell me what you think you want to do and let's see if we can make a workable plan."

Ellen glanced at Pop and cringed when she saw his red eyes and the deep circles under them. *Well, I think I would just like to die. Other than that, I have no plan.*

"I'll do whatever you and Mom think is best. I don't feel capable of doing anything else."

Pop cleared his throat. "Well then ... I think, Ellen, you should go back to school tomorrow and stay until Christmas vacation. During vacation we will move you to the Springs. I've arranged to have a teacher tutor you, so you can continue your schooling and not lose the rest of the year. In the meantime, Mom and I will investigate adoption arrangements."

Pearl stared at Nate. "Did you just say you've hired a teacher? When? How did you find her? I'm surprised and a little confused. I don't understand how all this happened."

Nate explained. "As you know, the superintendent of schools is a friend of mine. I called him, explained my need, and he helped me find this teacher and made the arrangements. He agreed that Ellen should be able to continue her studies and not lose the time. He's a good friend and will not divulge anything to anyone."

"Nate, you are a wonder. I think this is a reasonable thing to do. She turned to Ellen. "Ellen, what do you think?"

"You want me to go back to school tomorrow? How can I go back to school? What can I tell my friends? This is awful," Ellen bawled.

Mom responded, attempting to calm Ellen's rising panic. "There's nothing to tell. Your friends don't know you're pregnant. You just had a bad case of the flu, so you'll be under the weather for a bit. You're an excellent debater, now you'll be an excellent actress. There really isn't that much difference."

"What can I tell my friends about not going back to school after vacation?"

"I'm working on that," Pop said. "Please just trust your Mom and me to figure it out."

Ellen continued to cry as she went back to her room.

～～

ON MONDAY MORNING, ELLEN resisted getting out of bed and ready for school, but her parents remained adamant. She had to return today. She dragged herself out of bed. *You can do this. Make your mind a blank. Don't feel anything. If you don't feel anything, it can't hurt you. Mom's right. Be an actress. Remember talking about façades in class? Well, just put on your school façade.*

She thought about Bev. She had avoided talking to her since the previous week. *Guess I'll just have to put on the best friend façade too.*

Mom called to her.

"I'll be down in a few minutes." Ellen peered into the mirror. *Funny, I don't really look any different. Somewhat pale, maybe, but certainly not pregnant. I don't understand it, I certainly feel different. I am different. I should appear different.*

When Ellen went into the kitchen and saw her parents sitting and eating breakfast, she felt extremely sad. *My God, they have aged over the weekend. It's all my fault. Look what I've done to them. They were so vibrant just last week.* She stifled a sob. *Get yourself together, Ellen. Remember, don't feel anything.*

She sat down for breakfast. Pop folded up the paper and prepared to go to work. "You'll be okay, Ellen. It will all work out."

"I'll be okay, don't worry."

Nate sighed. "I do worry, but I'll try not to."

He told Pearl it would be a good idea for her to drive Ellen to school.

Just then, the phone rang. Pearl kissed Nate, told him to call her later, and went to answer the phone. It was Bev.

The moment Ellen had been dreading arrived. Mom had been putting Bev off. Nothing to do now but talk to her. Ellen told Bev that Mom was taking her to school, so they arranged to meet at lunch. Ellen felt grateful she would be spared talking to Bev until then.

Somehow, the morning passed. Ellen tried to concentrate on her classwork. It amazed her she was so far behind after only two days off.

As lunchtime approached, she tried to ready herself mentally to be with her friends and act normal. When Bev caught up with Ellen, she grabbed her and hugged her.

"I'm so happy to see you. Wow, you look awful. You're so pale. We'll find a table, and you can sit and rest while I get your milk."

Ellen was content to let Bev take care of her and do all the talking, as she was extremely tired after her morning classes. She sat quietly while the girls gossiped about the weekend. Relief washed over her when lunch ended. Bev told Ellen to meet her at the end of the day and she would drive her home as usual.

~

STANDING UNDER THE CLOCK at their normal meeting spot, Kenny saw Ellen before she saw him. He prayed she would at least say hello before she headed to the parking lot. His heart filled with dismay at how pale and ill she appeared. Even from a distance, he could tell she wasn't feeling well.

Unfortunately, the gods didn't seem to have heard his plea. Maybe it was because he hadn't had the courage to call her over the past four days. He honestly hadn't known what to say after realizing how he'd messed things up by suggesting the abortion. *But what else can we do? I am definitely not ready to be a father.* As she continued on past where he stood, he might as well have been invisible. Not only did she not look at him, she seemed to look right through him. What a creepy feeling.

Ellen felt a swell of anger well up in her chest when she spotted Kenny. *It's because of you that I'm in this trouble. I'll never speak to you again and I'll hate you for the rest of my life for doing this to me just for some sex. You obviously didn't love me, or care about me at all, since all you wanted me to do was get an illegal abortion. I don't ever want to see you again, Kenny Johnson.* With that pronouncement, she walked by as if he didn't exist.

~

ELLEN SURVIVED THAT FIRST day back at school. Nobody seemed to notice anything different, other than when a few made comments about how she still appeared pale. On the way home,

Bev wanted to make plans to see each other that afternoon, but Ellen begged off. When they reached her house, Ellen embraced Bev. "You are definitely the best friend a girl could ever have. Thanks for being so special."

Bev beamed. The sun shone on her face and highlighted her freckles, making her look quite sweet and motherly. She hugged Ellen back and promised to pick her up the following morning. Ellen ambled into the house, threw her books down, and collapsed on the couch.

Mom heard the door slam, came into the living room, and saw Ellen sprawled on the couch. She sat down beside her and patted her hair. Finally, she said, "So, how did the day go?"

"It was hard, Mom, really hard. And I have a ton of work to make up too."

Pearl clucked sympathetically. She told Ellen to have some milk and cookies and then rest for a while before doing homework.

Ellen got up, went to her room, and put on her favorite cuddly pants, a shirt, and fluffy slippers. She realized she actually was hungry, and milk and cookies sounded good.

As the days passed, Ellen became more and more disconsolate. In her mind, she was no longer a person. She functioned on autopilot. She functioned, but she didn't feel. She became colder and colder on the inside. The world seemed to move farther away.

Her parents decided she would tell her friends she had a wonderful opportunity to do a semester of independent study with their old friends Dede and Chuck Torrance. They had both been college professors, who, having tired of academia, had instituted their own program on their ranch in Montana. Each year, they took a few good students who came to live at the ranch. In addition to regular studies, the students learned survival skills, and when the group became a team, the students explored their passions. One group studied the Inuits in Alaska, while another group went on a dig in Egypt. It sounded so fantastic that Ellen wished this flawless plan was actually true.

"I can't believe I'm not going to see you for a whole year," Bev lamented. "What will I do without you, my best friend?"

"I know. It's going to be hard for me too," Ellen answered, as she grabbed Bev and gave her a big hug. "I'm going to miss you so much."

Ellen's other friends were all envious she was going to live "the great adventure," as they called it. And all the time, a fetus grew inside her as she shriveled up, dying inside more and more each day. *Some great adventure. Yeah.*

⁓

IT WAS GETTING LATE. Time to leave the park, go home, and get ready for another day at Titillations. Once again, Ellen wept for quite some time. On this night, however, she realized they were tears of self-pity and sadness for all she'd lost.

NINE

SUMMER WOUND DOWN. BUSINESS at Titillations slowed, as parents got their children ready for the new school year, which allowed Ellen more time to think about completing her arrangements for college. She had received her dorm room assignment and all the forms that needed to be filled out and returned upon her arrival at the university.

Instead of being energized and excited, Ellen felt even more depressed. The thought of leaving home again frightened her. She moped about the shop all day and was moody at dinner. She couldn't wait to go to the park each night, where she could sit and brood without the endless questions and conversation from her parents.

She thought about the transition from Denver to Colorado Springs.

~

THE DAY FOR THE move to the Springs came. A typical Colorado day, bright with sunshine, crisp air, blue sky. The family engaged in the usual Sunday morning breakfast ritual, pancakes or French toast. The previous day, Ellen had bid goodbye to her friends, spent some extra time with Bev, and now had to say goodbye to her home. She choked up as she wondered what it would be like when she returned.

The car was packed and ready. Pearl, Nate, and Ellen had nothing left to do but put on their coats and go. Without speaking, they stepped into the car. Ellen saw her house disappear from view.

Tom and Ginny were waiting for them when they arrived. They had the spare bedroom cleaned and ready for Ellen and greeted her warmly with hugs and kisses. Ellen was like a beloved niece to them. They had known her since the day she was born. When Ginny led her to the bedroom, she offered, "I kept the dresser top empty so you would have a place to put some of the things you like to look at. Please, make yourself at home."

Ginny departed, and without a word, Pearl helped Ellen unpack and put away the few things she had brought with her.

In the meantime, Nate and Tom sat on the back porch and discussed the arrangements Nate had made for Ellen.

"We came down early so Ellen wouldn't have to endure vacation at home ... and so she could have a couple of weeks to adjust. Mrs. O'Connor, the teacher I hired for Ellen, will come by tomorrow to meet her. She'll draft a curriculum and get an okay from the superintendent in Denver. By the time vacation is over, she'll be ready to begin."

"That sounds just fine, Nate, but have you made any plans for Ellen during vacation? You know the holiday drill here. We're busy until Christmas. We won't have too much time to spend with her, but we'll do our best. I know Ginny has put some ideas together already."

Nate ticked off the plans he and Pearl had made. "She has

a doctor's appointment on Thursday, so Pearl will drive down and spend a long weekend with Ellen. They'll go shopping, have lunch, go to the movies, and spend some time together. I'm not sure about the following week. As much as I'd like to have planned more things for her to do, I think it's best for Ellen to figure out some of this herself. Pearl and I know she's still trying to come to terms with her situation, so some free time may be good for her right now too."

Tom remarked, "Don't worry, Nate. It'll all work itself out. Let's see if the girls are ready for lunch. I sure am."

GINNY HAD PREPARED A pleasing lunch that included stew, a garden salad, and freshly baked rolls. For dessert they had Ginny's famous red velvet cake with ice cream. Ellen felt sure they all noticed she didn't eat much, but nobody said anything.

Finally, Pop stood up. "Well, Pearl, it's getting late. Time for us to head back. Ellen, I have a surprise for you. When Mom comes back on Thursday, I made reservations at the Antlers Hotel for you two. Mom is going to stay until Monday morning."

Ellen smiled and embraced Nate. "Thank you, thank you, Pop." She clung to Pearl as they kissed. "See you Thursday, Mom."

Ginny kept Ellen busy for the rest of the afternoon. After dinner, they all settled down to listen to the radio, since television had just become available in the Springs and Tom and Ginny had not yet made the decision to purchase a set. Ginny took out her quilting materials. Fascinated, Ellen observed her as she worked.

"I didn't know you quilted. How long have you been doing this?" she questioned.

"Oh, my grandma taught me when I was just a little girl. We used to quilt on Saturday mornings. She saved all the scraps of material for me to cut up. Then as I got older, she taught me how to create designs and sew them together, and most important, she showed me the quilting process. I find it relaxing to quilt and listen to the radio. I do it almost every night."

They continued to sit and listen to the radio, and Ellen was mesmerized as she watched Ginny quilt. At nine thirty, after Tom and Ginny's favorite program ended, they said their good-nights and everyone went to bed.

Ellen went to the room that was to be hers for the next several months. It seemed so plain and dreary compared to her room at home, and she felt extremely weary. Every muscle ached. It had been difficult all day to keep from crying. She felt as though she had lost everything—her life, her parents, her home, and her friends. Finally, she couldn't hold it in any longer. She crawled into bed and cried as noiselessly as she could. She didn't want to bother Tom and Ginny. They were both being so good to her. She cried until she finally fell asleep.

WHEN ELLEN GOT UP the next morning, Ginny had already left for work. Ellen stopped in Tom's workshop, greeted him, and then meandered into the kitchen for some breakfast. Still having morning sickness, she was acutely aware of what she put in her stomach. As she ate, she read the note Ginny had placed on the table asking her if she would mind doing the few chores she had listed. Obviously, Ginny thought this would keep her busy so she wouldn't sit around and feel sorry for herself.

Mom came on Thursday. The visit to the doctor went fine; the pregnancy was going along as expected. They shopped, and

Mom bought her some maternity outfits, which really made Ellen want to throw up. Instead, she thanked her. Over the next couple of days they went to lunch, the movies, and the ballet that was in town for the holiday season. The Broadmoor Hotel had a special Christmas program. They took Tom and Ginny to that one. On Monday, Mom prepared to go back to Denver.

Remembering Mom's advice, Ellen became the consummate actress as she prepared for Mom to leave. "Thanks, Mom, it's been a really wonderful weekend. Give Pop a kiss, and tell him how much we missed him."

Mom patted her cheek. "I'm glad I came. I'll call you next week. I won't be able to come back until after New Year's. Besides Pop's annual Christmas party for the employees, we have several holiday parties to attend. You know, busy time."

"I know. It's okay." *It's really not okay, but it's obvious I'm not as important as business and holiday parties.*

LATER, MRS. O'CONNOR CAME over with the curriculum she had put together, to be approved by the Superintendent before the holiday break was over. She and Ellen reviewed the list of studies, discussing it in detail.

Feeling rebellious, Ellen shrugged. "This seems like an awful lot of work to me. I really don't think there's enough time to do all the things you've listed."

Mrs. O'Connor scrutinized Ellen as she cleared her throat. *I need to help this child move on. I can't let her spend her time moping. That wouldn't be helpful. If that means I have to be stern, so be it. I can't let my personal feelings get in the way.* "I'm going to be blunt, Ellen. You have no friends here. There will be no parties, no extracurricular activities, and no sports. You will have nothing but time on your hands. Make the most of it. It can be important to you. Being pregnant is difficult. Your studies can help you through this trying period. If you persevere, you will be the better for it." She looked into Ellen's eyes. "Don't allow this to ruin your life."

AFTER WINTER BREAK, ELLEN began her studies with Mrs. O'Connor. The days came and went. She functioned at robot level. She did as she was told. She felt nothing and didn't let herself think about Kenny. She didn't allow herself to think about anything or anybody. She just existed.

One evening as they listened to the radio and Ellen helped Ginny cut up pieces for her latest project, Ginny said, "Ellen, I've been thinking. Maybe you'd like to make a quilt for the baby so you can send him or her off into the world with a little piece of you."

"Could I Ginny? I'd love to do that."

Ginny helped her design the quilt. It was so precious. It had a soft green border, with the interior divided into squares. Each square was a different color. She alternated yellow, pink, and blue. In each of the squares, she sewed the scraps together to look like objects that had been meaningful to her as a child, like her red rocking horse, her playhouse, her kitten, and her Scottie dog. She hoped her childhood memories would form a connection with her baby that would tie her to him in some small way. During the hours Ellen spent working on the quilt, the lump in her chest didn't seem as large, and she even experienced a measure of peace.

Each evening they gathered around the dining room table— Ellen with the baby quilt, Ginny with one of her projects, and

Tom with his polished stones that he set into jewelry. They listened to their favorite radio programs.

On one particularly cold evening near the end of January, the phone rang at exactly eight o'clock. It startled the three of them, since the phone seldom rang in the evening. Ginny answered.

"Hello. Pearl, is that you? What did you say? Oh, God, is he going to be okay?"

Ellen jumped up and ran to the phone. "Ginny, what's the matter?"

Ginny put her hand over the receiver. "It's your mother. Your dad has had a heart attack. Here, talk to your mother."

She handed the phone to Ellen.

"Mom, what's happening? Is Pop okay?"

"Calm down, honey," Mom sounded weary. "Early this morning your father started having terrible chest pains. I took him to the hospital. Oh, Ellen, he's had a serious heart attack."

"He is going to be okay, isn't he?"

"Right now he seems to be stable, but we'll just have to wait and see. There's nothing any of us can do. I'll call as soon as I know anything. In the meantime, I'm staying at the hospital. I'm in the second floor waiting room, the number is East 5665, if you want to reach me. We probably won't know anything until after nine tomorrow morning. That's when the doctor said he'll update me on Pop's condition."

Ellen wailed. "Oh, Mom, I'm so sorry, it's all my fault. I just know it's all my fault."

"It's not your fault, Ellen. That's not why a person has a heart attack. Please, don't make it any more difficult for me than it already is. Please."

Ellen pulled herself together. "Okay, Mom. I know Pop will be okay. He's tough."

"That's better. I'll talk to you tomorrow."

Ellen hung up the phone. "Oh, Ginny, what am I going to do?" she wailed inconsolably.

By this time, Tom had wheeled around to the phone, and the three of them huddled together.

"I'm so sorry, Ellen," Tom said. "But I know Nate. He's a fighter, he'll be okay."

They got ready for bed. Cold permeated Ellen's every bone. She pulled the covers around herself and wept. *Oh, God, please, please, let Pop be okay. Will my world ever be right again? Why did this all have to happen? I never thought I was a bad person.* The thoughts whirled relentlessly around in her head as she tried to go to sleep. She slept fitfully.

They were all up early the following morning. Tom and Ellen went about their business. Ellen gathered up the breakfast dishes, filled the sink with hot soapy water, and began the daily cleanup. When she finished, she went to her room to study the day's lessons.

When Mrs. O'Connor arrived, the first thing she did was clasp Ellen in her arms. "I'm so sorry. Ginny called to tell me about your father. I know the next few days will be extremely difficult, so I think we'll make a slight change in our plans." Mrs. O'Connor shuffled her papers. "Here's what I want you to do. I want you to write a paper. I want this paper to be about your father, and about your relationship with him. I want you to write about all the things you've done together through the years. Write about the things he's done for you. Find out who your father really is, besides being your father. He's a husband, a friend, a businessman, a community leader. I want you to explore all these aspects of your father's life and write about how they impact you."

Just then, the phone rang. Ellen leaped up and ran to answer it. "Mom?"

"Yes, Ellen, it's me." She sounded exhausted. Ellen held her breath.

"Your father is holding his own. The doctor seems to think he has a better than even chance of making it. The next couple of days will be critical. We'll know better after the next forty-eight hours."

"Have you been able to see him or talk to him?"

"I can see him for five minutes every hour, providing he remains stable."

"Will you tell him I love him and miss him?"

"Of course, darling. He knows that, but I'll be sure to remind him. I'll call again this evening when Tom and Ginny are home. Do your best not to worry. We will get through this. I know your father will be okay. He's a strong man." Pearl's voice faltered. Ellen heard her swallow. "I love you, Ellen. I'll call you later."

The next few days were a nightmare. Tom, Ginny, Mrs. O'Connor, and her husband, Greg, all stayed close by to support Ellen. Miraculously, Nate began to recover.

In the meantime, Ellen found solace in the paper she was writing. It amazed her to find out how little she actually knew about her dad. After learning Nate was doing better, Ellen called her mom and asked her for some stories about Pop. As Pearl sat in the waiting room, she made notes about Nate, his family, and what she knew about his early life. She related these stories to Ellen in their conversations. Ellen found great comfort in these nightly tidbits.

The day came when Pop was able to go home, and for the first time Ellen was able to talk to him. A weight lifted from her shoulders. She could almost breathe.

Her days resumed their usual rhythm. That is, if you could call being unwed, pregnant, and away from home usual. Even though she ate little, she gained weight. Her waist had thickened, and she definitely had a belly. The time had come for her to wear the maternity tops and pants so she would be more comfortable. Recently, she had begun to feel some little scratches in her stomach. She nearly passed out when she realized it was the baby making his presence known.

TEN

ONE SATURDAY MORNING, ELLEN decided to spend the day reading the book Mrs. O'Connor had given her. Because it was an historical romance novel, Mrs. O'Connor felt it would help take Ellen out of the present and allow her some surcease from her present troubles. *Lorna Doone* was a formidable looking book, and it would probably take eons to read. She had just settled down in her favorite chair when the phone rang.

"Hi, Mom. What are you doing home on Saturday morning? Did you change your hair appointment?"

"Honey, I have something important to discuss with you. Stay calm and wait until I'm done."

Suddenly, Ellen felt hot, and she began to tremble. "Okay, Mom. Shoot," she said, in as ordinary a tone of voice as she could muster. She heard Pearl take a deep breath.

"First, your dad has sold Gordon's. Anderson's Bridal Shops has wanted that location for some time, and Mr. Anderson offered an excellent price, so Pop decided to sell the business."

"What will Pop do if he isn't running Gordon's? It's his life. I can't imagine him without the store."

"That's the second thing, Ellen. We're moving to San Diego as soon as the deal is closed. He's anxious to make a fresh start. He knows it will break his heart to see what they are going to do with the shop. So, the sooner, the better."

Speechless, Ellen could barely comprehend what Pearl told her. She moaned. "But what about me, Mom? Are you just going to leave me here by myself?"

She panicked at the thought of her parents moving hundreds of miles away. *How can they do this to me?*

"Ellen, I know this is a big shock. We hate to do this, but right now your dad's health is the most important thing. He needs to live in a lower altitude. Thank God, you're with Tom and Ginny. We know you're being taken care of. As soon as you have the baby, you'll come to San Diego and go to school there. When you get a chance to think it over, you'll realize this is the best thing. You won't have to go back to the same school and face your old friends and bad memories."

Thoroughly unnerved, Ellen could feel her whole world spinning, her life being taken away from her. *Oh, God, what's to become of me? What's happening?*

"I know this is hard, but it'll work out, you'll see." After a long pause, Pearl continued, "Ellen, say something."

Ellen swallowed hard and tried to compose herself. "I understand, Mom. But you'll call me and write to me, won't you?"

The tears came then, and she blubbered. That opened the floodgates, and Pearl cried too. Together they bawled for some time, and then Mom gurgled, "I wonder how Pop will look in Bermuda shorts and sandals."

It seemed so weird and out of nowhere Ellen laughed hysterically, and then Mom joined in. When they were finally exhausted, Ellen said quietly, "I know you have to do this. Please don't forget me, though. I'll miss you so much."

"Ellen honey, we could never forget you. We'll call and send pictures of the new house. You know how Pop has always loved San Diego and wanted to retire there. The weather is beautiful all the time, and you'll see the ocean. It'll be wonderful."

"Of course, Mom, wonderful." Almost mechanically, she echoed Mom's words.

Pearl paused. "Honestly, Ellen, I really don't want to leave you, my home, my friends, or Denver. But I have to do what I have to do for Pop's sake. I must be strong."

Ellen didn't have the strength to talk another minute. "Give my love to Pop. Let me know when you move."

~

ELLEN WORKED DILIGENTLY ON the essay assignment. She found her mother's reminiscences fascinating, and she thoroughly enjoyed the task, especially since it kept her mind off her parents' move. She hadn't realized her father was active in the downtown retailers group and served as an officer. When called upon to help some needy person or a social cause, he was always ready to donate time and money. Mom told her that Pop was much admired by his fellow retailers, who often sought him out for advice. When Ellen finished her essay, she felt satisfied she had done a creditable job. She confessed to Mrs. O'Connor that she was almost sad she had finished.

"That's a good sign, Ellen. The next logical assignment is to do an essay about your mother," replied Mrs. O'Connor.

"But I had Mom to help me write about Pop. Now they're both gone, and there's no one to help me."

"Nonsense," Mrs. O'Connor responded briskly. "You have Ginny and Tom here to help you. Plus you can write to your dad for stories about your mom. I'm sure he'd be pleased to help."

"Yes, I'll do it." Writing another paper excited her.

She realized she hadn't felt complete after she finished the paper about Pop—like there was something more she needed to do. Besides, it would give her a chance to have some communication with Pop.

A few days later when Mrs. O'Connor arrived, she appeared visibly excited. "Ellen, this paper about your father is one of the best pieces I have ever seen written by a student. It is a pleasure having a student of your abilities."

Since Mrs. O'Connor was not one to hand out compliments, this was indeed high praise coming from her. Impulsively, Ellen embraced her.

"Thank you, thank you. That means a lot to me."

Mrs. O'Connor didn't want Ellen to know how moved she was. In a neutral voice, she responded, "Okay, Ellen." She gave Ellen a squeeze and added, "Time to get back to lessons now."

The rest of the day followed the regular routine, but Ellen basked in the glow of the praise. It was a lift she needed badly. There were precious few moments when her heart felt lighter than stone.

~

ELLEN FINISHED HER PAPER about Mom. She was even more excited about this essay. This paper had been a revelation to her. *My mother, I thought I knew her, but I don't really. She has always been the one who took care of me, scolded me when I behaved badly, hugged me when I needed it, and kept me from harm. But she has so many other facets to her life too. She's more than a mother to me and a good wife to Pop. She's also a good friend to many, a leader among women, a gracious hostess, and a tireless volunteer. I've had so many bad thoughts about her lately. I should have realized she's only interested in doing what's best for me.*

Ellen presented the paper to Mrs. O'Connor. "I hope you'll like this paper as much as you did the one about my dad. I really learned so much about my mom."

"I'm eager to read it, Ellen. I'm sure it will live up to my expectations. It's almost the end of the term, and you've done well, even though it hasn't been easy. I'm proud of the way you've handled yourself during this difficult time."

Ellen beamed. "Thanks to you."

Mrs. O'Connor continued. "I also know you've reached the point where doing anything is becoming difficult. The last weeks of a pregnancy can be challenging. Since there's only a couple of weeks before the end of the semester, I thought I'd let you choose what you'd like to do."

Mrs. O'Connor was right. Ellen had reached the point where she was so large that there was no comfortable place to be. She was always tired, and her back ached constantly. The baby was quite active and the constant kicking and moving only reminded her of the impending birth. Thinking about giving birth and the actual birth process really frightened her. She wasn't sure she could do it. Tom, Ginny, and Mr. and Mrs. O'Connor all tried to be supportive and helpful, but all the support in the world didn't help how uncomfortable and scared she was beginning to feel.

"Thanks," Ellen said gratefully. "I think I would just like to read and discuss an interesting book."

"A perfect way to end the school year. I'll see what I can find, unless you already have a book in mind."

"I'll let you decide. I don't really know what I want to read."

The next day, Mrs. O'Connor gave Ellen *Gone With the Wind.* "I think this will make for an interesting read and discussion."

"I agree. I've been wanting to read it for some time."

As she read the book, Ellen couldn't help but compare herself to Scarlett. *I had the best of all worlds, and then this awful thing happened. Scarlett seemed to be a strong woman who conquered her troubles and still had hope and determination. Will I get through this? Is tomorrow really another day? I don't know if I'm as strong as Scarlett was. I don't know if I can make it.*

On the morning of June 6, Mrs. O'Connor pronounced school over. "It's been a pleasure working with you, Ellen. I hope you'll keep in touch with me."

Ellen hugged her. "Thanks for all your help. I couldn't have gotten through the last few months without you. I'll always be grateful."

Mrs. O'Connor hugged Ellen and gave her a card with her name, address, and telephone number on it. "I mean it, Ellen, keep in touch. Please call me after the baby is born and let me know what your plans are."

She gave Ellen one last squeeze, gathered up her belongings, and departed. Ellen, bereft, sat on the sofa with her head bowed. Once again, someone she loved, someone she'd come to count on, someone who'd become important in her life, was deserting her.

~

ELLEN SWIPED AT HER tears and realized it was time to leave the park and go home. The memories were still so fresh and painful. Once again, she felt the bitter taste of those tears, and once again she felt no healing.

ELEVEN

ELLEN LET HER EYES wander around her room. She could hardly move around, it was so jammed with things for college. Mom had certainly gone overboard buying her new clothes and other necessities.

Admittedly, the new outfits pleased Ellen. Somehow, after she'd had the baby, her figure was not quite the same. She had lost all the weight she had gained, but she found subtle changes in her body. It was softer with more curves and less angles. She had matured after the birth, and her new clothes reflected those changes. She also was ready to rid herself of her old clothes with their old memories.

Will getting rid of these things really make the memories disappear? Or am I just kidding myself? Oh, God, I need to get rid of this pain.

Ellen spent the morning packing. She had a lunch date with Pop at one. This was officially her last day at Titillations. At noon she paused in her packing, washed up, put on some make-up, and went downstairs.

As she wandered into the kitchen, the smell of fried chicken cooking made her mouth water. Pearl looked up from the frying pan. "You're ready to go? The keys are on the hall table. Enjoy yourself, but don't eat too much. Please save some room for fried chicken tonight."

Ellen kissed Pearl on the cheek. "Thanks, Mom, I will. See ya later."

Ellen had mixed emotions about today. She had enjoyed working at the store, but it still hurt and made her ache seeing the children day in and day out. She would miss Max and his stories, but she was ready to commence learning again. As much as it made her stomach queasy to think about leaving her comfortable surroundings, she knew she had to get on with her life. She tried to sort out all these feelings as she drove, when she suddenly realized she was already at the store.

Pop had been watching for her. As he waited for Ellen to arrive, he smoothed out his curly hair, tucked his shirt in, and hitched up his pants. He gave Ellen a kiss as she got out of the car.

"The usual, or would you like to go someplace different today?"

"The usual. I couldn't miss saying goodbye to Max. He'd never forgive me."

As they sauntered to the coffee shop, Nate inquired, "Did you finish packing yet?"

"Almost. I should be done this afternoon."

Nate nodded. Max was waiting for them at the door and gave Ellen a bear hug when they entered the shop.

"Nu, is the college girl ready to go to college?"

Max took their order, then came back to the table, and they sat and reminisced.

Ellen turned to her father. "You know, I never did hear your version of how you came to open a store here."

"You remember when you were little and we used to just take off in the car and drive to different places to see what interesting things we could find?"

Ellen giggled. "How could I forget our adventures? We ended up in some very strange places."

"After we arrived in San Diego, I drove around the different beach towns every morning. Somehow I always ended up here on Mission Beach, where I *kibbitzed* with the various storeowners. One day I noticed that my friend Jack was having a liquidation sale, so I said to him, 'You're going out of business?' He said he was getting old and tired, and his wife wanted him to retire. He wanted to make his wife happy, so he was going to do it."

Nate closed his eyes, remembering that day. "So then I asked him if he would miss being here. I told him, 'Since I stopped working, the only thing keeping me from going crazy is coming down here to see you guys every day.'"

Max broke in. "It was obvious to all of us that Nate was like a man without a country. We weren't surprised when he rented Jack's place."

Nate told her how he thought about Jack's shop as he drove home, and that's when Titillations was born. "Your mom knew as soon as I came home that something was up. I'll tell you, she's one sharp cookie."

"As if I didn't already know that," Ellen said.

"She wasn't easy to convince, though. I had to swear I would keep it a relaxed kind of business, not the kind of hustle that Gordon's was. Finally she agreed, and that basically is how I got started."

Max interjected. "What we didn't realize was what a fantastic businessman Nate is. He's brought a tremendous number of people to the area. I haven't worked this hard in the last five years. Not that I'm complaining, you understand."

Ellen chortled. "I believe you. Thanks for making my favorite lunch, Max. But as much as I'd love to just sit here with the two of you all afternoon, it's time for me to get home and finish packing."

"Before you leave," Max said, "I want to remind you that going to college is going to be a fantastic experience for you. Take advantage of every opportunity that comes your way. And don't forget to think about old Max from time to time."

Then Ellen kissed and hugged Max, who blushed bright red.

"Pop, would you walk me back to the car?"

Once they got to her car, Nate said to her, "Ellen, I just want you to know how much I've loved having you at the store this summer."

"Thanks, Pop. I've enjoyed it too." She blew him a kiss as she drove off.

After dinner she headed to Balboa Park. *This is my last time at the park for a while. I hope I can find a place like this near school where I can get away.* She settled down and once again went back to the day just a few months ago when Mrs. O'Connor left.

ELLEN WAS STILL CRYING after Mrs. O'Connor departed, when the phone rang. "Hullo," she sniffled.

"Ellen, is that you?"

"Mom, is that you?" Ellen bawled into the phone.

"Honey, what's wrong?" asked Pearl. "Is everything all right? Where is everyone?"

"Everything's fine. Tom and Ginny are at work, and Mrs. O'Connor is gone. School is over, and I feel awful. I just wish it was all over."

Pearl sounded relieved. "I just called to tell you I'm coming out to be with you until the baby is born. I'm taking the train. I'm leaving on Wednesday and will be there Thursday. I hope Ginny can pick me up."

"Oh Mom, I'm so glad you're coming. I need you so much. I'll have Ginny call you."

"I've missed you so much, honey. I can hardly wait to see that beautiful *punim* of yours."

"Gosh, Mom, I look just like an elephant, and I'm miserable."

"Shh. It'll be okay. Now stop crying, put your feet up, have a nice glass of milk, and then take a little nap. I'll say goodbye now. I love you. Oh, and your dad sends his love too."

"Okay, Mom. Tell Pop I love him too." For some reason after Ellen hung up, she felt more forlorn than ever.

Later, when Tom and Ginny got home and Ellen shared her mom's plans, they were pleased with the news that Pearl was coming.

"I wonder why Nate isn't coming with her," Tom mused. "If Pearl is coming alone, then Nate must be doing okay."

"Let's call now to get the details," said Ginny.

"Of course." Tom handed her the phone.

"Hello, Pearl. This is Ginny. We're excited you're coming. Just give me the time, and I'll be at the station."

Pearl gave her the arrival details.

"Do I understand that Nate isn't coming with you?"

"That's right. The shop Nate opened is wildly successful, and until he finds more help, he can't get away, so I'm coming alone."

"How exciting. Well, we look forward to seeing you."

Ellen was disappointed. She desperately wanted to see her dad. Not having seen him since before he had the heart attack, she needed some assurance that he really was okay. However, now that plans had been made and her mom would be there in a matter of days, she felt relieved.

Ginny commented, "Ellen, we'll need to plan a special dinner for your mom. What do you think she'd like? Tomorrow we'll go shopping."

After she hung up, Pearl sat by the phone for several minutes, sadness permeating her being. She knew the real reason Nate wasn't coming was because he didn't want to see Ellen pregnant. He would see that she was taken care of, and he would do everything in his power to protect her. However, his disappointment and the reality of the situation were more than he could bear.

Pearl felt sick about it, but she understood Nate's feelings and deemed it best to leave well enough alone.

PEARL WAS HAPPY TO be on her way to Colorado. She loved San Diego, but it wasn't home. Not really. She longed to smell the crisp, fresh air of Colorado, to gaze at the clear blue skies and drink in the beauty of the mountains.

As the train chugged along, she focused her thoughts on Ellen. Pearl tried to visualize how she would look, but somehow the image of Ellen that stuck in her mind was the picture Nate had taken of her last summer in her bathing suit, posing with a beach ball. So young, so carefree, so beautiful. Pearl's heart ached for her daughter. Her life was now irrevocably changed. She would never again be that young, innocent, carefree child.

Pearl looked out the window as the train pulled into the station. She could see Tom in his wheelchair and Ginny behind him. *And, oh my God, a little girl with an enormous stomach!* Her heart sank. *Oh God, look at her, poor child.* She took a deep breath, collected her thoughts, and pasted a smile on her face. She readied herself to get off the train.

"Mom, Mom, oh Mom." Ellen hugged her mother and clung to her as though she would never let her go.

"Darling, you're squeezing the breath out of me." She stared at Ellen. "I'm so happy to see you, you're positively radiant." She reached out to Tom and Ginny. "It's good to see you two, I've missed you both."

The girls, Ginny and Pearl, kissed, and Pearl shook Tom's hand. They picked up Pearl's suitcases, got into the car, and started for home. Ellen didn't speak during the trip. She hung onto Pearl's arm and stroked it, as if to make sure she wasn't dreaming. Pearl sensed how much Ellen had needed and missed her. She was suddenly overcome by guilt. How could she have left her child the way she had? *Poor Ellen,* she thought, *no wonder she felt abandoned. She had been.* Well, she would do her best to make up for it now. Thank God, Nate was doing well. She could give her full attention to Ellen for the next month or so.

When they reached home, Ginny said, "While you unpack, Pearl, we'll get dinner ready. Ellen and I are making some special dishes for you."

Pearl was touched. *Tom and Ginny have taken such good care of Ellen.* "Thank you. Just show me where to put my things, and after I unpack, I'll help."

Tom had cleaned out his office for Pearl. She unpacked and went to join the girls in the kitchen.

Over dinner, Pearl told them with genuine enthusiasm about the shop. "Ellen, I know you'll enjoy working there."

"I'm sure I'll love it," Ellen said politely.

~

WITHIN A COUPLE OF days, things quickly fell into a rhythm. Tom and Ginny went to work. Pearl tidied up the house and shopped for and cooked dinner. Ellen observed her stomach expand even further as she waited.

Dr. Burke now saw Ellen weekly. He indicated in a cheery voice that he was delighted to see Pearl. "Come in, Mrs. Gordon. Have a seat in my office. We can have a chat while Miss Morris is checking Ellen."

He settled back in his chair. "Ellen will be having her baby soon now. It's time for you to get in touch with the proper social service authorities to make arrangements for the adoption. I assume nothing has changed and Ellen still plans to give up the baby." He waited for Pearl to answer.

"Yes, that's not going to change. I'll contact Jewish Family Services. Both Nate and I want the baby to be adopted by a Jewish family. And I'm sure Ellen does too. How soon do you think Ellen will have the baby?"

"As you know, first babies are unpredictable, but I think we can safely assume it will be within the next two to three weeks. Any time after the fourth. Well, it's time for me to check on Ellen. Make yourself comfortable, and we'll both be back shortly."

Dr. Burke finished his exam and helped Ellen up. "Looking good, Ellen. I spoke with your mother about making adoption arrangements. She's going to contact Jewish Social Services. Is that what you want?"

She cringed. "Whatever Mom said is okay," she answered in a small voice. She swallowed hard. "Is it going to be pretty soon?"

"I can guarantee that. By mid-July you will have a baby."

"I'll be glad when it's over."

Studying her for a moment, Dr. Burke spoke in a reassuring voice. "You can get dressed now, and we'll all meet in my office and have a visit." He patted her on the arm and left the room.

Ellen joined Mom and Dr. Burke in his office. "I just gave your mother the necessary papers to start the proceedings. Are you sure this is what you want, Ellen?"

She nodded. Ellen kept her head down, so Mom and Dr. Burke couldn't see how upset she was feeling.

"Usually once you contact the people at the agency, they will get in touch with you within the week. The social worker will want to get the details worked out before the baby is born. In the meantime, take it easy, and I'll see you next week."

Now that the actual commitment had been made, Ellen's stomach shuddered. Her head ached, she felt like vomiting, and she could feel sweat flowing out of every pore. She had always known she couldn't keep the baby, but until now, she hadn't had to face the reality of that decision. For the first time in months, she thought about Kenny, and she wondered what he would have thought at this point. She remembered with revulsion their last meeting when he had said those detestable words. It made her shiver just to think about it. She sighed. *I wish it could be different, but there is no choice besides adoption.*

As Dr. Burke predicted, Jewish Family Services called and scheduled an appointment for the following week. Ellen's blood ran cold at the thought of actually discussing the details.

Pearl surmised what she was thinking. *I know how hard this is for Ellen. It just makes me so sad.* "It'll be all right, Ellen. Once the arrangements are made, you'll feel better knowing you've done your best for your baby." *For some reason, I can't help feeling like we're making a mistake, but there really is no other option.*

JENNY GOLDSTEIN SEEMED LIKE a caring person. She stood at the door, introduced herself to Pearl and Ellen, and after being let in and seated, studied Ellen.

"So now, Ellen, are you certain you want to give your child up for adoption?" She looked directly into Ellen's eyes.

Ellen choked. "Yes," she replied. She struggled to keep from shivering.

Jenny took out her checklist. "Please answer the following questions as fully as you can."

Ellen responded in a monotonous voice to each of the questions. She gave short answers until Jenny asked, "What is the name of the father?"

Ellen expressed alarm. "Do I have to answer that?" she asked with obvious fear in her voice. She had never told anyone who the father was.

Pearl intervened. "You don't have to answer, Ellen."

"No, but any information you can give us will be helpful."

"He's not Jewish," Ellen replied in a shaky voice, avoiding all eye contact.

Ellen continued answering the questions, but Jenny could see that she answered mechanically. Trembling and obviously upset, she kept her head down throughout the rest of the interview process.

Jenny finished with the questions as quickly as she could. "Okay, here's what will happen. After you have delivered and the baby has been examined to make sure it is healthy, you will be given a short time with your child. Then, one of our people will come, have you sign the final papers, and take the baby. I want to stress that it will only be a short time. The sooner we take the infant, the better. Your identity will be kept secret, and the identity of the adoptive parents will be kept secret. That's basically it. Do you have any questions?"

Jenny glanced at both Ellen and Pearl.

Pearl stood, obviously unnerved. "I think we've covered enough for now. If we have any questions, we'll call you. Thanks for your help."

Jenny rose. "We'll be in touch, Mrs. Gordon. Good luck, Ellen. I hope you'll have an easy labor. We'll make sure your baby has a good home with parents who will love and take care of your child the way you would."

Most of her interviews were like this, so she knew when to quit. With one rapid movement, she gathered up her papers and left.

~

AS SOON AS JENNY had gone, Ellen bawled. "It's so awful, Mom. It's just awful. I don't think I can bear it."

"Shh, it'll be okay. I know it's hard. Just remember, we all love you, and we're doing what we think is best."

The days dragged by. Tom, Ginny, Pearl, and Ellen celebrated the Fourth of July without any fanfare. They talked briefly to Nate, who was in the midst of a busy holiday season.

"I'm looking forward to you coming home," he said to Ellen.

"Me too."

Ellen's only thoughts at the moment were to get this pregnancy over with. Everything else was unimportant.

On July 9, Ellen woke up, and she could barely drag herself around. There was no satisfactory place to sit. She wasn't relaxed lying down, and she couldn't walk because the baby pushed so hard on her legs.

"This could be the day," Pearl proclaimed. "I think that baby is telling you it wants to come out."

Ellen sighed. "I hope so. I don't think I can stand this much longer."

Just after lunch, she had her first labor pain. When Tom and Ginny arrived home, the pains were coming regularly. Mom announced to everyone, "I think it's time to call Dr. Burke."

When Miss Morris answered, Pearl told her that Ellen was having labor pains. "When the pains are three minutes apart," she instructed, "take her to the hospital. It could be hours yet. Once you get to the hospital, the staff will check Ellen and let Dr. Burke know her status. Give her my best."

Mom and Ginny finished packing Ellen's suitcase. Ginny folded up the quilt Ellen had made, wrapped it in tissue, and put it in a box. Then they had a light dinner. Nobody felt hungry.

After dinner Tom announced, "Time for our favorite radio shows." Trying to bring some levity and distraction to the situation, he turned on *The Shadow*, which was followed by *Mr. District Attorney*. In the meantime, Ellen whimpered and clung to her mom, as Pearl kept track of her daughter's pains. By ten o'clock, the contractions were coming every three minutes. Ellen, frightened, complained about how miserable she felt.

"It looks like it's time to go to the hospital," Mom said.

"I agree," Ginny replied as she went to get her purse. "Are you coming with us, Tom?"

"Of course. I couldn't possibly stay home. I'll just grab some of my journals to keep me busy."

Upon their arrival at the hospital, a nurse pointed Pearl, Ginny, and Tom to the maternity waiting room and whisked Ellen to the maternity floor in a wheelchair. For Ellen, the rest of the night was a blur. The nurse gave her a shot to help relieve the pain. Finally, at 7:06 a.m., the baby was born.

"It's a fine baby boy, Ellen," Dr. Burke announced. "He has ten fingers and ten toes, and he seems to be just fine. Now, open your eyes and look at him." With that pronouncement, he laid the baby on Ellen's stomach. "We'll cut the cord, clean him up, weigh and measure him, and soon we'll bring him back to you."

Exhausted, Ellen opened one eye and then the other. She gazed at her baby in wonder. *My life will never be the same.* It was strange seeing him. He had been inside her for so long. *I often wondered what he would look like, and now here he is. God, he is so tiny.* She felt tired and grateful when the nurse picked him up. Then she felt herself being rolled somewhere. When she opened her eyes, she was neatly tucked into a hospital bed, where she immediately dozed off.

Suddenly, Ellen felt herself being shaken as a nurse said, "Ellen, wake up, here's your baby." Instantly, she was awake.

"I'm going to leave him with you. The folks from Social Services will be here soon to have you sign the final papers." She handed the infant to Ellen.

As she gazed upon her son, Ellen realized she needed to give him a name. Now. Knowing how difficult his life might be, she decided to name him Daniel, remembering the story of Daniel in the lion's den. Tenderly, she swaddled him in the quilt she had made for him and kissed the top of his head.

Just then Pearl came in. She was stopped momentarily when she saw Ellen holding her baby. There was no holding back the tears now. Both Ellen and Pearl cried as they looked over the baby, stroked him, and kissed him.

It seemed only seconds before there was a knock on the door. "Come in," Ellen said, her voice quavering.

It was Jenny. Jenny came to the side of the bed. "It's time, Ellen. Are you ready to sign the final papers?"

"Yes," she sobbed.

Pearl put her arm around Ellen's shoulders protectively, then grabbed her hand and held her close.

"You are aware you are giving up all rights to your baby and that you are doing it voluntarily without any coercion from anybody?"

"Yes," Ellen whispered.

Jenny took the documents from her briefcase and handed them to Ellen. "Sign here at the bottom, and put today's date underneath."

Trembling, Ellen signed her name.

"It's time," Jenny stated in as gentle a voice as she could muster. These situations were always difficult.

Ellen picked up Danny, caressing him one last time. Handing

him to Jenny, she told her, "Make sure his quilt goes with him. I want him to know his mother loved him."

"I'll make sure it goes with him. Goodbye now. Take good care of yourself. I promise I'll take good care of your baby." She took Danny and departed.

Ellen's chest burned with excruciating pain, and she wailed. Pearl tried to comfort her, holding her and patting her back, as though she could assuage the pain Ellen felt.

By the end of the week, Pearl and Ellen were ready to leave for San Diego. Ellen was anxious to escape the place where she had experienced so much sorrow. Ginny and Tom took them to the train station. They all embraced, and then Pearl and Ellen got on the train, trying to get away as quickly as possible from a chapter in Ellen's life that they both wanted desperately to forget.

~

COMING BACK TO THE present, it was time for Ellen to bid farewell to the park and say goodbye to the spot where she had spent so many evenings during the last year. Once again, she wept an ocean of tears. This time her tears, still filled with bitterness, were because she had been so naïve and stupid. The pain still burned hot inside her. And, once again, there was no healing.

PART TWO

TWELVE

AS ELLEN WATCHED, SHE couldn't decide who was more excited, Mom or Pop. Pop kept scratching his head as he tried to figure out how to cram all the boxes and her suitcases into the car. Mom bit her pencil in between checking the list and observing Nate pack and repack.

"Mom, Pop, relax, we're not going that far. It's only a few miles. If I forget anything important, you can always bring it to me."

"You're right, dear," Pearl said. "I'm just so excited for you. I know how wonderful this experience is going to be. I always wanted to go to college, but, of course, it wasn't possible. I'm just so happy you're able to go."

Ellen's stomach churned as the butterflies fluttered around, making her nauseated. She wanted to go to college, but she was also apprehensive. Now that the time had come, she wasn't certain she wanted to go through with it. Yet, here she was, packed and ready to go, so it really was too late to change her mind. The decision had already been set in motion.

After a short drive, they reached the campus. The first time they visited early in the summer, Ellen felt awed by the sense of timelessness the buildings inspired in her. Once again as they approached, the feeling of timelessness and serenity calmed her. Pop slowed, as they weren't quite sure where her dorm was located. Finally, Ellen saw it ahead. "There, Pop, there it is."

Relieved, Nate drove up to the dorm. There were several other cars already parked, spilling out parents, girls, dogs, cats, little brothers and sisters, lamps, suitcases, and other assorted items.

"First we should check in and find your room, and then we can carry things in," Nate instructed.

Pearl nodded in agreement. "Good idea, Nate. Come on, Ellen, let's go check in."

Pandemonium. Parents yelling, kids crying, students running around. Girls carrying pillows and suitcases. Exhausted counselors desperately trying to establish order and give directions.

As they stood trying to decide what to do next, Nate scanned the room, stepped in front of the check-in tables, and announced in a booming voice, "Attention, please."

He paused and then repeated himself. "Attention, please." The crowd looked around to see who had spoken, and when they noticed Nate, everyone quieted down.

"Now, folks, if you haven't yet checked in, please form lines in front of each table so the clerks can register you and give you directions. Thanks for your help."

He turned to the counselors. "I hope you didn't mind my butting in, but the situation seemed to need someone with a loud voice. Permit me to introduce myself. I'm Nate Gordon, father of Ellen Gordon, one of your new students."

Several of the counselors smiled as one said to him, "Thanks for the help. We seem to have needed your voice."

As Ellen observed this scene, she felt the blood rush to her face in embarrassment. Not appreciating the attention suddenly being directed at her family, she watched as Nate gave the counselors his most charming smile.

"I'd like to check in my daughter, Ellen Gordon."

Ellen stepped up to the table. Checking her list, the counselor greeted Ellen. "Welcome to the university, Ellen. I'm Mary Jo, and it just so happens I'm the second floor counselor, where your room is. Your roommate will be Myra Kahn. You're lucky. Room 203 is an end room. They're the largest and have two windows. Here's a key to your room and a booklet that tells you everything you need to know. Good luck. We'll have a meeting later, and we'll get better acquainted then."

Nate found the stairs. "First, let's find the room, and then we'll go back to the car and start unloading."

Pearl and Ellen followed Nate up the stairs.

"Aha, here it is, the first one. Conveniently located, Ellen." He took the key and opened the door.

It was a typical college room, painted puke green with a carpet of an indeterminate beige color. It certainly wouldn't show any dirt. The drapes were beige drab. The normal assortment of non-descript chests, beds, nightstands, desks, and chairs completed the room. To Ellen, it seemed dark and foreboding.

Taking note of Ellen's unspoken reaction, Pearl commented first. "Once you get settled and you and your roommate get all your own things in, I'm sure the room will look much more cheery."

Ellen stood rooted to the floor. Once again her stomach churned. She wanted to go home. Now.

"Okay girls, enough looking. It's time to bring things in."

They hurried back to the car. Ellen still hadn't spoken.

Nate and Pearl chatted. "Nate, I hope you gave Ellen enough money to fix up her room and get supplies."

"Don't worry, Pearl. If I didn't give her enough cash to get started, she can write a check."

"You opened a checking account for her?" Pearl blurted out.

"Why on earth did you do that?"

"Just in case, darling. I opened it at my bank. That way if she makes a mistake and is overdrawn, John Goody will call me and I can take care of it."

Ellen finally spoke. "Thanks Pop. I'll try to be careful and not cause any trouble."

Because it was moving-in time, boys were allowed to be in the girls' dorm, and several milled around, eager to help. When the boys saw Nate unloading, two scurried over to the Gordons' car.

"Hi folks, can we help you unload?"

"Thanks, we'd appreciate any help you can give us."

Nate turned to Ellen and Pearl, "You go on ahead. I'll help the guys, and we'll see you in a few minutes."

Nate handed suitcases and boxes to the boys, as Pearl and Ellen strode back to the dorm. Ellen and Pearl directed the boys where to put things, and after four trips, they had all Ellen's possessions in the room. Ellen surveyed the scene.

"I think I can safely proclaim this a disaster area. Guys, we couldn't have done it without your help. Thanks so much."

"Glad to be of help. If you need anything else, let us know."

"Just a minute, fellas." Nate pulled out his billfold and handed the boys some bills. "You saved this old man from a wicked backache. Thanks."

"Thank you, sir. Not necessary to pay us, but we sure do appreciate it. Thanks again."

"Well, Ellen, it's time for us to go too. I know you're eager to get settled, so we'll let you get to it." Nate took Pearl by the arm. "C'mon, honey, let's go."

"But, Nate, shouldn't we help Ellen unpack?"

Ellen sensed Mom's reluctance to leave, and she didn't want her to go either. It was hard to part again, as she thought of the months she had spent feeling alone and deserted during her pregnancy while she was with Tom and Ginny. She wanted to say, "Don't go yet, I need you," but she remained silent.

Nate remained firm. "No, Pearl, Ellen needs to unpack herself. If we help, she'll spend the next few days trying to find things."

"Yes, dear, I suppose you're right." Pearl opened her arms to Ellen. "Have a wonderful time during rush, dear. Call whenever you want. We'll be happy to hear from you."

She kissed Ellen and embraced her in a bear hug.

"Okay, kiddo, have a great time." Nate embraced Ellen. "Bye now."

As they walked back to the car, Nate remarked to Pearl, "It worries me. She thanked them, but she never even asked any of the boys their names and didn't so much as smile. She really didn't show any emotion at all."

Pearl sighed. "I know. It worries me too. I wish I knew what to do, but I have no answers."

"I guess we'll just have to trust in the powers above." They took one last look at Ellen's dorm, got into the car, and drove home.

～

AFTER THEY LEFT, ELLEN sat down on the bed and cried. *I hope I can do this. It's just so hard. I feel so alone.* She sat that way for ten minutes. Then she wiped her eyes and explored her dresser, desk, and closet.

Well, I guess I might as well get moving. If I can get all my stuff in what's here, I'll consider myself a miracle worker. She unpacked, folded and hung, arranged and rearranged. She re-folded and rehung. Finally, she had her things put away.

The handbook instructions said to tag boxes and luggage with name and room number and put them outside the door, where they would be picked up in the next day or two. She did as instructed.

As she closed the door, she couldn't help but wonder what would happen next. *Will a new door open for me, or will things remain the same?*

THIRTEEN

AFTER ELLEN FINISHED PUTTING away her things, she plopped down on the bed, pooped. Time to take a breather. She checked her watch and was surprised it was already after noon. *It's no wonder I'm starving.* She really wanted to move and get some lunch, but somehow she just couldn't.

Someone knocked on the door, and before she could say come in, the door opened, and a tall, stunning redhead burst into the room. As Ellen rose from the bed, this person flung out her arms, grabbed Ellen, embraced her, and said, "You must be Ellen. Hi, I'm Myra." She let go and stared at Ellen. "Darn, I'm in trouble. You're gorgeous. Just so you know, I planned to be the popular one and have all the boys hanging on my every word. I certainly wasn't planning on someone like you."

Ellen was taken aback, but she laughed and said, "I don't think you need to worry, since I don't date. You're welcome to all the boys."

Myra's big blue eyes got even bigger. "Well, we'll just see about that."

Myra turned her attention to the room. "My God, this place is awful. We have to do something right away. Ellen, can you get a pencil and a piece of paper? We need to make a list."

Before Ellen could say another word, a gang of boys arrived with Myra's stuff, and she began directing them. "Steve, please put those suitcases by the chest. Rick, those suitcases go by the dresser. Bill, please put those boxes by the closet with the biggest one at the bottom." When they finished, she gave each of them one big hug.

"Now, which one of you hunks is going to get us some lunch?"

They all yelled at once. Rick held his hand up for quiet, and in his best Clark Gable imitation of Rhett Butler, said, "Now Miss Myra and Miss ... ," he looked at Ellen. Myra prompted, "Ellen." He continued, "Miss Ellen, please permit me the pleasure of providing the lunch."

Both girls giggled.

"I'd be pleased to have all of you bring lunch. Treat's on me." Myra took some bills out of her purse, handed them to Rick, and said, "Go." The boys made their exit.

As Ellen observed this flurry of activity, she felt hot and her stomach lurched. *Who is this person? Is she always like this? I'm not ready for this.*

Myra whipped a tape measure out of her purse. "Now, back to the list."

Ellen wondered why she had a tape measure in her purse. *What kind of wild women is she?*

First Myra measured the windows, then each piece of furniture, and then the room. She measured the closets. Then she found her own paper and pencil and began making some sketches as Ellen wrote down the measurements.

"Okay, I'm ready. We'll need bedspreads, matching material for drapes and pillows, two bulletin boards, and stuff for decorating and trimming. We'll need a throw rug, a couple of lamps for more lighting. Light bulbs. Shelving material and lining for the closets. A rocking chair, a couple of door mirrors, some framed pictures, a couple of vases, and some flowers or plants. Can you think of anything else?"

Ellen, too dumbfounded to speak, just shook her head.

"Okay then, organize the list by hardware store, department store, et cetera, so we'll have some idea of how many stops we'll have to make. By the way, I have about one hundred and fifty dollars to spend on this stuff, how about you?"

"Uh, that's about what I have too."

Myra grinned. "Great. We're going to have a super room."

"When are you planning to do all this?"

"Why today of course. We have to get it all done. Rush starts the day after tomorrow. We have to be finished by then."

The boys returned with lunch, and they all sat around munching their hamburgers and fries, drinking their Cokes, talking, and getting to know each other. Except for Ellen, who sat without saying a word and just observed.

After they finished lunch, Myra asked who owned the truck. Steve raised his hand.

"Good, I hope you know the area. Ellen and I need to go shopping. We'll need one other strong guy to help." They were all eager to help Myra. She chose Rick. "Rhett Butler was always so helpful." All the boys chuckled, and Rick turned red.

Myra thanked the guys again and grabbed Steve, Rick, and Ellen. She instructed Steve to take them to the local Penney's, Sears, or Wards, whichever was closest. Then she took the list and checked the items on it. Steve, Myra, and Ellen squeezed into the cab, and Rick sat in the bed of the truck.

"Ellen, since you're sitting by the window, see if you can spy any antique stores or secondhand stores on the way. Check for any other stores that might have more interesting things for our room."

"O-kay." Ellen wasn't exactly sure why she was doing this at all, but since she was, she would do as she had been bid. She peered out the window, noting the various stores and names of the streets. During the ride, Myra peppered Steve with questions. Ellen noticed how delighted he was to be the object of Myra's attentions.

As they parked in front of Penney's, Myra handed Steve a list of things to get from the nearby hardware store. "When you're finished, come back and pick us up." She blew the boys a kiss and dragged Ellen out of the truck.

Myra went to the store directory. "Second floor. There's an escalator."

"Uh, do you have some idea of exactly what we're looking for?" Ellen asked.

"Oh, we'll know."

Shopping with Myra was like being in a whirlwind. She flew around choosing the items on their list and checking them off. Finally, Myra asked Ellen to find a cash register where they could dump everything until they finished.

"Yes, boss," Ellen cracked, "I live to serve."

Myra cackled. "Do I detect a note of sarcasm? I guess I'm getting a bit overbearing. I sometimes do that."

"Oh really. I hadn't noticed."

Myra grabbed Ellen and squeezed her. "I'm sorry, just hit me over the head when I get to be too much."

"Don't worry, I will."

Myra will always be too much, and I'm not sure I can live with it. I guess we'll see.

"When you've set everything down, meet me in the gift department."

By the time Ellen got to the gift department, Myra had picked out the rest of the things on the list. She sought Ellen's opinion. Ellen liked everything except the color of the frames on the pictures Myra had picked out.

"Don't worry, we'll paint the frames."

Ellen paid while Myra went to find the boys to carry their purchases to Steve's truck. By the time she finished, Myra returned with Steve and Rick.

The guys groaned as they picked up the mountain of bags. They had all the items on Myra's list and hoped they were finished.

"Ellen, did you see any antique shops or secondhand stores on the way?"

"I did." She gave Steve directions.

Steve pulled out, holding his nose as he stuck out his tongue. This gave his otherwise handsome face a comical look. "Yah, I remember seeing that place. Are you sure that's where you want to go? Looked like a real dump to me."

Myra stuck her nose up in the air and fluttered her long black eyelashes as she sniffed. "Just remember, one person's junk is another's treasure. And a junk shop is just the place to find such treasure."

They drove up to the antique store. "This is not a dump, it's quaint," Myra commented.

"Quaint, shmaint, it's a junk shop," Rick guffawed.

Myra gave him a withering stare as they got out of the truck and walked into the store. A miniature bell tinkled when they opened the door, and a short lady carrying a broom and a dustpan came out of nowhere in response to the bell.

She inquired if she could help them, and Myra said, "Yes, I'm looking for a rocker and some kind of floor lamp. Do you have anything like that?"

The shopkeeper told them where to find the rockers. "I know I have a wonderful deco torchiere somewhere. While you're looking at the rockers, I'll see if I can find it."

Myra pulled out two rockers and turned them around and then upside down. "They're both sturdy. We'll try them both out and then pick one."

Ellen frowned as she held her nose. "Kinda musty and yucky, don't you think?"

"Don't worry. We'll clean up and paint whichever one we choose. You'll never recognize it when I'm finished."

After they decided which rocker to buy, Myra instructed, "While we're waiting, let's check around. You never know what you'll find."

"More yuck, if you ask me," muttered Rick.

"All right guys, enough of the yuck. There are some interesting pieces here." Myra spied a chest. "Aha, here's a great chest. We could put tons of stuff in it." Myra took out her tape measure, measured, and consulted her sketches. "Yep, it'll work."

"Are you serious?" Ellen asked. "That is just disgusting."

"Ellen, you have no imagination. Cleaned up and painted, it'll be perfect. Trust me."

Gawd, she's a real know-it-all. I'm not sure how much more I can stand.

At that moment, the woman appeared with a lamp in tow. "Sorry I took so long. Couldn't remember where I'd put this." Cautiously, she placed the lamp on the floor.

"By the way, I'm Alice, and I own this shop."

Myra held out her hand. "I'm Myra. This is my roomie, Ellen, and our friends, Rick and Steve. This is our first year, and we're trying to find some things to make our room more livable."

"I suspected as much," Alice said. "I suppose that means you don't have much money, either."

Myra nodded.

"Okay, I'll keep that in mind. Now, how about this lamp?"

Myra examined the lamp. It stood about five feet tall. The base was marble and brass, and it had a deco bowl. "Does the lamp work?"

Alice took the cord. "Let's find a plug and check it out."

Myra looked at Ellen. "I think the lamp will work, what do you think?"

The expression on Ellen's face said, "Who are you kidding?" She knew both Alice and Myra had caught the look.

Alice plugged in the lamp, and it worked. She faced Ellen. "With some cleaning up, this could be a great lamp."

Myra considered her next words. "So how much do you think you could sell the lamp for?"

Alice cast her eyes on Ellen. "Would ten dollars be too much?"

Ellen gave Alice a definite *no* face.

Alice got the message. "How about five?"

"Ellen, I think that's a fair price, and we could sure use the light."

Ellen agreed.

Alice directed them back to the rocking chairs. "Did either of these work for you?"

Again, Myra was the spokesperson. "Ellen thought this one seemed a bit more comfortable," she said, indicating the smaller rocker.

"A good choice," Alice responded. "It's in good shape."

"I don't know. It looks to me like it will need a lot of work to clean it up," Ellen said.

"I can make you a good deal. How about twenty?"

Ellen could see that Alice thought she was a pain in the ass. She shrugged her shoulders and looked at Myra.

"Okay, ten," Alice said.

"Ellen, I think that's a good price." Turning back to Alice, Myra told her, "I saw one last thing that might work for us." She led Alice to the chest.

"Yes, now you've found the best piece in the shop." She rhapsodized about what a marvelous piece it was and said she could give it to them for the special price of seventy-five dollars.

Ellen could tell by Alice's body language that she really wanted to get rid of this piece. What Ellen didn't know was that Alice thought the piece a monstrosity—it had been in the shop for far too long, and she'd be happy to get rid of it at any price. Ellen was having a good time now. She knew this game. Based on her gut, she decided to play it cool. She let her face drop.

"Myra, that really is way more than we can afford. Let's get the lamp and rocker and be on our way."

Myra agreed. She shrugged her shoulders. "Thanks anyway, Alice. I guess we'll just pay and be on our way."

Alice inquired, "How much do you think you can pay?"

Ellen looked intently at Alice. "Twenty dollars, tops. That's it. That's all we have."

Alice grunted. "Okay, I have a soft spot for college girls. It's yours for twenty."

They paid Alice, and Steve and Rick moved the items out to the truck. As soon as they were out of sight of the shop, Steve parked the truck, and they all got out and burst out laughing.

"You two are the biggest con artists I have ever had the pleasure of meeting," he shrieked.

"I know, I know," screamed Myra. "How did you ever learn to do that, Ellen? I almost peed in my pants when you did your number on Alice with the lamp. I thought you were going to screw the deal for sure. I was dying because it's such a great lamp. And the rocker. Your face was priceless. And the chest, definitely the final stroke of genius."

"My dad taught me the art of good guy, bad guy bargaining a long time ago. We do it all the time, much to the dismay of my mom, who hasn't a clue how to bargain."

They climbed back into the truck and headed back toward school. They were happy, tired, hot, and sweaty, all except for Myra, who appeared as though she had just stepped out of a fashion magazine. Her auburn hair was perfect, not a hair out of place. Her make-up was still flawless, too, with not a smudge anywhere. Her yellow sundress was still crisp and perfect as well. It all made Ellen furious.

Since it was almost dinnertime, Myra asked the boys if they knew a good place to eat. "Ellen and I will treat."

Ellen was annoyed that Myra made an arbitrary decision about treating for dinner. Not that she minded treating. She just wanted to be consulted. *Gawd, she can be irritating.* On the other hand, she couldn't deny she'd had fun with Myra today.

Steve, always short on funds, liked having someone else pay for dinner, so he was quick to respond. "There's a good Chinese restaurant a few blocks from here. Would that be okay?"

They all concurred. During dinner, Ellen was subdued. Myra and the boys had a swell time laughing and shooting the breeze. Finally, it was time to go.

"Steve, do you have a place where we can clean up and paint tomorrow? We can't take these things into the dorm until they're cleaned and painted."

"Myra, Myra. You could become a real pain in the butt," he said. "We'll leave the stuff in the truck tonight. Tomorrow we can paint in the backyard of the frat house."

～

WHEN STEVE DROPPED THEM off, Myra thanked them

both. "You and Rick have just been super. Couldn't have done it without you."

Rick gave them both his broadest grin. "Don't think we don't know that, Myra. You're gonna owe us big time."

Each boy grabbed a couple of bags and marched to the girls' room. "Well, girls, it's been real, but it's time to hit the sack. I'm beat. How about you, Rick?"

"I'm past beat. See you tomorrow, girls. What time do you want us to be here?"

Myra thought about it and then told them ten in the morning. She gave both of them a hug and waved as they took off.

As Myra closed the door, she turned to Ellen. "I need to sit down for a minute, and then we'll get started."

Ellen groaned. "What do you mean, get started? I'm ready to die now."

"Just rest for a few minutes, and then we'll discuss it."

They both collapsed onto their beds. Ellen was almost asleep when Myra shook her.

"No, no, no." Ellen tried pushing Myra away with her hand.

"Okay, I'll do it myself. Never mind."

Myra unpacked everything they had bought. Then she went to the boxes the boys had unloaded earlier in the day. When she found the one she wanted, she opened it, pulled out her portable sewing machine, and set it on the desk. After cutting and measuring the drapes, she flipped on the sewing machine.

Ellen popped up. "What in the hell are you doing?"

"Making swags, some pillows, a covering and ruffles for our bulletin boards, and ruffles for the lamps." Myra cleared her throat. "Then I'm going to take the stuff from the hardware store and make some shelves, and then I'll be ready to unpack."

Ellen moaned. "I've got a mad woman for a roommate. Can't any of this wait?"

"Nope, gotta get it done. We have to have it all done, so that when classes start, we're ready. I don't want to have any of this left to do. It'll just stress me out." Myra proceeded to sew and hum at the same time.

Grumbling, Ellen got up. "All right, what can I do to help?"

Myra directed her to a box that held some tools and paper to line the shelves. "Can you use a hammer and nails?"

"I'm no expert, but I can do some simple things."

Myra instructed her to hang up the swag holders and put up the nails for their bulletin boards. They worked until three in the morning. By that time, Ellen was down on her knees pleading for mercy.

"Please Myra, we can finish tomorrow. I can't do another thing."

Myra yawned. "You're right. It's time to quit. I'm pooped myself."

And that was Ellen's introduction to Myra. She wondered if she could spend an entire year with such an overwhelming personality. On the other hand, she hadn't thought about Danny all day. She had even felt some stirrings of the old Ellen, the one who joked and always had fun. *This has been some day. Not at all what I expected. It's actually been a pretty good day. I didn't want to, but I think I really like Myra. It promises to be an interesting year … that's for sure. I wonder what's next.*

FOURTEEN

THERE'S AN EARTHQUAKE GOING on in my bed, and I don't even care. I just can't move.

"Ellen, Ellen, time to rise and shine."

Nuts, it's not an earthquake. It's Myra. "Go away, I don't wanna get up. I'm too tired. Go away." Ellen turned to her other side, but Myra persisted in shaking her. "All right, what time is it, anyway?"

"It's seven thirty. There's a lot to do before the boys come."

God, she sounds so cheerful and wide awake. How disgusting.

Ellen moaned. "Are you trying to kill me so you can have the room to yourself?" Her eyes seemed to be glued shut. "You win, I'm getting up."

Myra giggled. "If that's your idea of getting up, you're never gonna get anywhere. I'm going to get some breakfast. I'll bring you something back. What do you want?"

"Coffee, cream, two sugars, toast. Thank you."

Myra chuckled. "Okay. Don't forget to get up."

Now she had no choice. She had to pee. Now. Ellen leaped out of bed, put on her robe and slippers, and ran down the hall to the john. By the time she finished, she was awake. As she sauntered back to the room, Myra came up the stairs.

"I brought you two cups of coffee. I thought you might need more than one. I also brought some cereal. I thought it might taste good."

Ravenous, Ellen attacked the food. "You're a good woman, Myra Kahn. Mmmm, this does taste good."

As Myra sipped her cup of coffee, she gave Ellen the plan for the day. Ellen was to get the room organized while Myra finished unpacking. Then when the boys came to pick them up, Ellen would be dropped off to pick up desk supplies.

"Oh, yes, we'll also need some paper goods and snacks for the party tonight."

"What party? Who's having a party?"

"*We're* having a party. We need to meet the other girls in our dorm. The most efficient way to do that is to invite everyone to our room to get acquainted."

Ellen frowned and groaned. "I can't believe what I'm hearing. I don't want to have a party. And I don't want to meet anyone else."

"Of course you do," Myra said. "Wait and see ... it'll be fun."

Ellen was too tired to argue, so she simply grunted, "Yes."

As Myra unpacked, Ellen tried to make some sense out of the mess. After she made the beds, she put all their purchases in place. When she put down the throw rugs, she was amazed. They weren't even finished, and the room was already transformed. The chintz bedspreads with the flowers and the leaf green accents brought out a glow in the room. *Myra does have a flair for this sort of thing.*

"Not bad, girl." Myra took a moment to admire what they had accomplished so far. "It's shaping up. Okay, stop gawking. The boys will be here soon, so help me lug these boxes and suitcases into the hall, and then we'll be ready."

They heard someone shout the familiar words, "Men on the floor." They greeted Steve and Rick as they approached.

"We'll just grab our purses, and we'll be ready to go."

The boys stood at the door, dumbfounded at the change.

"Wow, you must have stayed up all night."

"Pretty close," growled Ellen. "Myra is a slave driver."

Myra gathered up a bag of tools she had brought with her from home. "Okay, I'm ready."

"Where did you get all those tools?" inquired Steve.

"They're mine. I never go anywhere without them. You never know when you're going to need them."

"Now I've seen everything." Rick chortled. "Have tools will travel. That's our girl Myra."

Steve gave Ellen the telephone number for the frat house as they dropped her off at the dime store. "If you can't find what you want here, just walk up and down the street. You're sure to find everything eventually."

Ellen was glad to be alone, so she could shop at a leisurely pace, since she was still exhausted from yesterday. As she checked items off her list, she felt a sense of accomplishment. Tick, tick, tick. All she had left to buy were snacks for the party. She spotted a store whose sign advertised cold drinks and snacks.

The shop, pleasantly cool, had a counter where one could sit down and have a cold drink. She ordered a cherry Coke. As she drank her Coke, she inspected the shop. Instead of the usual packaged snacks, everything was bulk, and it all looked yummy. She finished her drink, walked around, and after much contemplation, made several purchases. Then she called Steve and asked him to pick her up. She strolled back to the dime store, found a shady spot, and settled back.

In a short time, Steve pulled up, parked, and loaded her bags into the truck. "I thought you bought out the town yesterday, but I guess I was mistaken."

"It does seem like a lot of stuff, doesn't it? How are you guys coming along?"

She hoped to keep him talking so she wouldn't have to carry on a real conversation. She wouldn't know what to say.

"Like gangbusters. You know Myra. She has all the guys in the house working for her now."

When they reached the house and went out back, Ellen could not believe her eyes. There must have been twenty boys all vying to be near the Queen. Myra was busy supervising, putting a touch here and a touch there. The lamp was finished. Ellen was shocked. It looked fabulous. The boys had polished the brass until it shone, and the marble was actually white, not gray.

Myra had painted the rocker a velvety off-white. What a difference a little paint made. Myra worked on the chest, repairing broken drawers and tightening loose pulls. She stopped for a second to find out if Ellen had finished shopping.

"I did."

"Good. I knew I could count on you. Would you and Steve mind getting all of us some lunch now? By the time you get back, I'll have the chest ready to paint. We can get the entire job finished after lunch."

"What am I," Steve quipped, "the local *shlepper*? I know … the answer is yes. And you, Ellen, you look like the *shlepper's* helper, so let's go." Steve good-naturedly swung his thumb over his shoulder.

Ellen felt her face grow warm. Why was Myra throwing her with Steve? She didn't like it, not one bit, but since she didn't know how to get out of it, Ellen shrugged and went with Steve. They bought fried chicken, mashed potatoes, slaw, beans, and Cokes from a local takeout place. When they got back to the house, the hungry hordes attacked the food. In no time at all, they demolished all of it.

"Okay, back to work, guys." Myra gave Ellen a drawer and showed her how to trim it.

Ellen did as Myra instructed and found pleasure in the finished product.

"Did you expect anything else?" inquired Myra.

Before long, they were done. The boys agreed to bring the chest and rocker over at five that evening.

Myra gathered up the picture frames. "Ellen, when we get back to the dorm, we'll make some signs announcing that the party will be after the floor meetings. Then we'll hang the pictures. I'd also like to stop and get some flowers on the way back," Myra added.

"There's a flower shop on the way," Rick told her.

Feeling ready to call it a day, Ellen commented, "I hope we'll have time to take showers, Myra. I'm hot and sticky and generally stinky."

"Don't worry, we'll have time."

They finished hanging the pictures and placed the lamp, then stepped back to observe their handiwork, as Myra asked Ellen, "Well, what do you think, kiddo?"

The delicate watercolors looked beautiful in the soft white frames, and the green walls made a perfect background. The appearance of the room was now bright and cheery, with the colorful bouquets they had bought adding an additional burst of color. The dreary room that had made Ellen so despondent the first time she saw it was gone.

"You're a genius, Myra. I never would have believed this room could look so cool."

Someone knocked. "Come in."

It was Mary Jo. "I'm dropping off schedules for the first day of rush. We'll have a floor meeting after dinner, and I'll go over the schedule. Have your questions ready."

"Thanks. Ellen and I are planning to have a get-acquainted party after the meeting. Would you let us make an announcement at dinner?"

Mary Jo noticed the room while Myra talked. "Wow, what have you girls done? This is spectacular. Most of the rooms are still a mess. Of course you can talk about the party. Wow, how did you get this all done in just two days?"

"Everyone isn't as fortunate as I am to have a dynamo for a roommate," Ellen said with an expression that belied her words.

Myra punched Ellen in the arm. "C'mon, you're glad to have it done."

Ellen rolled her eyes and raised her eyebrows.

Mary Jo laughed. "Okay, you two, I'll see you at the meeting."

~

AFTER THEY FINISHED THEIR showers, Myra noticed that Ellen seemed even more quiet than usual. She wondered if Ellen was just tired or if something was bothering her. *I'll figure it out, sooner or later.* She was already fond of Ellen. What she had noticed so far was the pain in Ellen's eyes. She also noted that Ellen seemed uneasy around boys and didn't say much. *I wonder what could have happened to her. God knows she's pretty, petite, and extremely smart. Not everyone goes to college on a full scholarship. So, it can't be her* looks, *her figure, or her brain.*

To Ellen, she suggested, "Let's check our schedules and compare. Tomorrow is the open house where we get a chance to visit all the sororities."

"I'm dreading it. I really don't want to go through rush, Myra."

Perplexed, Myra frowned. "If you didn't want to go through rush, why did you sign up? Don't you want to join a sorority? I think it'll be a total blast."

"I'm doing it because my mom insisted. I'm not comfortable smiling and making small talk with people I don't know and don't care about. I just wanna go to school."

Very *strange. There is something going on here I obviously don't know about. Ellen is a girl much like my friends and me, and this is just not typical behavior.*

Aloud, Myra said, "I think you should just give it a try. It may not be as bad as you think. You can always quit at any time. Now, let me see your card."

Ellen handed Myra her schedule. Myra checked both and announced, "Well, kiddo, we have pretty much the same schedule, so you can stay with me most of the time. That'll be okay, won't it?"

"I guess."

Myra checked the time. "It's about time for the boys to be here."

She opened the door and saw Steve and Rick carrying the chest, and she directed them where to put it. Puffing, they eased the chest against the wall. Then they brought up the rocker and put it in place.

Myra took out the cushions she had made and tied them on. "Perfect." She admired her work.

"Looks great, Myra. Hope you're finished. You wore us out," Steve said.

Myra gave each of them an affectionate squeeze. "Couldn't have done it without you. Thanks a million."

The boys blushed. "Aw, Myra, we loved doing it. It's time for us to go. I know you're not supposed to talk to guys during rush, so we'll try to find you, and you can wave to us," Rick added.

FIFTEEN

DINNERTIME HAD COME, WHICH presented Myra and Ellen with their first opportunity to meet the other girls in the dorm. After they got their dinner, they searched for a table. They found one with a few empty seats and sat down. Myra handled the introductions.

"Hi, I'm Myra, and this is my roomie, Ellen."

One girl had long blonde hair and blue eyes, the color of a summer sky. She wore a pink pastel plaid skirt, pink blouse with a peter pan collar, and a pink cardigan sweater draped down her back with the arms tied around her neck. "Hi, I'm CeCe," she greeted them.

God, she's preppie, Ellen observed.

Another girl had black, curly hair, dark brown eyes, and an olive complexion. "I'm Joanie," she said in a friendly and warm way. "Welcome to our little group." She seemed the typical Chicago girl from Skokie.

Patty Murphy, tall, lanky, and Irish, sat next to Joanie. She chuckled. "Imagine a nice Irish girl like me in the midst of a bunch of Jewish girls. Mary, Mother of God, what have I done?"

The girls roared. She embellished every story in such a way that she had the girls constantly in stitches. There were other girls at the table, but this group of five bonded immediately.

After dinner, the girls convened for the dorm meeting. The advisors introduced themselves. Then Mary Jo passed out copies of the dorm rules and explained them. Andrea, the Panhellenic rep, covered rush week procedures, after which the girls were given an opportunity to ask questions and make comments.

Myra raised her hand. "Hi, I'm Myra, room 203. This is my roomie, Ellen. After the meeting we're having a party in our room. We have plenty of snacks, and we hope you'll all come and have a super time. Thanks." As she sat down, everyone clapped.

"Thanks, Myra. I declare this meeting over." Mary Jo concluded the meeting.

Ellen and Myra hurried back to their room to prepare for the party. "Um, delicious yummies, Ellen," Myra said as she munched on them as fast as she put them out.

After twenty minutes, girls began swooping into the room. *Wow!* was the first reaction of most of the girls. Myra was gratified. Soon the room was jammed with girls all talking at once. Ellen retreated to a corner, where she sat listening to their chatter. Myra noticed, but she said nothing.

Finally at midnight, Myra yawned. "Okay, okay it's time for everyone to go. We have to be bright and charming tomorrow for rush."

The girls said their goodnights. It still took fifteen minutes for everybody to leave, as they continued talking about rush and getting acquainted. In the meantime, Ellen started to clean up the mess.

"That was a blast." Myra's eyelids drooped, and she yawned again. "Let's get this finished up as quickly as we can. I'm pooped."

When the room was clean, they fell into bed.

There's a lesson here today, Ellen. The room as you first saw it seemed dark and dreary, just like your life. Then Myra came and gave it a fresh look. A fresh start, Ellen, aim for a fresh start.

~~~

THE ALARM WAS SET for seven thirty, so Myra and Ellen could get up early for their first day of rush. Chaos reigned, with girls trying to take showers, wash and set their hair, and put on make-up. Fortunately, Myra had had the foresight to buy a small make-up mirror she and Ellen could use, as well as a full-length door mirror. As soon as they completed their showers, Myra and Ellen retreated to their room.

They finished dressing and stood together, admiring themselves in the mirror. Myra, with her mane of auburn hair, cerulean blue eyes, and a sprinkling of freckles on her face, was definitely the lioness. Ellen, with her short, curly, black hair, green cat's eyes, and beautiful delicate complexion, personified the kitten. Myra wore a kelly green suit trimmed in white; a white blouse and a white scarf with kelly green polka dots completed the outfit. Ellen wore a navy blue suit and a powder blue blouse with white polka dots on it and a bow. Both girls looked crisp and appealing.

Myra nudged Ellen on the shoulder. "Well, aren't we just gorgeous? We'll be a hit, I promise you."

I'm not what you think I am. "Do I really have to do this, Myra? I'm too tired. I would just like to stay here and rest."

"Oh, no, you don't. Just stick with me, kiddo. We'll have a great day, so pull your behind together and let's go."

For Ellen, the day seemed like a nightmare. *What do I have to talk about with these girls? Maybe after they share all the fun*

NO OTHER OPTION | 133

they had during their first year of college, I can share all the fun I had being pregnant. She tried to appear interested in the conversations and did her best to be perky, but she knew she was a dismal failure. Myra tried her best to include Ellen in some of the conversations, but she did not succeed in getting Ellen to participate.

"Wow! What a fantastic day," Myra said, obviously exhilarated by the day's events.

Ellen was in hell. "I hated it, Myra, I just hated it."

Myra doesn't know and doesn't understand. I had a baby. A bastard. I had to give it away. I don't care about something as trivial as sororities. Mom said the past is the past and can't be changed. I have my whole life ahead of me. I'm trying, Mom, but I'll never be able to finish the week.

Every sorority wanted Myra. Only Sigma Delta Tau and Alpha Epsilon Phi invited Ellen back.

"I guess they need someone with a scholarship," Ellen ventured. "I'm sure it's not because of my sparkling personality."

Myra didn't comment. "So, what's it going to be? I can go whenever and wherever you want."

"I don't want to go back to either."

"Okay, I'll pick. Tomorrow, we'll go to SDT for lunch and AE Phi for dinner."

"What about the rest? Aren't you going back to any of the others?"

"Oh, sure, I'll go to a couple of them. Probably the Pi Phi's and the Tri Delts. I'll do them the day after tomorrow."

"Okay, I guess if we do both tomorrow, I'll be able to stay home after that."

The second round of rush proved to be not much better for Ellen, although she did feel slightly more relaxed because there were a few familiar faces. At the end of the day, though, she was exhausted.

"This is such a blast," Myra declared at the end of the day. She was clearly in her element and having a great time. "So which sorority are we going to pick, SDT or AE Phi?"

"*We* are not choosing either. *You* can choose whichever you want. I only promised Mom I would go through rush. I didn't promise I would actually join a sorority."

Myra didn't say anything.

Ellen enjoyed the respite the next day. She spent her time alone reading and resting. Myra came back exhilarated as usual.

"I met some super gals today. It was so much fun."

That night when preference cards were delivered, Myra asked Ellen again, "So, kiddo, what's it going to be, SDT or AE Phi?"

"Neither, I told you I don't intend to join. I'm going to be an Independent."

Myra tried her best to get Ellen to change her mind. Eventually she realized it was hopeless. "Okay, we'll be God Damn Independents. No problem." She hugged Ellen. "Whatever my roomie wants, she gets."

Ellen, horrified, screeched, "Oh, no, I don't want you to do that. You want to join. I don't want you to give it up for me."

"I would be giving up my chance to have my roomie as my very best friend. Being close to you is more important than any sorority. I guess you just don't know me very well yet. I'll still be able to be friends with the girls I choose to be friends with. No sorority can stop me from doing that. Being a GDI will be interesting. I'm sure we'll meet people we probably wouldn't get to know if we were part of the Greek world."

Overwhelmed, Ellen began to cry. "I've never met anyone like you, Myra."

"Dry your eyes, and let's get these preference cards back and be done with it."

Myra turned the cards in and came back to the room. "Well, let's just relax. Tomorrow is a new day. We'll get to know the campus and some of the people." As soon as she finished laying out their plans, a knock came at the door. "Come in."

It was Mary Jo. "I just reviewed your cards. Are you sure this is what you want?"

"Yep, we're sure," Myra responded. "We think the Greek system is not for us. It's too confining. We want to experience all the kids on campus."

"Okay, girls. Just wanted to make sure you weren't overcome with the emotions of the week. Just so you know, I made the same decision you're making, and I've been happy with my choice. Good luck."

They got into their PJs, and again there was a knock on the door. This time, it was CeCe.

"Just thought I'd drop by and see if you've made your choice yet."

Just as she finished her sentence, in popped Joanie, followed by Patty.

"Well, it looks like we're about to have a talk-fest," Myra giggled.

CeCe told the group, "I've chosen AE Phi."

"SDT for me," Joanie announced.

"My choice is the Pi Phi's," Patty added. "How about you guys?"

They were devastated when Myra told them the news. "Now don't fuss, girls. We'll all still be friends. No different than if we were all in different sororities. We'll still have time for each other."

The three girls mulled it over.

"I, for one, would rather spend more time with you and Ellen than the AE Phi's," declared CeCe. "I think I may reconsider."

There was silence for a minute. Then both Joanie and Patty chimed in, "Me too."

Ellen and Myra cheered. "Okay, girls, we'll be our own sorority," Myra said. "We'll be The Club."

They spent the rest of the evening chatting about themselves and their families. Ellen even joined in the conversation. *I guess this is probably the happiest I've been in a long time. It feels good to listen to girl talk, even if I don't have much to say.*

THE HUSTLE AND BUSTLE of rush week was over, and the girls tried to set their class schedules. Ellen, fretting, told Myra, "I'll absolutely die if I don't get Professor Stanford for Humanities. I've heard so much about him during rush from lots of the girls."

An outstanding professor, he also was one of the oddities on campus. He didn't adhere to the standard dress code of the times; instead he wore jeans and sandals. Yet, he was one of the most respected professors on the campus, by both faculty and students.

"You're a scholarship student. I'm sure you'll get every class you want. Stop being a baby, and let's get this done. Now if I could just figure out when I'm going to take psychology I'd be finished," Myra scowled.

Ellen took Myra's schedule. After spending several minutes cross checking the time schedule and reworking it, she let out a triumphant cry. "I've got it!"

She pointed out the class to Myra. "Good. Done. Let's go to the Phi Sig house and get together with the guys. Steve has been pestering me to come over."

Ellen and Myra went over to the house and spent the rest of the afternoon teaching Ellen how to play bridge.

The next day they signed up for classes, purchased their text-books and supplies, had lunch at the frat house, and prepared to start classes. *Now, if I could only learn to follow suit like I learned in bridge and just be a regular person, I might be able to get on with my life. I'm trying, Mom. I really am.*

SIXTEEN

FROM THE MOMENT JONATHAN Friedman stepped into Professor Stanford's class and saw Ellen Gordon, he knew she was his *bashert*, his fate, his intended, his karma, whatever you wanted to call it. He knew it by the way the hair stood up on his arms and the back of his neck. He knew it by the way his heart contracted when he looked at her. He knew it by the way his stomach churned. Jonathan Friedman was smitten. He couldn't get enough of looking at Ellen Gordon.

He also realized it was not going to be easy to get to know this girl. Her eyes said it all. He could see the sadness. He could see it in the barely discernible droop of her shoulders and the way she kept her head down slightly. She rarely spoke to any of her classmates. She only became animated when Professor Stanford called upon her to respond to a question.

The class had been given an assignment to write a paper about *Madame Bovary*. On this particular morning, Professor Stanford singled out one report that exemplified what he wanted in a quality paper. He called upon Ellen to read hers.

When she finished, Professor Stanford told the class, "This is what it's all about. This is what you should be striving for. Thank you, Ellen, for your most excellent work."

Ellen blushed. "Thank you v-very much."

After class, several classmates approached her and congratulated her. Terrie, one of her classmates exclaimed, "To receive such praise from God himself is a huge accomplishment."

John didn't have the guts to talk to her yet. He spent the next few days learning her schedule. He determined his best bet for a chance meeting was the library. She went there most evenings from seven to nine. She even had a favorite cubicle. Afterwards, he watched her walk home.

On the following Tuesday, John chose a cubby where he could observe Ellen coming down the stairs. He calculated that he would have enough time to get to the stairs and accidentally run into her when he saw her approaching. As excited as he was to finally meet her, he couldn't believe how nervous he felt. *Why am I so nervous? She's just a girl. It's not like I haven't gone out with girls before. It's not like I never met a new girl before.* But in his heart he knew this was different. Ellen wasn't just a girl. She happened to be a very special girl.

Ellen gathered up her books and papers at nine on the dot. She headed toward the stairs. He picked up his books and did the same. As usual, she was preoccupied and didn't see him coming. The plan worked. They collided and all her papers and books flew across the floor.

"Oh, I'm so sorry. Please excuse me. I didn't see you," John said as he knelt next to Ellen. "Here, let me help you pick up your books and papers."

She squinted at him, confused for a moment. "It's okay. I wasn't paying attention to where I was going either."

John peeked into her green eyes, and his heart thumped. He was sure she could hear it going ca-jump, ca-jump, ca-jump.

"I know you," he said. "You're Ellen Gordon. You're in my lit class with Professor Stanford. Your report was excellent. *Madame Bovary* was one of those books I found difficult to read. Incomprehensible, really."

She smiled. "It just so happens it's my kind of book. Thanks for helping me pick up. G'night."

"Wait a minute. Can I drive you back to your dorm?"

"Thanks, but I can walk. I do it every night."

"But you shouldn't be walking alone at night. Haven't you heard? There's been a couple of incidents, you know."

"I know, but I can manage. Thanks anyway."

John felt desperate. Damn, she didn't even ask his name. Well, he wasn't going to let her get away, so he followed her.

She walked. He followed. She turned around.

"Are you following me?"

"Yes," he explained. "If you're walking, then I'm walking. I told you, it's not exactly safe for a girl to be out alone after dark."

He could see her amusement, and he could see that she was searching her mind for his name. Finally she said, "Well, John, you might as well walk with me instead of following me. If a campus cop comes by, he'll think you're up to no good."

Elated, John said, "You know my name?"

"Yes, once you mentioned we were in the same class, I remembered you."

"Can I carry some of those books for you? Seems like a pretty heavy load."

Ellen worked hard to contain a giggle before she said, "Thanks, that would be nice."

"Do you go to the library every night?" he asked, desperately searching for something to talk about.

"Yes."

They strolled along in silence for a few minutes. *Oh, boy. She isn't going to make this easy.*

"I'm from LA. Where are you from?"

"San Diego."

Guess I'm going to have to carry this conversation by myself. He made some small talk about his classes, before they reached her dorm.

"Thanks for escorting me. It's nice of you. See you in class."

"You're welcome, I was happy to do it. See ya tomorrow."

He waved as he left. Now he had to walk all the way back to the library to get his car, but he didn't mind. He'd finally made contact.

~

ELLEN DIDN'T EVEN MENTION the encounter to Myra. She figured she had put him off with her attitude and he wouldn't bother talking to her again.

"I met him," Myra announced after they had put on their PJs and settled down for their nightly exchange about the day's events. The events were usually Myra's, but Ellen liked to listen.

Ellen, startled for a moment, thought Myra meant John, but she quickly realized that wasn't possible as she questioned, "Him who?"

"The man I'm in love with, that's who."

"And who might that be? Does this man have a name?"

"Of course he has a name. It's Robert Snyder. He's a Phi Sig. Somehow we just happened to miss each other these last few weeks. I met him when I went to the house to play bridge today. He was my partner. Just looking at him made me melt. I almost forgot how to play. So, what do you think? Have you ever met him or heard anything about him?"

"Can't say that I have."

"You're no help at all."

Exasperated, Myra twirled a curl at the back of her head. She did that whenever she was agitated.

"You didn't ask for my help. You asked if I knew him. I don't. Did he ask you out?"

"No, but he said he would call me. I'll just die if he doesn't."

"Don't worry, he'll call. Anything else?"

"Not really."

Ellen wondered as she settled down to sleep if the collision with John really had been an accident. He followed her and insisted on walking her back to the dorm. He kept trying to make conversation. Hmm … did it mean something?

~

THE NEXT DAY, JOHN stopped to talk to her after class and accompanied her to her next class. "Are you going to the library tonight?"

"Probably." Suddenly she felt a slight shiver go up her spine.

"I'll probably be there too. I'll walk you home if I'm there."

"Okay, thanks." She knew he would be there. He was obviously trying to make a move on her, but she was having none of it. She had no intention of going out with him … or with any other boy. *Thank you, but I'm here for an education. I have no time for boys. Hell, admit it, Ellen, what boy would want to go out with you if he knew what you had done?*

Yet Ellen couldn't help being flattered by his attention. She also couldn't help noticing his big dark brown eyes, curly brown hair, and boyish grin. She also noticed how muscular he appeared to be under his T-shirt and khakis.

ONE THING YOU COULD say about John Friedman ... he was patient. He had an older brother, Josh, and an older sister, Ruth. He had a younger brother named David. He was a middle child. As a middle child, he had to be patient. It seemed he was either too young or too old for whatever it was he wanted at any given moment. "Be patient," his dad always told him. "You'll get what you want when the time is right."

So he practiced patience, and slowly but surely he became friends with Ellen. Every night he escorted her home from the library. He even stopped taking his car, so he wouldn't have to run back to the library. Instinctively, he knew he shouldn't ask her for a date yet. *Just be a friend for now,* he reminded himself.

SEVENTEEN

AS ELLEN, FEELING REASONABLY happy, sat waiting for her friends to arrive at Pete's Pizza Parlor, she thought about what a wonderful group of friends they'd become. She considered how each of them had brought something different to her life.

Myra. How could I have ever thought I wouldn't like Myra? Now, she's my best friend. She constantly cajoles, confronts, and challenges me. She defends me, listens to me, and loves me. I could never imagine not having Myra in my life now. Like when she dragged me to that lecture about politics that I didn't want to go to and it turned out to be so exciting and stimulating, I talked about it for days.

CeCe. With all her wealth and designer clothes, she never flaunts that wealth. She's a simple, down-to-earth person. She's generous with herself and her money. I remember when I was complaining to her about a girl in my class who was always harassing and being nasty to me. 'Ellen, just listen to her and be gracious. Don't respond to her taunting. Be above it all. Try to be her friend. I'm guessing she's just jealous and wants your friendship.' CeCe was so right. I'm grateful for her friendship as well.

Joanie. Miss Adventurous. Or should I say, misadventure. She's always fooling with her hair. Oh, God, that beehive. Thank goodness that didn't last long. And the poodle and the ponytail. That girl will try anything. I have so much fun going to the beauty shop with her. We just laugh and laugh. When she starts trying on wigs, I usually end up on the floor giggling. She's always so warm and friendly to all of us. You just can't help loving her.

And Patty. I never really had any good friends who were both Irish and Catholic. How much I've learned from her about Catholicism. In one of our discussions about divorce, she told me she believes in divorce. She couldn't fathom being excommunicated. The way she told the story was hysterical. A deep subject, one she was serious about, but she could still find humor in it. She's so much fun. She's definitely given me a new sense of humor.

Looking around the pizza parlor, she smiled, realizing the five of them ate a lot of pizza here and always had fun when they were together. And Myra, ever passionate about the issues of the day, constantly challenged all of them. Consequently, they had some interesting discussions as they ate.

On this particular night, after the girls arrived and they'd ordered their pizza, the conversation turned to another pressing issue.

"It makes me furious when guys ask me if I'm going to be a teacher, a nurse, or maybe a librarian. They seem to think that's all women can do." Myra fumed as she worried the curl at the back of her head. "That's one of the reasons I'm considering poly sci as a major. I love decorating and sewing, but it's not enough for me."

"What's even worse," griped Patty, "is when they assume you're in college to find a man and get an MRS degree instead of a bachelor's. I'm thinking about going into finance. Not definite yet, but leaning that way."

"What really gets my goat is when my dad or one of my uncles says 'a goil needs to know how to type and take shorthand,'" said Joanie, mimicking her uncle's New York Jewish accent. They all giggled. "Well, I'm going to be a CPA, and I'll need a secretary. I won't be one."

"What about you, Ellen?" Myra asked. "What do you think you want to do?"

"I don't know. Right now I don't seem to have a real calling. But I do know it's still a man's world. If you're not a member of the good ol' boys' club, forget it. Last time I checked, I don't qualify. So, I guess I'll have to be a teacher, a nurse, a librarian, or some such thing."

"Man, I hate when you talk like that," Patty growled. You're so darned smart. You could run those good ol' boys around in circles. We women need to do something to change things."

"True, true, but right now I need to get back to the dorm and study, or the only thing I'm going to change is my status on campus," added CeCe, who planned on becoming a psychologist.

They finished their Cokes and sauntered back to the dorm, all except for Ellen, who left for the library. *Is Patty right? Should I be striving for something more? Just because I had an illegitimate child doesn't mean I don't have something to contribute. I probably should have some higher aspirations. Something to think about.*

Like always, after she finished her studying, John escorted her home.

EIGHTEEN

ABRAHAM FRIEDMAN HAD NAMED each of his boys after Jewish warriors, Joshua, Jonathan, and David, because, as he told his boys, life is like a war. While one may lose a skirmish or a battle, the object ultimately is to win the war of life. "Know your goals and achieve them, that's what's important," he always told them. In order to do this, one must have a plan. Each person must have a life strategy for himself. To Abraham Friedman, strategic action was all-important.

John realized the time had come to alter his strategy for winning Ellen. He had established a solid friendship with her. Now it was time for the next step ... getting a date with her. He knew if he asked her out, she would refuse. *What to do?* He scratched at his beard. Finally, he decided to enlist Bob Snyder's aid.

John explained to Bob what he wanted. "I know you've been dating Myra for a while now. I'm hoping you can figure out a way for us all to go out together without making it seem like a date."

Bob, happy to help, said, "I'll talk to Myra, and we'll work something out."

When Ellen came home that night, Myra met her at the door and threw her arms around her. "Guess what?"

"Guess what, what?" Ellen tittered. She loved to tease Myra.

Myra punched her in the arm. "Bob got four tickets to the Dave Brubeck jazz concert Saturday. Do you wanna go?"

"You bet. How did he manage to get tickets? I heard it's like pulling teeth to get them, and he got four? So who's going to use the fourth ticket?"

"Well, Bob thought he'd ask Johnny, since he's a friend of yours, and that way you won't be a third wheel, if that's okay with you."

Ellen thought for a moment. "Sure, why not?" After all, it wouldn't be like going on a date. She and John were just friends. They often studied together and sometimes even grabbed a burger or pizza while they studied. He'd never really made a move on her, and certainly he had never tried to kiss her.

Excited, Myra said, "I'll call Bob and let him know."

~

ON SATURDAY MORNING WHEN Ellen woke up, her first thought, as always, was of Danny. *I wonder what Danny is doing today. By now, he's a toddler.* She thought of all the adorable toddlers she used to see at Titillations. *I wonder who he looks like. Does he have Kenny's blonde hair and blue eyes? Or does he have my dark hair and green eyes? Or does he look like both of us? Oh, God, I hope he has a good home and parents who love him as much as I do.* The hurt and the ache were still there, but the intensity had lessened. Now, she could think about Danny and then get on with the rest of her day. But the first thoughts of the day were still always reserved for him.

Let's see. Today is Saturday. She spent the next few moments reviewing the things she had to get done. Wash clothes, get her hair cut, decide what to wear to the concert. It was pleasant just letting random thoughts run through her head.

Well, I guess I should get up and get started. She glanced at the clock. *Holy Toledo. It's later than I thought.* She jumped out of bed.

Seeing that Myra was still asleep, she tried to be quiet as she put on shorts and a t-shirt. She took her dirty clothes to the laundry room, and when she returned, Myra was beginning to make waking-up sounds.

"Are you awake?" whispered Ellen.

"No, I'm still sleeping. Don't talk to me."

"Okay, I won't talk, I'll whisper. I'm leaving to get my hair cut. My clothes are in the washer. In twenty-five minutes, will you put them in the dryer?"

Myra snorted. "Thanks, kiddo, I'm awake now. Yes, I'll take care of your clothes. Go get gorgeous for tonight."

Ellen wasn't really thinking about getting gorgeous. Her mop of hair just needed cutting. *Oh, ya. For John, I don't need to get gorgeous. He's my friend, not my lover, for gosh sakes.*

To Myra she replied, "Thanks, roomie, love ya, see ya later."

Myra put the pillow over her head and mumbled something that sounded like goodbye.

Later, after Ellen returned, a loud buzz could be heard throughout the dorm as girls got ready for the concert. They all wanted to look good for their dates, whether it was a date with a new guy or a date with a steady.

CeCe dropped in to see what Myra and Ellen were planning to wear. Ellen folded her laundry as she pondered the question. "I haven't really thought about it yet."

"I'm going to wear the new turquoise blue pants and blouse I bought with the big white patent leather belt," Myra responded in her usual bubbly take-charge way. "And Ellen's going to wear that great-looking kelly green outfit she looks so cute in."

"I am? Okay. Sounds as good as anything."

CeCe smiled. "Okay that will help me decide. Thanks," she said and left.

~

MYRA AND ELLEN WERE ready and standing in the lobby when the guys arrived.

"You girls look great," Bob said.

John echoed the compliment and then added, "We're going to Mama's for dinner."

They escorted the girls to the car. Mama's, a local restaurant hangout, was a favorite of the college crowd. As they walked into Mama's, it was like stepping into a place out of the past, with its black-and-white tile floor and family pictures in their old-fashioned frames covering the dark green walls. White lattice panels formed booths along the walls with various colored grapes hanging from the tops of the latticework.

Papa was the maitre d', cashier, host, dishwasher, janitor, and the doer of whatever other jobs needed doing. The waiters were students from the music school. They all loved working at Mama's, because once all the customers were served, Papa and the waiters entertained the guests by singing songs from various operettas, Broadway shows, and hit tunes of the day.

Mama did all the cooking. Mama's calzones were to die for, but everything she prepared was fabulous and over the top. Mama believed in *abundanza*. A spaghetti and meatball dinner might fill a person up for a week. And, to top it off, Mama made the best cheesecake ever. When Mama finished cooking, she joined Papa and the waiters, and they sang as long as the guests wanted them to.

Tonight Ellen's group didn't stay for the singing, since they needed to get to the concert. Stuffed, they waddled out of the restaurant and strolled toward the student union, where the concert was being held.

As Ellen headed to the ladies room before the concert started, she ran into Steve and Rick. "Hey guys, long time no see."

"Well," answered Steve, "since Myra started going out with Bob Snyder, there's been no room for us. So we've been exploring greener pastures. Good seeing you, Ellen. Later."

Rick, who had been shaking his head in agreement the whole time waved. "Later, Ellen."

Experiencing a sense of well-being as she sat down, Ellen smiled. *I didn't realize how long it's been since I've been out on a date. Did I just think "date"? This isn't a date, this is John. Actually it is kinda like a date, being with Bob and Myra and John and me. Anyway, I'm glad I'm here.* She turned her attention back to enjoying the quartet. Dave Brubeck was fantastic.

Afterwards they all went to the A&W drive-in and got Cokes and fries. "Why are we eating more? I'm still stuffed from dinner," Ellen complained as she felt her stomach.

"Because that's what we're supposed to do," John answered.

It was a beautiful moonlit night as John drove along the beach. Myra and Bob were busy necking in the back seat. Ellen's stomach clenched. She moved over nearer to the door. *Hold on Ellen. Don't let yourself get involved.* She couldn't help but think about Kenny. *No, no, no, Ellen. Not again. Remember how nice Kenny was. Remember what happened? Just because John is charming doesn't mean anything.* Her stomach slowly relaxed when John tuned in on a jazz station and talked about the concert.

After a while, Ellen yawned. "Okay, you guys, I'm ready to call it an evening. I've been stuffed, entertained, stuffed again, and lulled by the drive. Now I'm ready to sleep."

John chuckled at her description of the evening. "You're right, and as it is, we're going to *just* make check-in."

Myra and Bob groaned, but they knew it was time to go. They drove up to the dorm just as Mary Jo stood ready to shut the doors.

"Hurry up, you're about to be late."

"Thanks guys, it was a fantastic evening." Myra gave Bob a quick kiss, and Ellen waved to John as they ran into the dorm.

They had just settled down, when Mary Jo knocked on the door. "Have you girls seen Cary anywhere?"

Cary had the room next to theirs.

Myra called Cary "the little imp," because with her honey-colored hair, azure blue eyes, sharp nose, and petite stature, she looked like one. And, like an imp, she always found ways to have fun and stir up mischief. Some of her friends referred to her as Bubbles because, like a boiling pot, she always bubbled over with good humor and a multitude of ideas.

"No, but did you check with Anita?"

"Not yet, but I will. That girl will be the death of me yet." Mary Jo resumed her search.

"I know she's out with Mike again tonight. I hope she doesn't get in trouble. This will be the second time she's late. I wouldn't wanna be in her shoes," Myra added.

Just then, the phone rang. "Hello, this is Myra."

"Myra, this is Mike. I have Cary's laundry down here in the front hall. Would you and Ellen come and pick it up?"

"Cary's laundry? Why do you have Cary's laundry?"

"Don't ask questions, Myra, just hurry up and come get this laundry."

The light dawned. "Be right down."

She turned to Ellen and burst out laughing. "If I'm not mistaken, Cary's just arrived. Mike has her downstairs in a laundry bag, and we have to pick her up."

"I can't believe it. Only Cary would come up with a scheme like this."

The girls hurried down to the lobby to be greeted by an unhappy senior advisor, Jennifer. "Hurry up, girls, men are supposed to be out of the building by now."

Myra and Ellen each picked up one side of the bag and raced for the stairs. As soon as they were out of Jennifer's sight, they opened the bag, and out popped Cary, who squealed, "I thought you guys would never figure it out and come down and get me."

Myra yelled at Cary. "What is the matter with you? Are you out of your mind? Mary Jo is searching all over for you right now, and she's not happy. You'd better find her and have some great story."

"Don't worry, I can handle Mary Jo. Thanks." She blew the girls a kiss and ran up the stairs.

"That girl is going to give us all a nervous breakdown." Ellen rolled her eyes and yawned. "Let's get back to our room. I'm pooped." *Cary always seems to make everything exciting. Maybe it wouldn't hurt if I tried to be a little more adventuresome instead of ... what? Boring. I used to be more fun, I think.*

As they were getting ready to fall asleep, Ellen whispered to Myra, "Thanks, roomie, for including me tonight. I had a wonderful time. It's been a long time since I've had so much fun."

Ellen sensed Myra's smile as she said, "There's hope for you yet, Ellen Gordon. You're welcome. We did make a congenial foursome. I had fun, too, and you know, I really do like Johnny."

NINETEEN

THE SECOND SEMESTER WAS almost over. Myra, packed and ready to go home, announced, "Thank God. My last final is at ten o'clock. I'll be able to spend the rest of my time with Bob."

Ellen checked her schedule for the umpteenth time. "Mine's at eleven. I'll have plenty of time to finish packing afterwards. Mom and Pop aren't going to pick me up until tomorrow. The only thing I have left to worry about is my grades."

"Yeah, some worry. Are you going to receive all As or A plusses? My heart really bleeds for you."

"So, like you're failing. What, you got one B plus? What a tragedy."

They both knew they were just covering up their emotions. Ellen would be lost without Myra. Myra was her best friend. She couldn't imagine a whole summer without Myra to talk to. Would things still be the same next year? Would Myra come back to school? A knot formed in her stomach. She tried to keep her lips and her voice from trembling as Myra left for her date.

JUST AFTER MYRA DEPARTED to spend her last evening with Bob, John called. "Hey, Ellen, how about one last dinner at Mama's?"

He held his breath. As hard as he had tried, he still hadn't made any headway with Ellen. Sometimes he thought he had won her over. Then there were the other times when she seemed as remote as ever. He vowed to himself that someday she would tell him what it was she was afraid of. *Somehow I've got to convince her I'm trustworthy.* Wrapped up in his thoughts, he almost missed her reply.

"I'd like that. Actually, I'm ready now, so come by anytime."

"Just so happens I'm downstairs in the lobby. Thought I'd take a chance."

"I think you have my number, Jonathan Friedman. I'll be right down."

At dinner they discussed their plans for the summer.

"I'll be working at Pop's store, and then we'll probably take a driving trip up the coast. Pop loves to play tourist, and we have a lot of fun doing it."

"I'll be working in my dad's law office. He always has a lot for me to do. I don't mind, though, because it's interesting. He does quite a bit of work for actors, producers, and directors, and I get to meet them. I may have a chance to get down here this summer, since we usually come down and spend a few days with my aunt, who lives in Coronado. I hope I'll see you if we do."

"If we're in town, it'd be fun to see you and meet your family."

John was pleased. Even though his aunt always asked them to visit, they never did, so John felt certain he could wangle an invitation and have a chance to see Ellen during the summer.

He rubbed his stomach with a satisfied grin. "It's time for me to finish packing so I can get an early start in the morning. Have a good summer, Ellen. If I write, will you answer?"

"Of course I'll answer. What kind of question is that? Aren't we friends?"

John's face fell. "We are, Ellen, we're friends."

Damn, after all this time, she still thinks of me as her buddy. Why do I keep trying? She's not the only girl in this world. Will I ever get her to think differently? Crap, I probably should start walking and keep on going. But in his heart he knew the answer. She was the only girl for him. He held back a sigh as he put his arms around her and embraced her.

"See ya."

Ellen looked surprised, but she hugged him back and said, "Sure, looking forward to it."

~

EMOTIONS RAN HIGH IN the dorm, and the air was filled with hormones as all the girls ran around crying, kissing friends goodbye, and generally feeling weepy. By the time Ellen got to her room, she was red-eyed. When Myra came into the room, Ellen was bawling. "This is awful. I never cry when saying goodbye. Now I can't stop."

"I know. Me too. I didn't realize how much I'd miss you all."

The morning passed all too quickly. Bob came to pick up Myra promptly at eight thirty. She kissed Ellen, promised to write, and then she was off.

Ellen kept packing. As she looked around the room and its decor, she thought, *I'm so lucky to have made so many wonderful friends. I'm glad Mom and Pop talked me into going to college.* When she finished packing, she couldn't help but notice how empty the room felt. It gave her a shiver. She hadn't been finished for long when Mom and Pop came to the door.

"Yoo hoo, Ellen, are you there?"

"In here, Mom, and ready to go." She gave the room one last

fond look, grabbed her cart, jammed her suitcases into the car, and they were on their way.

~

FOR THE MOST PART, the summer proved to be uneventful, with the exception of working at Titillations. Much of the melancholy returned as she watched the children come and go. One small toddler in particular made her think of Danny. Funny, though, her memory of how Danny looked began to fade. *How can that be? I felt certain his face would stay burned into my memory forever. I guess memories aren't what they're cracked up to be.* It frightened her to think she was losing the memory she'd held so dear. *Please, don't let me forget. I mustn't forget.* She attempted to throw off the fear.

A couple of weeks later John called and said he had come to visit his aunt for three days. Mom invited him to dinner.

As Ellen listened to the conversation over their dinner table, she realized how much she had missed him. *He has a good pun-im, a good face. I'm pleased he came to visit. Look at Mom and Pop.* You'd *think he was the King of Siam or something the way they're making over him. And check him out, he's eating it up. Too bad we're leaving tomorrow. It would have been fun to spend the next two days together.*

"So, Johnny, you're having a good summer?"

He grinned at her. Ellen knew it tickled him when she talked like a little old Jewish lady. A real *balaboosta*, he would say.

"So, I'm having a good summer," he responded in kind.

After dinner they walked to the park and caught up with each other and whatever news they had from their friends.

"I'm glad I had a chance to see you, Ellen. You're looking great."

"Thanks for the compliment. You're looking good yourself." *What a nice guy he is. I wish he would find some fabulous girl for himself.*

When he bid her goodnight, he hugged her. This time she wasn't surprised, and she hugged him back.

"I won't be visiting San Diego again, so I'll see you at school."

"Planning on it," she said as he drove off.

As John drove, he thought about their visit. He'd wanted to kiss her so much. He had tried to figure out a way to make it happen while he was there. But, as always, Ellen was just being friendly. No sexual hints or come-on from her. He scratched his head. *Guess I'll just have to keep on being patient.*

He wasn't exactly sure what he was feeling. He felt happy because she'd seemed sincerely glad to see him, and she had actually hugged him. On the other hand, his heart remained heavy, because he still hadn't made any substantial headway, and he wasn't going to see her again until school began.

PEARL WAS EXCITED. "SUCH a nice boy, Nate. I couldn't be more thrilled. Maybe it won't be long before we can make an announcement."

"Now, Pearl, don't get your hopes up. It didn't look to me like Ellen was serious about this boy. Patience, darling. I'm just pleased she even has a boy who's a friend."

When Ellen came home, Pearl said, "Such a nice boy, Ellen. I really liked him. Can we expect to see more of him?"

"Johnny is a good friend, Mom. We have some classes together, and we all chum around together. So, I suppose you'll see him again. You sure did make over him at dinner. I mean, really, he's nothing special, just a friend."

Pearl was disappointed, but she kept it to herself. "I'm sure all your friends are just as nice. Such a pleasure getting to meet one of them."

But I'll still hope for more as long as I'm alive.

TWENTY

THE DORM WAS FILLED with excitement. Friends clasping each other, glad to be together again. The members of The Club were back together for the 1957 fall semester.

Myra was high-spirited, as usual. "It's so good to see all of you. I was afraid maybe someone wouldn't come back." She squealed as she embraced each of them.

Joanie became serious. "Someone didn't come back. You remember Cary?"

"Who could forget Cary? Remember when Mike brought her back that night in a laundry bag?" Myra chortled.

"Unfortunately, Cary won't be back," Joanie advised. "She got pregnant. So they had a quiet wedding, and Mike is working for her dad. They're living in Sacramento."

Ellen could feel the blood drain from her face and her heart flip-flop. *Oh, my God. Poor Cary.* The sweat poured from her armpits. *Get hold of yourself, Ellen. You don't want to give away your secret. Compose yourself. Just be quiet and listen.*

Myra lamented. "Why does it have to be this way? Such a waste for both of them. Mike shouldn't be working for Cary's dad. He should be in college studying to be an accountant. And Cary, she so wanted to be a teacher. Maybe this is what she wants, but knowing Cary, I don't think she was ready to settle down and be a married woman and mother yet. She had such plans. She may have acted goofy sometimes, but she really was quite serious about having a career. Damn. I'm guessing the decision was made by their parents, not by them."

"What are you saying, Myra?" CeCe asked.

"I'm saying, she should have been able to have an abortion if that's what she wanted. That's what I'm saying."

The girls were shocked.

"Myra, are you saying abortion should be legal?" asked Joanie.

"That's exactly what I'm saying. Do you have a problem with that? When I was in high school, two girls had back alley abortions. One died, and the other will never be able to have more children. I barely knew them, but I felt sick inside that one girl had to die and another had the rest of her life ruined. I believe a woman should be able to decide what she wants to do with her own body."

"I have a problem with it morally," responded Patty, "but maybe that's just me. I could never morally, legally, or otherwise have an abortion. But then, I'm a Catholic, so what do you expect?"

Gently Myra grasped Patty's hand. "I don't have a problem with that. That's your choice. This country was founded on freedom. The government is not supposed to be making social choices for us. So, if for some reason a woman chooses to end a pregnancy, it should be her business, not the government's. It's a personal issue, so it should be personal."

Both Joanie and CeCe had mixed reactions to her statement.

"I think there are times and situations when I would want to see abortion be legal," Joanie said. "What about rape? Shouldn't a girl who's been raped be able to have an abortion?"

"Absolutely," responded CeCe. "And Patty, what about if having a baby would threaten the mother's life? Would you be in favor of an abortion then?"

"Now you've found my open wound. I don't agree with sacrificing the life of the mother for the child. No. A child needs its mother. A husband needs his wife. I feel strongly about that part of the issue. That's different. That's not terminating a pregnancy just because of the woman's wishes."

"What kills me," CeCe continued, "is that they were having sex, and I'm thinking Mike couldn't have been using rubbers, or we wouldn't be having this conversation. We all know that every guy carries rubbers in his billfold. What could they have been thinking?"

"It's obvious. They weren't thinking," Joanie snorted.

The conversation made Ellen extremely uneasy, but at the same time, she could empathize with Cary. How well she remembered what it was like to be in the throes of love and be carried away by the passion and heat of having sex. A chill ran through her body and caused her to get goose bumps. *Control yourself, Ellen, control yourself.*

"So, Myra," Joanie said, "what wonderful advice about sex did your mother give you?"

Myra giggled as she got that expression on her face, the one the girls called the Myra's-up-to-something face, where the corners of her mouth turned up and her eyes crinkled and she had that mischievous look.

"This is what my mother said." She posed, hands on her hips, and then pointed her finger and said, "Myra, just remember, you can run faster with your skirt up than he can with his pants down."

The girls exploded with laughter. Joanie laughed so hard that the Coke she was drinking came out her nose. CeCe, Patty, and Ellen cackled.

Myra directed her gaze to CeCe. "So what advice did your mother give you?"

"Well, my mother gave me an aspirin. She told me to keep it in my purse and if I ever had any thoughts about having sex, I should put it between my knees and hold it there."

Again, the girls doubled over laughing.

When Myra stopped laughing, she pointed to Joanie. "You're next."

Joanie took a breath. "My mother said if I ever think about having sex, just remember that a moment of pleasure can bring a lifetime of responsibility."

Ouch, that hurts like an arrow right on the bulls-eye.

This time the girls didn't laugh. "A sobering thought," Myra said. "Patty, how about your mom?"

"Being a tight-lipped, tight-assed Catholic, the only thing my mom ever said was that nice girls don't. Now I'm not sure what she meant. Nice girls don't talk about sex, don't think about sex, or don't have sex? I guess she meant all three."

"I guess you'll just have to figure it out," Myra said. "How about your mom, Ellen?"

Ellen thought about it. Had her mother ever told her anything specific? And, if she had, what had she said? Obviously she had ignored it, whatever it was, because hadn't she gotten pregnant anyway? What could she say?

Ellen paused, swallowed, and tried to get some saliva back in her dry mouth. Then she said, "Never do anything you'd be ashamed to tell your mother about."

The girls all nodded as they digested that thought. Joanie said, "Enough deep thoughts for today. Time to hit the books."

After the girls left, Ellen realized what a revelation the conversation had been. It had never occurred to her that she should have been able to determine what she did with her body. She had never considered she might have alternatives or choices. Abortion was illegal. End of story. Personal choice? Something to think about.

The ringing of the phone interrupted her thoughts. It was Johnny. "Pizza tomorrow night with Myra and Bob?"

Myra signaled yes. "Myra will set it up with Bob. We'll see you then."

After she hung up, Myra asked, "So are you two becoming an item?"

Ellen blushed. "Oh, no, we're just good friends."

Myra chose not to pursue it further.

~

A FEW DAYS LATER, the conversation about abortion led Ellen to the synagogue library. She wanted to find out what Jews believe. According to what she read, life begins at birth, when God gives the baby a soul. She also found in the books she looked through that abortion was permissible should the mother's life be threatened in any way, stating that, although the unborn child is a living being, it does not yet have the status of personhood equal to its mother.

So, she concluded, rape and incest would certainly qualify as threatening a mother's life. Under ordinary circumstances abortion is prohibited. *Protection for both. Interesting.* She needed to think more about this. But not yet. It was still too soon. Still too painful. She wasn't yet ready to think about abortion as a choice.

September and October flew by. Myra persisted in *shlepping* her to lectures, meetings, and social events, which in her own modest way she enjoyed. She also enjoyed time with Johnny.

Ellen and Johnny had several classes together. They both still went to the library every evening. This year she allowed him to drive her home instead of walking her home. She enjoyed the walk, but this made it far for him to go back home. She felt she could make this small concession as long as she didn't have to make any others.

TWENTY-ONE

THANKSGIVING HAD COME. NATE and Pearl told Ellen to bring home as many friends as she thought they could stuff into the house. With that invitation, the members of The Club and their boyfriends went to the Gordons' house for Thanksgiving dinner.

After dinner, as they sat in the living room, where the aroma of turkey, stuffing, and side dishes still lingered, Nate, now divested of his coat and tie, told his stories. Nate loved company, and he loved entertaining.

"So, Pearl is driving, and her Mah Jongg ladies are in the back. And a cop stops them. Pearl asks the cop what's wrong. And he says, 'Ma'am you're driving too slow.' Pearl points to a sign and says, 'No, I'm not, the speed limit is 22.' Now the cop is ready to crack up. 'Lady, that's the route sign, not the speed limit.' Now Pearl is embarrassed, apologizes, and the cop says okay. Before he leaves, though, he looks in the back seat, and the ladies are all sitting there petrified. 'Are your friends okay? They look pretty frightened,' he observes. Pearl looks at him with a straight face and says, 'We just came off the 101.'" The kids howled. Nate bowed, loving all the attention.

The smell of coffee brewing filled the room. Pearl smiled indulgently at Nate as she kept busy. First dinner, now coffee and dessert. No one could ever say they didn't get enough to eat at Pearl Gordon's house.

"Some cake, Patty, a cup coffee? Joanie, you need some ice cream with your cake. CeCe, here's some cream and sugar for your coffee."

Johnny and Ellen kept just as busy helping Pearl. She was a regular dynamo, and they were hard pressed to keep up with her.

"Darlings," she said, "sit. It's okay. I'll take care of everything. Just enjoy your guests."

At the end of the evening, Ellen realized she'd had a wonderful time. *Johnny is so sweet. He is just so* haimish. *I have to admit that I'm happy he hasn't found anyone yet. If he had a girl, I'd probably lose him as a friend. That wouldn't be good at all. I guess I'll worry about it another day ... or not. Tonight I'm beat.*

THE END OF THE semester neared, and the holidays were approaching. Johnny asked Ellen if she wanted to come up to Los Angeles for a couple of days, meet his family, and see some of the holiday shows.

"I think I'd enjoy that. I'll check with Mom and Pop. I'm not sure when the best time would be for me to come. What about your parents? What would be most convenient for them?"

"Mom told me anytime. This time of year is chaos anyway. Josh and Sylvia's kids and Ruth and Ted's kids are out of school. David and I are out of school. Between the grandchildren and our friends, there are always a ton of people at the house. One more or less doesn't matter. No one will even notice."

They decided Ellen would visit between Christmas and New Year's. As the time drew nearer, she wasn't sure she was looking forward to it. *Whatever possessed me to say I would go? All those people. It'll be awful. But, then, if I back out, Johnny will be crushed, and I can't do that to him. He's such a good friend. He's just trying to reciprocate for last summer and Thanksgiving. I owe him that.*

Myra planned to spend the holidays with Bob and his parents, while CeCe and Joanie planned to be at home with their families. Before they all left, they had a farewell dinner at Mama's, where they exchanged gifts and wished each other a Happy New Year.

<center>~~~</center>

AFTER STANDING IN FRONT of her closet for an hour, Ellen phoned Johnny. "I'm trying to pack. What should I bring? I have no idea what I'll need. Help!"

"Like I know what a girl needs. I guess you'll need a couple of fancy dresses for the parties. A swimming suit for sure. If it's warm, we'll spend some time at the pool. And just regular clothes for the rest of the time."

"I guess that's helpful. I'll do the best I can. What time are you going to pick me up?"

"Around nine. I want to be home by lunchtime."

"I'll be ready. See ya then." *Ready, shmedy. I'm a nervous wreck. I wonder if I can hurry up and get sick so I don't have to go.*

Out loud she screamed, "Mom, come help me, I don't know what to pack."

As Pearl went to help Ellen, Nate could see she was *shmeltzing.* Her Ellen was going to spend a few days with the Friedmans. He knew that she thought things looked good.

Nate was shrewder. John seemed smitten with Ellen, but it appeared she only looked upon him as a friend. *Good luck, John,* Nate thought to himself. *He seems to be a* mensch, *and he's good to my daughter. Well, time will tell. In the meantime, I need to keep Pearl from reading too much into this relationship.*

With Pearl's help, Ellen was packed and ready when Johnny knocked at the door. He grunted when he saw the suitcases. "Are you planning to move in? Or is this your idea of a few *shmattas*?"

"I beg your pardon. You're calling my clothes rags? And I'm not planning on moving in. These are just a few necessities. But, of course, you wouldn't understand. You're a man."

They had a pleasant ride to LA. Johnny entertained her with stories about his family.

"It must be wonderful to have family all living near each other. It's always been kinda lonesome for us, with me being an only child. Pop's family is in Chicago, and I have just one aunt and uncle in Denver."

"It goes both ways. We've always had a lot of fun together. But then there are those days when you wish everyone would just go away."

"Well, anyway, I'm excited to meet your family."

"And they're looking forward to meeting you."

When they drove up to Johnny's house, the four grandchildren were waiting outside for them.

"Uncle Johnny's here!" Rob shrieked.

The children rushed over to the car and jumped all over Johnny. He punched the boys, kissed baby Linda, and rolled around in the grass with them. Ellen watched with amusement. This was Uncle Johnny, not the same Johnny she had become accustomed to. He seemed like one of the kids.

Finally, he shouted, "Okay, stop. I give. You win." And one by one they tumbled off of him.

"Line up now for introductions." The children lined up according to age. Rob, Ruth and Ted's son, was the oldest. Then came Steve, Josh and Sylvia's firstborn, and then Jay, their baby. Last, Linda, the princess, who was Ruth and Ted's baby.

"Ladies and gentlemen, I'd like to introduce my friend, Ellen Gordon."

"Are you Uncle Johnny's girlfriend?" asked Rob.

The children all giggled. "Hi, Ellen Gordon." Then they attacked her. Embarrassed by the question and the assault, Ellen stepped back, tripped, and fell to the ground.

"Whoa, guys, Ellen is breakable, remember? You can't all jump on a person at once."

"We're sorry," they said in chorus, "are you okay?"

Ellen checked herself. "I seem to be in one piece. I guess I'll survive."

She was more shaken than she wanted to let on. The proximity of all these children was more than she was prepared to deal with. Even after all this time, she was still fragile with the memory of Danny.

Johnny's mother, Bessie, came out of the house. She appeared to be an attractive woman, not what you would call beautiful, but not ugly. Her aura suggested a warm, comfortable, welcoming, energetic person. She had brown eyes and dark brown hair that she wore in a French twist.

"What's all the commotion about?" When Bessie saw Johnny, she wiped her hand on her apron and ran over to embrace him. Then she turned to Ellen.

"Excuse my bad manners. You must be Ellen. I'm Jonathan's mother. You can call me Bessie. Everyone does."

"It's so nice to meet you. It's kind of you to invite me."

"It's my pleasure. I'm always thrilled when the kids bring friends home for the holidays. Then I don't have to entertain them. They entertain themselves." She chuckled. "Did that sound selfish? Anyway, welcome. Jonathan, put Ellen's things in the corner guestroom, and David's friend, Sid, will be in the next room."

The guestrooms were Josh's and Ruthie's old rooms. They were the same now as when they had left to get married. Ellen loved Ruthie's room, decorated in shades of pink and purple. It smacked of Ruthie's girlhood and of decorator touches.

After she unpacked, Johnny took her on a tour of the house. She noticed that each room contained dozens of family pictures, from the time the children were infants and in various stages of their growth to more recent pictures of the grandchildren. Ribbons, trophies, and works of art by the children accompanied the pictures. In the basement was an enormous rumpus room, with a pool table and a ping-pong table. At one end was a bar with six bar stools tucked underneath. Trophies the boys had won covered all the available table spaces and walls in the room.

A lump rose in Ellen's throat as she realized these were things she would never experience with Danny. No pictures, no memories, only a single picture in her mind of a newborn baby that was becoming more and more difficult to recall. As they walked upstairs, she took a deep breath and tried to regain her composure. When they joined Bessie, she said, "Your home is beautiful. I enjoyed the tour."

"Thanks, we like it. It's an excellent house for entertaining and for grandkids. You must be starving by now, it's way past lunchtime. Come, have a little something."

The kitchen smelled delicious with the various aromas of chicken cooking, cookies baking, and a fresh-baked chocolate cake being frosted. Bessie, a typical Jewish mother, could always be found in the kitchen making her mouth-watering delicacies. Ruby, the maid, washed dishes and cleaned up.

Not quite what I'm used to, but very nice.

That night the whole family and their guests gathered for dinner. Ellen, nervous, sat with her hands tensed under the table. She watched as Abe presided, a regular chairman of the board, the epitome of the successful LA lawyer, in his beautifully tailored pinstripe suit, custom-made shirt with initials on the cuffs, and silk tie. He stood about 5'10" with dark hair graying at the temples and gray eyes. *He has a distinguished air about him.* He gave each family member an opportunity to report on his or her recent activities. Even the grandchildren amused everyone with their reports.

"Grampa, I swimmed with the goldfishes today," reported Linda to the family.

"Did not," Josh corrected Linda. "You're in the goldfish class."

"Thank you Linda and Josh. Any announcements anyone wants to make?" Abe asked.

He made sure dinner proceeded smoothly as he mediated the minor squabbles that inevitably go on between siblings and cousins.

It's no wonder he's a successful lawyer. See *how he manages the family. This could be total chaos. And Bessie. She makes sure everybody has enough, and she covers up all the minor faux pas so they go unnoticed. She makes me feel welcome; she is such a gracious hostess. That's why Johnny is so* haimish. *The family is all that way. I'm actually glad I came. I think this visit will be okay.* Ellen prayed as she felt her hands and her heart unclench.

TWENTY-TWO

ELLEN FELL INTO BED exhausted and didn't wake up until the enticing smell of fresh coffee brewing dragged her out of her stupor. After the previous night's dinner, she had thought she wouldn't be hungry for at least a week. Now her stomach rumbled.

She got out of bed, washed up, and put on a pair of jeans and a white t-shirt. She heard Johnny fly up the stairs, presumably so he could escort her down to breakfast.

"I take it you slept well," he said.

"Like a log. I literally passed out. The smell of delicious coffee woke me up."

"Wait till you taste the cinnamon rolls Mom made to go with that coffee."

Abe had already gone to work. Bessie and Ruby were busy preparing food to keep in the fridge in case somebody got hungry and needed a *nosh*. Bessie paused to ask about their plans for the day. She reminded them that the adults planned to go to the country club for dinner that evening and afterwards they had tickets for the theater.

"I thought we'd do the usual," said Johnny. "Farmer's Market, Knottsberry Farm, Santa Monica Pier, whatever."

"Be home early enough to give Ellen time to rest and get ready for this evening."

"Yes, Mother."

"Don't give me the *yes mother* bit. Just don't wear Ellen out."

"I'll have her home in plenty of time. Tomorrow Scott is having all the guys over to his house. So we'll just sit around the pool and relax."

Ellen observed the exchange between mother and son. *It's pretty obvious they are fond of each other. How pleasant this is.* For some reason, this made her think of Denver and her old friends. Her thoughts drifted back to her past. *I didn't realize how much I've missed Bev and my other friends these past two years. I really don't have any old friends anymore. I wonder if Mom misses having my friends and me around. Stupid, of course she does. Remember how happy she was at Thanksgiving, busy fussing over all of us? I'm sorry I never made any friends that last year in San Diego, but I'm grateful for the good friends I've made in college. I can't imagine not having them in my life.*

They had a fun day wandering around LA. As planned, that night the adults had dinner at the club and attended the Community Playhouse production. Abe commented, "The usual holiday production, don't you think?"

The family members all agreed, adding that it was entertaining but certainly not memorable.

The week went by quickly, and Ellen found herself enjoying every moment. At least for this week, her first thoughts in the morning were not of Danny, which made her feel guilty. *I wonder if someday I'm going to forget Danny all together.* Her heart thumped. *I could never forget Danny. Never!*

In honor of New Year's Eve, everyone was attending a big party at the club. She and Bessie were going to the beauty shop to get their hair and nails done in the morning, then they planned to have a peaceful afternoon and rest.

After they arrived home from the beauty shop, Ellen went to the library. She called home to wish her parents a Happy New Year.

"Are you having a good time, Ellen?" Pearl inquired.

"Yes, the Friedmans are very special. I'm having a wonderful time."

She realized what she had just said was absolutely true. Then she spoke with Pop and wished him the same. After she hung up, she sat there feeling just a bit sad, as she recalled the fun times she'd had in Denver with her friends.

Just then, Johnny came into the library. "Are you finished talking to your parents?"

"Yeah, they're going to a party tonight with their friends."

"Just thought I'd let you know I'm going to relax around the pool, if you want to join me."

Ellen thought about it. "No, I don't want my hair to get all sweaty. I think I'll relax and read a book."

After reading a few pages, Ellen, tired, went to her room and took a nap. When she woke up, it was time to shower and get dressed. Pearl had picked out a beautiful, soft turquoise chiffon dress for Ellen. The halter-top twinkled with seed pearls and rhinestones. Pearl had given Ellen her diamond-and-pearl necklace to wear with the dress. A dainty necklace, it went perfectly with the turquoise chiffon. She wore tiny diamond-and-pearl earrings to match. Ellen peered at herself in the mirror. *Well, I guess I look presentable. I don't think I'll embarrass Johnny or his family tonight. Actually, I think I look quite good tonight. So there.*

She stuck out her tongue at the reflection in the mirror. This was the first time in a long time that she had looked in the mirror and thought pleasant thoughts about herself and her appearance. Usually, she deemed the person in the mirror unworthy. One who had given up her child. What kind of person does that? Certainly not a good person. But tonight, under the spell of the magic of the week, she did not have these thoughts. She twirled, picked up her white fox stole and purse, and glided out the door. Waiting downstairs, Johnny heard her coming and went to the foot of the stairs to meet her. She saw him catch his breath.

In his most lighthearted voice, he said to her, "You are looking quite lovely tonight, if I may say so."

"You may say so. You look quite handsome yourself."

They went into the living room to wait for Bessie and Abe, who came in shortly. Abe carried his camera, and they spent the next few minutes taking pictures.

～

THE CLUB SHIMMERED LIKE a fairyland. All Johnny's friends and their dates had already arrived and were chatting as they ate and drank. They exchanged greetings as Johnny and Ellen joined them. Soon they all got up to dance.

Johnny loved dancing with Ellen. It gave him a chance to hold her close, feel the warmth of her delicate body fitting perfectly into his, and breathe in her fragrance. *Mom was right. The dancing lessons paid off. See how well we dance together.*

At midnight, the band played New Year's tunes. Johnny kissed Ellen lightly on the lips. He felt her stiffen in his arms, as she stood there without returning the kiss. Damn, she looked so beautiful, he just wanted to hold her in his arms and kiss her. But it wasn't happening.

To say Johnny was disappointed would be a huge under-statement. Devastated was more like it. He had had such high hopes for this week. He had prayed that by the end of the week, Ellen would realize he was her knight in shining armor and would fling herself into his arms and make mad, passionate love to him. It didn't happen. She seemed softer and friendlier, but that was it. *Just remember, John, this is just one more battle. Tomorrow is another day. I will win this girl yet.*

———

THAT NIGHT IN BED Bessie said to Abe, "So, nu, what do you think about Ellen and our Jonathan? Is anything going on or not?"

"Well, it's quite obvious he's head over heels in love with her, but she seems somehow detached. That's how I would describe it. She seems to be genuinely fond of Jonathan, but she has this mantle around her. She's like a princess in a castle with an in-surmountable wall. I don't know what to think about her. I only hope she doesn't break his heart."

Bessie sighed. "I hope so too."

———

THE NEXT MORNING AFTER breakfast, Ellen packed and prepared to go home. When she finished, she went into the kitchen, where Bessie baked and cooked while Ruby once again cleaned up and put things away. It was obvious they had a well-orchestrated routine.

"Mrs. Friedman, I can't thank you enough for your wonderful hospitality. It's been a fabulous week, and I'll always remember it."

Bessie beamed. "Darling, it was entirely my pleasure. You should come anytime. As you can see, we have plenty of room.

We enjoyed having you. And I've never seen Jonathan have such a good time. Usually he holes up and doesn't do much. I liked seeing him get together with you and his friends, doing things. So, don't be a stranger. Come again." She gave Ellen a kiss on the cheek.

"Oy, I've left lipstick on your face." She wiped it off with a towel. "You're okay now, so go say goodbye to Abe. He's in the den."

Ellen was touched. She hastened to the den, where she found Abe reading the paper.

"Well, Ellen, ready to go?" he inquired.

"Yes, packed and ready. I want to thank you for a wonderful week. I had a marvelous time."

"We loved having you, my dear. I always like having family and friends together. Bessie and I hope you come again."

He clasped Ellen and gave her a kiss. Just then Johnny came into the room.

"Kissing my girl, Dad?" Johnny teased his dad.

Ellen turned crimson and winced.

Johnny felt like biting his tongue. *Damn, look at how upset that made her. I've gone and stuck my foot in my mouth. I'll have to figure out how to smooth it over.*

"You can't blame a man for trying." Abe punched Johnny in the arm. "Be careful driving back. Call me when you get there."

"Yes, Pop. I'll call. Ellen, I have your things in the car. Let's go."

Ellen gave Abe a final squeeze. "I'm ready."

ON THE RIDE HOME, Ellen sat as close to the door as possible, her mind reeling. *What did he mean by "my girl"? I'm not his girl. We're just friends. I'm not worthy to be his girl. Did I make a mistake visiting his family? I must have given the wrong impression. What can I do to make this right?* Silently, she sat there going over and over what had gone wrong. It left her feeling exhausted.

～

THE GORDONS WAITED ANXIOUSLY for Ellen to get home. "Oy, I hope everything's okay. I pray that Ellen had a good time. This is the first time she's done anything since ..."

"Pearl, don't worry. I'm sure Ellen had a good time. They'll be here any minute, and then you can ask her."

Pearl stood at the window until they drove up. She threw the door open and said, "Happy New Year, kids. Did you have a good trip? How was the traffic? Did you have a good time last night?"

"Mom, one question at a time. First we need to unload. Then we'll answer your questions."

Johnny unpacked the trunk. Ellen grabbed the small suitcase and her make-up case.

"Just dump everything in my room."

"Yes ma'am." He followed her up the stairs and put the suitcases down in the middle of the floor, so she would have room to open them.

Pearl tagged along behind them. "Now, you'll come downstairs and have some lunch and tell me about your week."

"Good, I'm starving, Mrs. Gordon. I've worked up an appetite *shlepping* Ellen's stuff around."

Nate waited for them in the kitchen. He hugged Ellen and shook Johnny's hand.

"Well, well, it's good to have you home. John, good to see you. Sit down, we'll have a little lunch."

After lunch Ellen announced she was ready to unpack.

"Thanks for a marvelous week, Johnny. I had the best time. Your family is lovely. I liked all of them ... your brothers, your sister, the kids, and especially your mom and dad. They're wonderful people. I'll see you back at school next week."

Reluctantly, Johnny got ready to leave. Pearl could see that he really wanted to stay longer, but obviously Ellen was dismissing him.

"I had a fantastic week, too. Thanks for coming."

He didn't know what else to say, so he picked up his jacket and strode out of the house.

Pearl scolded Ellen. "You couldn't let him stay awhile?"

"It's enough already, Mom. I want to unpack, relax, and get ready to go back to school."

Pearl knew when to quit. She went to the kitchen to wash the dishes as Ellen went upstairs. *Will Ellen ever come out of her self-imposed prison?*

~

AS ELLEN BEGAN THE task of putting away the clothes she wouldn't be taking back to school and repacking her suitcases, she contemplated what had happened. Now that she had calmed down, she saw things in a different light. *Maybe Johnny had simply been joking. He and Abe kidded each other all the time. Was that it? Was he just having a little fun with Abe ... and I'm reading too much into this? But what about the kiss? He kissed me on the lips. What did that mean?*

At the time, she thought it nothing more than a standard New Year's kiss, but now she wondered if it was more—and it frightened her. *Johnny is one of my best friends. Am I going to lose him? When I get back to school, I'll have to see what I can do to put our friendship back on track.*

TWENTY-THREE

THE SCHOOL YEAR PASSED quickly, and it was soon time for sophomore finals. The girls in The Club made plans for their farewell dinner.

Myra had an internship lined up with a political think tank in San Francisco for part of the summer, so she could be near Bob. She planned to spend the last few weeks at home with her parents.

Joanie had been dating a darling ZBT by the name of Stan Rosenthal. It just so happened he lived in Highland Park, so Joanie looked forward to being at home for the summer.

Myra commented, "That's what I call having your cake and eating it too."

CeCe had also met a delightful boy, Edward Abrams, from a wealthy East Coast family. His parents usually spent summers at their cottage on Martha's Vineyard, and CeCe's family spent the month of July there. Both CeCe and Ed were happy they could be together during the summer.

"And you, Ellen, what are your plans?" the girls asked.

"Same old. Working at Titillations. I don't know if we're going to take any trips this summer. Pop hasn't made any plans yet, as far as I know."

Myra turned to the girls. "It sounds like we're all coming back in the fall. Am I right?"

They all nodded. "I have an idea then. Instead of living in the dorm next year, let's all rent a house together. It would be so much nicer than a dorm, and we can all be together."

"What a super idea." They all loved the suggestion. "But who will find us a house?" asked CeCe.

"I figure Ellen could find us a place since she's so close," Myra answered. "I've been checking around, and there are many rentals available near the campus. I could come down from San Francisco and help Ellen decide on a place. Then, if it's okay with everyone, Ellen and I can make the arrangements."

Why is it Myra always volunteers my services without my consent? Reluctantly, Ellen agreed to take the lead in finding a house. The girls gave their approval with a noisy hooray and then spent some time making a list of what they wanted and how much they thought they could afford to spend on rent.

~

THE NEXT COUPLE OF days were chaotic as everyone prepared to go home for the summer. After a short period of cautious restraint when they got back from the holiday break, Ellen's relationship with Johnny had resumed. Both had carefully repaired the damage done over the New Year's weekend, and now Johnny planned to drive Ellen home for the summer. He also had agreed to get a truck and haul all The Club members' furniture to Ellen's house for the summer, since she lived closest to the campus.

The trip home turned out to be quite perilous. The furniture slid around in the truck, and Ellen and Johnny had to get out every few blocks and re-tie everything down. Finally, they made it to Ellen's house. Pearl made room in the garage while she waited for them, so all they had to do was put the furniture in the space she had reserved.

After they finished, Pearl invited Johnny in for a cool drink. "I'd love to have you stay for dinner. I have a brisket and potatoes already in the oven. With brisket there's always enough for one more."

"I'd love to stay, Mrs. Gordon, but I need to get home. However, I'll take a raincheck. I'll be spending some weekends here in town."

"Oh?" Ellen looked at him in surprise.

"Ya, didn't I tell you? My uncle wants me to help him out a few weekends over the summer, so he and my aunt can do some other things."

"That's nice. We'll get a chance to see each other this summer then."

"Plan on it."

Johnny had finagled his uncle into asking him to do some work for him around their house. He planned to spend as many weekends as possible in San Diego so he could see Ellen. He was making progress in his relationship with Ellen, but his goal was to get her to open up this summer so they could begin to have a real involvement. *This is it, Ellen Gordon. This time you won't escape.*

TWENTY-FOUR

ELLEN HADN'T PLANNED THAT this summer would turn out to be a summer of learning. June, Nate's gal Friday, broke her leg, which meant she couldn't drive. She was confined to answering the phone, doing paperwork, and manning the cash register.

"Ellen," Nate said, "since June broke her leg, I need you to pick things up from my artists and run errands. You'll have a chance to learn the city. I think you'll find it interesting, as well as a change from what you've been doing the last couple of summers."

Ellen chuckled. "In other words, I've been elected chief gopher."

Nate chuckled with her. "You got it."

Actually, this pleased Ellen. *Well, now, didn't I luck out this summer? I've always wanted to know more about Pop's artists.*

"I'll be happy to do whatever I can to help, Pop."

On the first morning of her new duties, Pop scheduled Ellen to go to Sue Ann's and pick up a fresh batch of Beachfits. She took a couple of wrong turns on the way and found herself in a distinctly poor neighborhood where the homes were shacks. Instead of lawns, the front yards consisted of dirt and mud. Children

184 | ROCHELLE PADZENSKY

played everywhere, some so dirty you couldn't even tell the color of their hair. Their tattered and torn clothes revealed skinny bodies. Nothing but skin and bones. The state of these children frightened Ellen, chilling her spine and causing her to shiver. It made her feel better when she found the right street and left that neighborhood.

Lesson number one. In this wonderful city, where it is almost always summer, with azure blue skies, exotic flowers, and the sun dancing on the water, there are hungry children. As Ellen thought about the adorable beach outfits created by Sue Ann, sadness permeated her body. Those children would never have anything like the Beachfits created by Sue Ann. They probably couldn't even imagine anything like them. *Please,* she prayed, *don't let my Danny be like one of those children.*

Ellen found Sue Ann interesting to talk to. They drank lemonade and gossiped about the shop. Soon the time came for Ellen to leave.

"It was delightful seeing you, Ellen. Give June my best, and tell her to get well quick. Say hello to your dad, and have him call me and let me know what's selling best, so I'll know what to concentrate on."

"Sue Ann, every outfit you make is a best seller, but I'll tell Pop to call you."

On the way back to the shop, she couldn't help but think about those poor children. It hurt her eyes just to picture them. She was glad she didn't have to see them again.

A few days later, Pop sent her to Dorrie's house to pick up beach toys. When she drove up the driveway, she found four small girls and one chubby little baby boy with big brown eyes and curly hair having a tea party in the front yard. The baby sat in a chair next to a big brown, raggedy teddy bear while the girls fed him and the teddy lemonade and cookies. It seemed to

Ellen that they were having fun, especially the teddy bear. She skipped up to the door and rang the bell.

"Children, please stop ringing the doorbell. Dorrie is trying to get something done."

"It's Ellen Gordon, Dorrie. I'm here to pick up the beach toys."

"Ah, Ellen. I'm sorry." Dorrie appeared at the door. She brushed a blonde strand of hair from her tired face.

"Come in and sit down. The order is almost ready. I just have to take the last toys out of the molds and clean them up."

Ellen managed to find a chair that was only partially covered with children's clothes and toys. She moved the pile of clothing onto another pile.

"Are all those children yours?"

"Oh, my, no. We're foster parents. We generally only have two children. This has been an unusually trying day. That's why there's such a mess. No, my husband and I never had any children of our own. What with the war and him being away all the time, it just never seemed right. Anyway, we both love children, and after the war it seemed like a good idea to be foster parents. We've been doing it ever since. That's actually how I got into making these sand toys. The reason I'm not ready today is because there was an unexpected crisis. Did you see the adorable little boy with the curly hair?"

"Of course I did. The girls are busy stuffing him with lemonade and cookies."

Dorrie smiled. "Bless his heart, poor baby. He's part of what happened. Apparently his mother abandoned him and his sister. No one knows how long they had been left alone. A neighbor discovered them when the sister showed up at her door with the baby. They were very hungry and extremely dirty. The sister told her their mommy had been gone a long time. The neighbor called Family Services."

"Did they check the children's house?" Ellen asked.

Dorrie took a drink of water, wiped a speck of dirt off the glass, and resumed. "Yes, and Family Services determined that the mother had probably been gone for several days. They took the children. All the foster homes and institutions are full right now, so they called me with an SOS. Of course, I dropped everything and picked up the children. It's taken all morning to calm them down. I also stopped to collect some things from their house for both of them. As you can see, they seem to be okay for the time being, so I came into the house to finish the order."

Amazed, Ellen wondered aloud, "How could anyone abandon their children? I just can't imagine anyone doing that."

"My dear, that's only the tip of the iceberg. You wouldn't believe some of the things that parents do. Some of the physical abuse I've seen tears my heart out. Some of these children will probably never recover from what's been done to them."

"My God, that's just awful. It's hard to understand people like that." Ellen shook her head in disbelief.

"Yes, well, Frank and I just try our best to love them. We also pray a lot. Often, after a period of time, they're returned to the same parents. It scares the hell out of me when I think about it," Dorrie confessed. Looking back at the work at hand, she exclaimed, "Enough! This isn't what you came to hear. You came to pick up an order. Now, then, it's almost finished."

Ellen experienced a sense of horror at what Dorrie had told her. *Lesson number two. Not all parents love and take good care of their children. Some torture them, abuse or abandon them.* It made her stomach queasy, like she was about to vomit. *Please let Danny be with a kind family, a good family.*

On the way back to the shop she thought about her own family. *I guess I've been lucky. I just never even thought about it.*

Over the next few weeks, Ellen became better acquainted

187 NO OTHER OPTION | 187

with Dorrie. They talked about many things. Ellen found Dorrie to be a loving, warm person. *Any child would be lucky to have her as a mother*, she mused. *Lesson number three. Not all newborns are adopted. Sometimes a physical or mental handicap, gender, religious preferences of prospective parents, and physical characteristics keep a baby from being adopted. And sometimes they just fall through the cracks in the system.*

"What happens to these babies?" she asked Dorrie.

"They end up being shipped from foster home to foster home, or they sometimes end up being brought up in an institution. It's a crapshoot. Some end up doing well. Many end up with lifelong problems. It's sad, but that's the reality," Dorrie concluded with a shrug.

All these revelations weighed heavily on Ellen. She began to have nightmares, dreaming of Danny being abandoned, or abused, or in an institution where nobody cared for him or loved him. She became even more depressed and retreated further within herself. Once again, that terrible hurt was reflected in her eyes, but she kept it all inside herself. No one could ever know.

TWENTY-FIVE

JOHNNY FROWNED, WHICH PUT a crease in his usually smooth forehead. Puzzled, he couldn't figure out what had happened to Ellen over the last few weeks. During the past several months she had begun to lose the deep expression of hurt in her eyes. She seemed more relaxed and laughed more easily. It gave him a reason to look forward to the weekends he spent in San Diego. Without the pressures of school, he expected to make headway with Ellen. Instead, Ellen seemed to have gone back to where she had been when he first set eyes on her.

Johnny knew the change had not gone unnoticed by Nate and Pearl either. They too seemed worried. Johnny endeavored to get Ellen to confide in him, but she remained mute.

"I'm fine, don't worry," she said.

Absently, Johnny scratched at a mosquito bite as he devised a plan. There was a lovely restaurant on Coronado Island that served incredible seafood, and Ellen loved going there for dinner. *If we go there about eight, we should miss the family diners and retirees, so it should be quiet. We can sit on the patio and look out at the water. And then I'll take her hand and gaze into her eyes and beg her to tell me what's wrong. I've got to find out. I'm going to call her right now and make the date.*

The evening was delightful, a pleasant breeze filling the air with the perfume of flowers. As Johnny had hoped, the restaurant had emptied of the early diners, and they were seated out on the patio, just as he had planned. The patio lights twinkled from the edges of the patio cover, adding to the relaxing mood as they sat and looked out over the water.

Johnny ordered all Ellen's favorite dishes. The food was a feast for the eyes as well as the stomach, but Ellen only picked at her food without speaking. Finally, they were through with dinner and Johnny ordered coffee.

He took Ellen's hand in his. He gazed into her eyes and queried, "Are we good friends, Ellen? And have I been a faithful and true friend since we met?"

Surprised, Ellen looked at him. "Of course, Johnny. You're, well, actually you're one of my best friends."

"Then I'm going to ask you to return the favor as a best friend."

"I don't understand. What do you want?"

"I've always known there is something bothering you. Something that makes you very sad. I need to know what it is, so I can help you. Ellen, please tell me, because I can't bear not to know. You're too important to me."

Ellen peered at Johnny and really saw him for the first time. First, she looked at his hands—strong hands, helping hands. How many times had he offered her those hands, helping her out of a car, down a steep stair, or up an incline? Too many times to count. Then she glanced up at his face, and she saw a genuine and caring smile. She saw his eyes—honest, intelligent eyes— and suddenly Ellen knew she needed to share her pain with someone. Instinctively, she knew Johnny was that person. Her body trembled, and then all her emotions tumbled out in a flood of words.

"Oh, Johnny, it's so awful. I had a baby, an illegitimate baby. And ... and I had to give him up. I'm such a bad person. How could anyone ever like someone so awful? That's why I never told you. I wanted you to be my friend. I never wanted you to know what a terrible person I am. Could you ever forgive me?" She coughed.

Johnny squeezed her hand in his as he looked into her eyes without wavering. Johnny's mind raced as thoughts flowed out like a waterfall rushing into a river, spraying everywhere. *This is not at all what I expected. Shit. Maybe I should just fold up my tent and disappear. Whoa, hold the phone, John. Let's see. I had sex with Julie when she was my girlfriend and that was okay, but it wasn't okay for Ellen? Think, John, think. You knew from the first time you saw her that she was meant to be your mate. You've pursued her all this time, and now you're going to walk. No. It's no wonder she's been so sad. Oh God, please let me say the right thing. Let me do the right thing. I'm so sorry.* His heart broke for her.

She finished. She left out no detail, including how she thought about Danny every day and how she worried about him. She stared down at her hands, and then she looked up at Johnny expectantly.

"I'm so sorry, Ellen." He paused. "I can't pretend to know how you feel, because I don't. I can see how it's tortured you. I know you well enough to know you blame yourself for what happened and you believe what you've done is unforgivable." Tenderly, he wiped the tears from her face with his finger. "You're wrong."

He continued speaking. "You're the sweetest, most wonderful girl I've ever known. You did what you believed was best for your baby. You also made the only choice you could under the circumstances. In spite of what you think, you're important to your parents, your friends, and you're especially important to me."

Inwardly, he shook, praying he had said the right thing. He hoped he had made the right decision for himself. What would his parents think if they knew? *Man, what a shitload this is.* He didn't let go of her hands.

Ellen felt relieved. In fact, she seemed downright lightheaded. *I can't believe how good I feel. Oh, my, look at poor Johnny. What a load to drop on him.*

She gave him a hint of a smile. "Thank you."

Johnny, dazzled, thought she had given him the most spectacular smile he'd ever seen in his life. His heart sang.

"Let's pay the bill and go for a stroll."

They ambled down toward the water. Carefully, Johnny put his arm around her shoulders. They walked silently for a while, and then he made small talk.

"I have a few things to do for my uncle tomorrow morning, but I thought we could have a picnic in the afternoon, if that's okay with you."

"I'd like that. Mom made some fried chicken today when she found out you were coming. She knows how much you like it. I'll make us a nice picnic lunch."

They found a little stone wall and sat down. He drew her close to him.

"Are you warm enough?" he murmured.

"It's getting just a little chilly," she replied with a suggestion of a shiver.

He kissed her tenderly. Suddenly, Ellen sensed light all around her, as though a thousand fireworks had exploded. Her heart pumped as it exploded too. No longer a lump of ice, it was a throbbing, pounding, roaring, very-much-alive heart. Then she heard music. *Oh, God, this is too much. I can't be hearing music.* In fact, she was. The restaurant across the way always had live music on the weekend. A laugh gushed up inside her.

"Kissing me is funny?"

"No, kissing you is wonderful. But, as we kissed I heard music, just like in the movies when the lovers kiss and the music plays. But it was the music from that restaurant."

Johnny roared. He had actually kissed Ellen. It tasted fantastic, sweet, and still a little salty from her tears. Then it dawned on him. *Did she just say kissing me was wonderful? Wow! God, I love this girl.*

"So, if kissing me is wonderful, do you want to do it again?"

"Yes, yes, I do." It seemed they spent an eternity kissing after that, but finally it was time to go home. At her door, Ellen put her arms around him, gazed at him adoringly, and said, "I'll never be able to thank you for what you've done. You'll never know how much your friendship means to me. I was drowning and you saved me."

He took her face in his hands and looked deep into the pools of her green eyes. "I love you Ellen. I've loved you since the first time I saw you in Stanford's class. I would give my life for you." He kissed her softly. "I'll see you tomorrow."

~

ELLEN COULD HARDLY CONTAIN her happiness and couldn't remember the last time she had felt this light. She experienced happiness welling up inside her as she danced around the living room. Knowing she couldn't possibly go to bed, Ellen went to the patio and noiselessly slid open the door. Once outside, she pirouetted around the yard. Laughing and giggling like a carefree young girl, she spun round and round until she finally fell on the ground exhausted.

Eventually, Ellen went back into the house and upstairs to her room. As she peered at herself in the mirror, she saw a girl she hadn't seen in a long time. The eyes of this girl and the girl herself were actually happy. She plopped into bed and fell into a healing sleep.

~

JOHNNY FELT LIKE HE could drive forever. *I'll never forget this night. This has been the best night of my life. Dad was right. I may have lost a few battles, but I'm going to win this war.* As he drove back to his aunt's house, he anticipated the wonderful days he and Ellen would have together. At the same time, he was sobered by what Ellen had told him, and it made him sad. *How difficult this has been for her. I don't know how she held it in all this time without going crazy.*

He realized a long road still lay ahead of him. This chapter would haunt Ellen for many years to come. There would be obstacles to overcome, but he felt certain that with patience he could help Ellen during this difficult period of her life. After these sobering thoughts, he once again felt elated. When he arrived home, he went into the backyard and gave way to his emotions. He did a wild dance, whooped a couple of times, and then went to bed and fell into a peaceful sleep.

TWENTY-SIX

WHEN ELLEN WENT DOWN to breakfast the next morning, Pearl recognized the difference in her. Ellen was humming. *Something has happened. I just know it. Ellen is beaming. There's an aura about her. It's got to be that darling Johnny. Bless him, he's finally captured her heart.*

Wiping her hands on her apron, she turned to Ellen. "Good morning. I take it you had a good time last night."

"I had a marvelous time. Is the food ready for lunch? Johnny will be here around eleven. Instead of eating here, we're going on a picnic."

"Not to worry, everything is ready. We just have to pack up. The only thing left for you to do is make some lemonade."

"Thanks Mom, you're a doll." She kissed Pearl and gave her a hug.

Plotzing, Pearl wanted to know what had happened, but she didn't want to sound as though she were prying. As she scrambled some eggs, she casually asked, "So how was the dinner? Is it a nice restaurant?"

"It's a wonderful restaurant, and the dinner was scrumptious."

"And?"

"And what?"

"And what else did you do?"

"Oh, we took a walk by the water and talked. Then we came home."

"Good, I'm glad you had a nice evening. Johnny is such a *mensch*. Your dad and I both like him a lot."

"Mmm, me too." By this time, Pearl had Ellen's breakfast ready. "Smells delicious, I'm famished." She gobbled down her food.

"I'm going to shower now and get dressed. Then I'll make the lemonade and pack the picnic basket." She floated out of the kitchen.

Pearl smiled a huge smile. *My God, she's floating. She's smitten all right.*

At exactly eleven o'clock, the doorbell rang. When Pearl answered the door, she could tell by the expression on Johnny's face that he was as happy as Ellen. They exchanged greetings as Ellen came out of the kitchen.

"Stop flirting with my mother and start *shlepping* this stuff," Ellen laughed. "Mom, I was just kidding, don't look so shocked."

"I beg your pardon. I flirt as I please. And, by the way, I please as I flirt!" And with that, Pearl flounced out of the room as she said, "Have a wonderful day."

Both Johnny and Ellen burst out laughing.

"I love your mother, but I never quite know what to expect from her."

"Neither do I, neither do I."

⁓

THEY HAD A GLORIOUS day. Ellen realized that as well as she thought she knew Johnny, she didn't know him at all. She had always been so preoccupied with her own problems that she had never really seen him clearly. She also recognized that in his concern for her, he had kept himself hidden. Even though she had always thought of him as a likeable person, she now discovered just how special he was. So smart and clever, and, yes, so dear.

For his part, Johnny was ecstatic. This was an Ellen he had never been privileged to see. What a sense of humor she had, and she had so much to say. She had always been so quiet that he hadn't realized the wealth and depth of her knowledge. She expressed her opinions with confidence and assurance. He didn't know she had once participated in debate, but he wasn't surprised by this revelation.

At the end of this exceptional day, Johnny felt sad when it was time for him to head back to LA. He kissed Ellen tenderly and promised to call when he got home. On the drive home, he reviewed the events of the past couple of days. He understood he would have to be careful with this relationship. He realized how extremely fragile Ellen was still. Any wrong move on his part could destroy her, as well as the relationship. As for himself, even though he felt certain he had made the right decision to stand by Ellen, there was still that little piece of gnawing doubt. Not an easy job to tackle. But, as his mom always told him, nothing worth having is ever easy.

THE TIME HAD COME to go house hunting for school. Johnny came to San Diego to help Ellen search for a house where the girls could live during the upcoming school year. They found a couple of places that would work. Ellen called Myra, who promised to come to San Diego the following weekend.

By the hugging and kissing that went on, anyone would think they hadn't seen each other in years. As Myra appraised Ellen, she immediately noticed the change in her, but she was shrewd enough to keep quiet for the time being. Ellen quizzed Myra about her summer.

"It's been fabulous. Bob and I have had a lot of time together, and I really like my job."

When they arrived at the first house on the list, Myra expressed indifference toward it. "It could work, but ..." she said.

"Never mind, I know your buts," Ellen said. "I think you'll like the second house we picked."

Indeed she did. She loved the house. "Perfect, just perfect. So charming, plus the stuff from our old room will work great. Of course, we'll have to go shopping again for more furniture, paint, material, and other stuff."

Ellen groaned as she turned to Johnny and griped. "Oh, God, here she goes again."

Mystified, Johnny said, "I don't understand what the big deal is here."

Ellen raised an eyebrow and looked at Myra as she explained to Johnny, "Wait, you'll be sorry you ever got involved."

They found their way to the rental office, signed a year's lease, and paid their deposit and first month's rent. The agent reminded them that damages would be deducted from their deposit.

After they finished and got in the car to leave, Johnny suggested, "Let's grab some food before Myra has to go back to San Francisco." He pulled up to a restaurant. "Is this place okay, girls?"

"It's fine," they responded in chorus.

After they ordered, Johnny excused himself so he could say hello to some people he knew.

"So, kiddo, what's been going on this summer?" Myra asked.

198 | ROCHELLE PADZENSKY

Ellen felt her cheeks flush as she told Myra about her expanded responsibilities at Titillations.

Myra nodded. "And?"

"And what?" Ellen answered, giggling like a small child.

"And what's going on between you and Johnny?"

After Ellen had been going on nonstop for fifteen minutes, Myra interjected, "Okay, I get the picture. I'm so happy for both of you. I always knew Johnny was the guy for you."

She patted Ellen. "It makes me happy to see you happy."

Johnny came back as their food was served. Myra told them she would come back the next weekend. "That way we'll have plenty of time to shop."

Ellen wrote the girls in The Club and let them know the house would be vacant in mid-August, so they could actually move in before school started.

The next couple of weeks were busy. Between phone calls, letters, and shopping, Ellen hardly seemed to have any time for Johnny. Yet, he remained his patient self. "I can't understand what the big deal is. It's just a place to live," he groaned. "But, I guess if it's a big deal to you, then it's a big deal to me."

"Thanks for being so much help. I really appreciate it. You're a great gopher," she said as she gave him a quick squeeze.

~

MOVING DAY ARRIVED. FORLORN, Pearl said to Ellen, "Are you sure you don't need any help?"

"Johnny's borrowed a truck, and between the two of us we can handle it." She gave her mom a hug. "It's okay, Mom."

Johnny drove up a few minutes later. In less than an hour, they had loaded up the truck and were ready to leave.

Ellen went to find her mother. "So, we're ready to go. I'll call you when we get there."

"Now Johnny," Pearl instructed, when she came out to see them off, "drive carefully, and take good care of Ellen."

"Don't worry, Mrs. Gordon, I will. And say goodbye to Mr. Gordon for me too."

They waved as they got into the car. Ellen was looking forward to the upcoming year. *New beginnings. A new relationship with Johnny and moving into a new house with all my good friend*s.

TWENTY-SEVEN

THE NEXT FEW WEEKS flew by as the girls settled into their new house and new schedules.

At breakfast one morning Myra proclaimed, in typical Myra fashion, "Girls, I think it's time to have our first party."

"Yes, our social majesty, and what did you have in mind?" CeCe inquired.

"Well, I thought we'd have a dinner party. We can invite all our boyfriends, and then each of us can invite one other couple. That will make twenty people, which is just the right size. Any suggestions?"

"Madam secretary, majesty, whatever, who is going to cook this feast? When do you plan to have it, and what kind of dinner party will it be?" Joanie questioned.

"One question at a time, girl. I thought we'd have it in two weeks. I've checked the calendar. It's a slow week on campus. We'll all be responsible for cooking a part of the dinner. We'll have it on the patio, have candles all around, and hang some flowers. First we'll serve soft drinks and chips 'n dip and some other appetizers. That's as far as my thinking has gone so far."

"I make delicious brisket and potatoes," Ellen volunteered.

Joanie spoke up next. "Umm, good. I make a great green bean casserole that would go with the brisket. How about you, CeCe?"

"I'm your salad queen."

"Well, if you do the salad, I'll do the appetizers," Myra contributed.

"I guess that makes me the dessert winner. That's okay. I do killer strawberry shortcake with ice cream and whipped cream," Patty offered.

Within the next couple of days, they extended invitations and began serious planning. Each of the girls had come to the new house with various household items, including an assortment of pots, pans, silver, and dishes. They found two glaring holes in their inventory. Their collection of dishes was a disaster, and they didn't have enough serving plates. The ever-inventive Myra came up with a perfect solution.

"We'll tell each person to bring their own dinner plate. It can be one they already have, or it can be a new one. The catch is that there has to be a story to go with the plate. For instance, if it's an old one, where did it come from, how did they get it, and what's its personal meaning? If it's new, what made them buy that particular plate, and what special meaning does it have for them?"

They all shouted in unison. "Great idea, Myra." Her idea would make it possible for them to pool their money and get some serving pieces.

The night before the party, everyone pitched in and cleaned the house from top to bottom. By the time they finished, the place sparkled. Commenting on their work, Patty observed, "We should have parties more often. The house looks super."

Ellen cooked her brisket in advance, since it always tasted better the second day. Between the smell of brisket cooking and the smell of a clean house, excitement built, and the girls could hardly sleep. They were all up early the next morning.

Johnny came over and sliced the brisket, so all Ellen had to do was pop it in the oven and reheat it. While the rest of the girls prepared their dishes, Ellen and Johnny set the tables. Surprised, Ellen saw that Johnny knew how to set a table correctly.

He explained that he often helped his mom so he could spend time with her. "She always told me, 'Now, Jonathan, you never know when it will come in handy to know how to properly set a table.'" He guffawed.

Ellen chortled at his excellent imitation of Bessie. Then they decorated the patio by hanging fishnets from the patio supports and filling the nets with flowers. Various shaped candles placed around the patio completed the decorations. They surveyed the results and declared them perfect.

Ellen went to the kitchen to get the girls. "Time for you to check out the tables and the decorations."

The girls oohed and aahed.

"It's cool, guys. Imagine what it's going to look like at night with the candles lit. It's going to be a super party," Myra exclaimed.

When the girls were all dressed, they gathered in the living room. With their scrubbed college girl beauty and soft pastel dresses, the group resembled a rainbow. After they finished complimenting each other, Myra set out the snacks and lit the candles. The Club was ready.

The doorbell rang, and their first guests for their first dinner party arrived. Johnny and Bob stood at the door, with bottles of wine in addition to their plates. Myra took the wine and burst out laughing when she saw their plates, but decided to say nothing. The questions would come later at the table. Soon, the rest of the boys and the other invited couples arrived, and the party was underway.

As the group chatted and munched on appetizers, Ellen and Johnny scurried into the kitchen to get the food ready. Ellen busied herself organizing the food, and Johnny couldn't help commenting, "You're just like your mother, a fantastic hostess."

He gave her a squeeze and kissed her on the back of the neck. Without warning, her body betrayed her. The kiss gave her such a sexual jolt of desire that it shocked her. Her lovemaking with Johnny had been confined to hand-holding and restrained kissing. What had just happened? It had all been so safe, so warm and comfortable up to this point. Until now, she really hadn't had the sexual longings she'd experienced with Kenny. She had done such a good job repressing her feelings that she hadn't realized she still had desires. The butterflies in her stomach threatened to come up to her throat. She struggled to regain her composure, and after doing so, decided to dismiss the incident.

Ellen could tell that Johnny saw her jump and knew something had just happened. Trying to prevent an awkward moment, he began to chatter and worked at getting the food together. She pulled herself together, and they finished getting the food ready. Just then, Myra came into the kitchen.

"It's time to have everybody sit down. The food is ready. Have the servers come into the kitchen please," Ellen instructed.

"Yes, boss," Myra responded before disappearing.

On cue, Joanie and CeCe came into the kitchen. "What do you want us to do?" they asked.

"Serve the salad. Then Johnny will pick up the salad plates so everyone can put out their dinner plates. We'll pass out the rest of the food family style."

While they ate their salad, Myra explained the rules concerning the plates. "Before you put any food on your plate, you must show it to us. After all the plates have been shown and everyone has been served, you'll tell your story."

Bob showed his plate with great fanfare and flourish. "Ta, Da." A Donald Duck plate with compartments. The group laughed and applauded. Johnny ducked under the table and held up his plate, which was a Dumbo Plate, also with compartments.

"Look, they're twins." More laughter.

As each person showed his or her plate, Ellen became lost in her own thoughts about what had happened in the kitchen. *I don't understand it. Why did that happen now? I just don't get it. What can I do about it?* When everyone finished showing their plates, the girls served.

Johnny stood. "Before we eat, I would like to give a toast." Everyone raised their glasses.

"To the best hostesses in California, we raise our glasses and say thank you from the bottom of our plates. Let's eat."

"Hear, hear." They all clapped.

"Now we're ready to hear your stories," Myra announced.

As the crowd ate and told their stories, Ellen picked at her food, still thinking about what had happened, until CeCe told her story.

"I'm not sure where this plate originally came from," CeCe explained, "but it was given to my grandma by one of her boarders when he couldn't pay the rent. He assured her it was valuable, and when he had the money, he wanted it back. Of course, he never had the money, and Grandma ended up with the plate. She liked it and always told her children not to give it away because it was valuable. They all thought the plate was double ugly and nobody wanted it. When Grandma died, the family decided my mom should get it, because she was the youngest. She couldn't give it away or throw it away, since it had belonged to her mother, and besides, she would feel guilty. So it's been sitting in our cupboard for years. When I went back to school this year, my mom gave it to me. Whether it's really valuable or not, no one knows. So here I am, stuck, as the newly appointed guardian of the plate."

The group acclaimed CeCe's story as winner of first prize.

Then the cooks were complimented. The guys all agreed they would vote for Ellen to make them brisket every week. Ellen, embarrassed by the attention, sat quietly. Finally, amid the calls for a speech, she rose. A tiny bit like the old Ellen who could win a debate hands down, with bravado, she raised her hand for quiet. "Thank you all for recognizing the superiority of my cooking." Then she blew Hollywood kisses in her best Marilyn Monroe imitation. More guffawing and applause.

After dessert, they cleared the table and moved it out of the way. Then they put on records and danced. As the evening came to a close, all the guys and girls agreed it had turned out to be one of the best parties ever. Once their guests departed, the girls went to change out of their party garb and Bob and Johnny began to clean up.

After they finished cleaning up, Myra and Ellen walked the guys to the car. When Johnny kissed Ellen, it happened again. She experienced such a flash of desire that it scared her. Again, Johnny felt her shudder and hastily let her go. He leaped into the car. "I'll call you tomorrow," he said as he drove off quickly.

"I'm so tired, I think I'll sleep all day tomorrow," Myra yawned, as The Club headed off to bed.

Ellen had nightmares all night long. She dreamed she was pregnant, alone, and cold, although she had vowed she would never be in that position again.

When she woke the following morning, she huddled under her covers and thought about the meaning of her dream. Her heart beat rapidly as she thought about how much she loved

Johnny ... but she couldn't let this happen again. She considered that maybe it would be better if she stopped seeing him, but the thought of that made her heart hurt even more. She would miss his warm, loving ways too much. Then she realized Johnny hadn't done anything different. He hadn't pressed her or done anything to cause this reaction. Her own damn body had done these things to her. *Damn. You mustn't, you mustn't.*

This newfound knowledge cast a pall over the day. When Johnny called, Ellen was less than enthusiastic, so he ended the call before any tension could develop between them. She spent the rest of the day moping in her room.

⁓

JOHNNY HAD HAD HIS own nightmares during the night. He had frightened Ellen, and she ran away, and he couldn't find her. He searched for her all night in his dreams. When he woke up, he felt exhausted and miserable. *Shit, is this how I want to spend my life?* Perhaps he should just abandon this relationship now. *Not yet. Be careful. Ellen is still too fragile.* He knew he must be patient.

When he called her and heard the lack of warmth in her voice, it scared the hell out of him. He spent the rest of the day trying to figure out how to get things back to normal.

TWENTY-EIGHT

MYRA AND JOHNNY SIPPED Cokes in the Student Union. "Has something happened between you and Ellen?" Myra asked. "Something's wrong, I feel it. She's more like when I first met her. Quiet, withdrawn."

Absently, Johnny swirled his Coke around with his finger, as if he would find an answer in its depths if he stirred it long enough. He could understand Myra's puzzlement, since she didn't know what had happened to Ellen. Unfortunately, he couldn't enlighten her, and besides, he felt glum himself.

He eyed Myra and responded, "I'm not quite sure what's going on." He sighed and continued, "All I can say is be yourself with her, and do what you've always done. Be her friend."

She held Johnny's hand. "It'll work out … I'm sure it will. I'll work on her." She checked the time. "I've got to go. Catch you later."

Johnny decided to start over with Ellen. He called her often. He drove her to and from the library. And he barely touched her. He continued to be patient and considerate, even though he was ready to kill himself. But he hung in there.

DURING THE NEXT FEW weeks, Ellen agonized over what had happened. As she analyzed the events of that night, she realized she already loved Johnny as a friend. They went to the library together, studied and sweated through exams together, went to the movies, read and argued over books, and sometimes just walked in companionable silence. She loved Johnny for the man he was, thoughtful and even-tempered. Compassionate toward others and passionate about things he cared about. He always treated her as an equal and challenged her when he thought she was wrong, but never in a superior manner.

Now, she realized she loved him with her physical being as well. She liked the way his body felt when it was pressed against her as they danced. She liked his touch on her shoulder. She loved the way she felt when he kissed her. She hit herself in the head, as she realized things were different this time. Johnny cared for her and was not just looking for sex. *Damn, I need to let him know how I feel, but I don't have the words, and besides, I don't know if I can say them yet.*

Instead, she tried to show him by the way she squeezed his hand, by the way she touched his arm, and by the way she gazed at him. He received the message. Another battle won. Their courtship resumed and continued to grow.

ELLEN HAD BEEN DOING some serious thinking. What did she want to do with her life? She reviewed the previous summer and decided she wanted to help children, like the unfortunate ones she had seen while driving. The next time Johnny drove her to the library, she discussed it with him.

"If that's your calling," he said, "then that's what you should do. Tell you what. Let's make an appointment with the head of the department. You'll be able to find out the requirements needed to get into the School of Social Work.

That's why she loved Johnny. He was a man of action. "Uh, ya, I guess that's what I should do."

Johnny had a mission now. If Ellen wanted to be a social worker, then by God, he would do whatever he could to help her. He took this as a positive sign that she was coming out of her shell again, and that made him happy.

Even though their relationship resumed where it had left off, Johnny kept his promise to himself. He behaved very carefully. They held hands in the movies, he held her close when they danced, but the only kissing he did was to kiss her goodnight. If only he could have read her mind. *What's the matter with Johnny?* she wondered. *Is he ever going to do more than kiss me goodnight? Are we ever going to get back to where things were with us physically?* If Johnny had only known what Ellen was thinking, he would have been enormously relieved.

THE HOLIDAYS RAPIDLY APPROACHED. Johnny called Ellen. "Mom just called. She's invited your parents to spend the holidays with us, and they accepted."

"That's great. Does that mean I'm invited too or just my parents?" she chortled.

"Of course you too. Let's ask your parents for some suggestions as to what they would like to do when they're here, so my mom will know what to plan."

Nate and Pearl, delighted at how well things were going with the kids, were excited at the prospect of spending the week with the Friedmans. At last they felt exonerated. Their decision to have Ellen's baby adopted had been right after all.

Although they never discussed it, they both knew it was always in each other's mind. Somewhere out there in the world they had a grandchild they would never know. They prayed often that this child would never want for anything and had found a good home. They were as haunted as Ellen by the experience.

Nate picked up Ellen from school and brought her home, so they could all drive to LA together. When Ellen went upstairs to her room and saw her bed full of new things, she hurled herself into Pearl's surprised arms. "Mom, you didn't have to buy me all those fabulous new things."

"It's okay. You wouldn't want for your father to be ashamed of us."

Ellen snorted. "No chance of that, Mom. Anyway, Johnny's parents are just like you guys, *haimish*. They don't put on any airs. The whole family is that way, except maybe for Ruthie, Johnny's sister. Sometimes she can be a bit pretentious."

The only thing left to do the next morning was for Pearl to pack up the goodies she had made to take to Bessie. The house gift she had purchased was already wrapped and packed.

That night Pearl tossed and turned. *Why did the Friedmans invite us? Do they want to check us out and make sure we're suitable people for their kind of crowd?* She hoped she would like Abe and Bessie and they would like her and Nate. As usual, Nate pooh-poohed her fears.

"Pearl, don't worry, we'll like them, they'll like us. What's not to like? They like our daughter, we like their son. Nu, that's it. Done deal. We're all happy."

Pearl couldn't help but laugh. Nate could always make things simple and straightforward.

They got up early the next morning. Nate griped as he packed the car. "You girls think you're going for a year? I don't understand why you need all this stuff. Where am I going to put everything?"

"Sha, it's okay. We need to be prepared. Of course, if you'd rather, I could just take underwear and buy as I go." She gave Nate *The Look*.

"Okay, okay," he grumbled. "I'll find room. It's bad enough that I know you're going to shop anyway. Just remember, there's a limit."

Pearl grinned. He could never refuse her anything.

~

PEARL AND ELLEN RELAXED during the ride. When they arrived at the Friedmans, Johnny flew out the door to greet them. He pumped Nate's hand, gave Pearl a hug, and kissed Ellen on the cheek.

"Welcome to the Friedmans. We're happy to have you. C'mon in and meet my mom."

As they walked into the house, Bessie dried her hands on a dish towel. She welcomed Nate and Pearl and gave Ellen a big hug.

"It's so nice to see you, Ellen. You're looking fantastic, as usual. You'll stay in your same room. I'm going to put your mom and dad downstairs so they'll have some privacy. Is that okay with you?"

"That'll be just fine."

"Jonathan, take everyone's luggage and put it in their rooms."

She turned to Nate and Pearl. "Nate, Pearl, Ellen, come in the kitchen. We'll have a little *nosh* and get acquainted. Abe should be home soon. He called and said he was on his way."

Pearl instructed Johnny to bring in the boxes of goodies. "Just a few cookies for your family, Bessie."

"That's sweet of you, Pearl. Thank you. We'll set them out on a tray. The rest of the family will be over later to meet you. Sit, sit. Ruby will take care of it."

She introduced Ruby to Nate and Pearl. "Without Ruby, I'd be a dead duck. She's my right-hand man." Ruby gathered up the packages and went to get a tray. At that moment, they heard the garage door open. "That must be Abe. He made good time today." She called to him, "Come, we're in the kitchen."

Abe entered, which called for another round of introductions and greetings. Bessie poured coffee and tea and put out some snacks. Ellen observed for a few minutes. When she sensed things were going well, she motioned to Johnny, and they left so their parents could get acquainted.

"I think our parents like each other," Johnny remarked.

"I hope so." She had been keeping her fingers crossed. "So what are we going to do?"

"I just got some new records. I thought we'd go downstairs, listen to music, and maybe dance."

In this way he could hold Ellen close and smell her wonderful fragrance. As they danced, Johnny felt his desire for Ellen making itself evident. He hoped she hadn't noticed. He rapidly drew apart from her and said, "I'm sure you probably want to unpack now."

"I do. And freshen up. What's the schedule for tonight?"

"The whole family is coming over for dinner. Casual tonight. Nothing fancy. Give the family a chance to get acquainted."

"That sounds perfect. It'll be nice to catch up, since I haven't seen anyone since last year."

Just then, Bessie brought Nate and Pearl downstairs. "We're going to get ourselves unpacked," Pearl told Ellen.

"Okay, I'm going up to unpack too and get ready for dinner. Do you need any help?"

"No, but thank you," Pearl responded. "We'll be up in a bit." Bessie showed them to their room, as Ellen and Johnny headed back upstairs.

Later, when Johnny's nieces and nephews arrived and saw Ellen, they immediately attacked her with hugs and kisses.

"Whoa, remember Ellen is breakable," Johnny chided the youngsters.

"It's okay. I know them now, and I was expecting it. I was almost ready."

They had a pleasant evening. The two families seemed to enjoy each other, and it was late when Johnny's siblings and their families departed.

Ellen yawned. "I'm exhausted. I need to go to bed now."

Johnny escorted her up to her room, put his arms around her, and kissed her a bit more passionately than usual.

Surprised and pleased, she murmured, "Um, you could do that again."

"I don't think so. You need your beauty sleep." He embraced her one last time and turned to go to his room.

She could have killed him. *If he doesn't do something soon, I'm going to explode. I want him to kiss me. I want him to touch me. I want ... what am I saying? I do need to go to bed, before I do something I shouldn't.*

TWENTY-NINE

THE WEEK PASSED QUICKLY. Abe took time off, so he could spend time with Nate. Bessie and Pearl were like old friends. On the day before New Year's Eve, the entire family knew Ellen was about to get an engagement ring. Ellen was the only one who didn't have a clue.

Bessie and Pearl could hardly contain their excitement. They anxiously waited for the time to come when Johnny would pop the question. Having planned to do it at a very special moment, Johnny thought he would have a nervous breakdown in the meantime. He felt nauseated. *What if she says no?*

New Year's Eve morning, Pearl, Bessie, and Ellen left for the beauty shop after breakfast to get ready for the party. They planned to get the works: hair, nails, pedicures, facials, and massages.

Ellen loved the pampering. This was a first for her. It felt so soothing. After they finished, they had tea at a charming teashop. Then they headed home for an afternoon nap.

"I feel like a dishrag, I'm so relaxed. I could sleep until tomorrow," Ellen said.

NO OTHER OPTION | 215

"All this beauty treatment and you want to sleep through the party? I don't think so. After a little nap, you'll feel like a million dollars," Bessie told her.

Before going to her room to lie down, Ellen checked in on the boys. She found them nonchalantly watching TV. Ellen had no idea that Johnny had had the shakes while they were gone and that Abe and Nate had been trying to keep him calm.

When Ellen got up from her nap, it was time to get ready. She checked her reflection in the mirror, and what she saw pleased her. A happy girl. A content girl. It had been a glorious week surrounded by people she loved.

Ellen never used much make-up. Usually, she just used mascara on her lashes, but tonight she decided to make an exception. After studying her eyes, she also used some eyeliner and a touch of eye shadow. The difference amazed her. Then she applied her lipstick to her lips, smeared some on her fingertip, and rubbed it on her cheeks to give her face a light blush. *Well, now, don't I look sexy? Maybe this will give Mr. Johnny a few ideas.*

Pleased with herself, she hummed and went into the bedroom to put on her dress and jewelry. Mom was right. The dress was gorgeous, peach organza with metallic silver flowers appliquéd from the bust line, following a line to the waist and down the full skirt. Simple but elegant. Nate had had Irene create an original necklace for her of filigree metallic flowers that matched the ones on the dress. A tiny peridot gemstone filled in the center of each flower. Matching earrings and a pair of shoes that Pearl had had dyed to match Ellen's dress completed the ensemble. Ellen felt beautiful. No, gorgeous. *Watch out Mr. Johnny, I'm out to get you. No goodnight pecks tonight. I expect some real kissing.* She sighed with anticipation.

New Year's Eve at the country club was always extraordinary. Ellen looked forward to a wondrous evening and an incredible new year. She did feel somewhat sad, though, because it meant getting back to the regular routine after tomorrow.

A knock on the door interrupted her thoughts. It was Pearl. Her mother squealed when she saw her daughter.

"You are absolutely breathtaking. The dress is perfect for this special night."

What does she mean by that?

"Because it's New Year's Eve," Pearl stammered, catching the look of confusion in her daughter's eyes.

Ellen hugged her and said, "Thanks Mom, and thanks for the dress. I love it. Irene did a fabulous job with the jewelry too. Hey, you're glamorous tonight too. This is the first time I've seen you in black. It's so sophisticated. Wow!"

Pearl preened. "Yes, I'm definitely the sophisticated lady tonight. Actually, I came up here to give you an evening purse. I packed it with my things."

Ellen kissed her mother. "Thanks for being such a wonderful mom."

Pearl's eyes welled up. She collected herself and asked, "Are we ready to make our grand entrance?"

"I'm ready." Ellen opened the door and walked toward the stairs. Bessie opened her door and joined them. She also looked glamorous tonight dressed in midnight blue lace.

~

WHEN THEY REACHED THE top of the stairs, Ellen called out, "Yoo hoo, we're going to make our grand entrance, please be ready."

Abe, Nate, and Johnny appeared at the bottom of the stairs. One by one, the women glided down the stairs—first Pearl, then Bessie, and then Ellen. When Johnny saw Ellen, he was literally dumbstruck. She was the most beautiful woman he had ever seen. He loved her so much, it hurt him to breathe. *Please,* he prayed, *let her say yes tonight.*

When she reached the bottom of the stairs, she gave him her most dazzling smile.

"I'm overcome by your beauty," he whispered.

"You're handsome yourself. Almost as handsome as our fathers."

"Well, I'm miffed," he said as graciously as possible.

As they complimented each other, Ruby came into the foyer with the camera, and after taking several pictures, Abe pronounced them ready to go.

~

ON THE WAY TO the club, Johnny had such dry mouth he could barely carry on a conversation. *I've got to relax, or I'm never going to pull this off.* It felt like the ring was burning a hole in his pocket. Fortunately, no one noticed he was unusually quiet as they chatted. By the time they reached the club, he managed to calm down and act like himself.

The rest of the family was already milling about. They all greeted each other, looking forward to the night ahead. When the entire family walked into the dining room, all the women oohed and aahed over the decorations.

The dining room was decorated like a winter wonderland with little twinkling lights everywhere. The artificial white trees sparkled with glitter, and jeweled birds glided among the branches. Yards of white chiffon floated around and above the trees. The tables were decorated with chiffon cloths, and tiny tapers rose above white roses frosted with glitter. The effect was breathtaking.

The waiter brought drinks as they settled into their chairs. The band played, and Johnny asked Ellen to dance. He whispered in her ear and told her how much he loved her. By the time they were ready to go back to the table, he could feel Ellen's heart pounding against his chest. *A good sign.*

While the waiter served appetizers, the women gossiped about the events of the last few days. When the servers brought the salads, Ellen noticed Johnny had hardly eaten a bite. "Are you okay? You've hardly touched your salad."

"Just saving myself for dessert. I have to watch my waistline, you know."

As they waited for their entrée, a trio of waiters marched up to their table. They each held up a corner of a gigantic box and stopped in front of Ellen.

"I believe this box is for you, Miss Ellen," the first waiter announced.

Ellen appeared surprised. "For me?"

"Yes, ma'am."

The waiters placed the box on the table. When Ellen got the box open, she stared into the eyes of a huge stuffed puppy dog. With Abe's help, she got the dog out of the box. "Oh, look how cute he is. Johnny, is this from you?"

He managed to croak out a yes. She hadn't seen the ring tied to the dog's bow yet.

"Well, he's very cute." She kissed Johnny on the cheek and put the dog back in the box.

Johnny felt dizzy. *How could she have not seen the ring?*

Everyone at the table was *plotzing.* "Ellen, I don't think you really looked at the dog, darling," said Pearl.

Ellen glanced at the family, confused. She opened the box again and stared at the puppy, trying to figure what she was supposed to be looking for, but she didn't have a clue.

"Did you notice what a beautiful bow the dog is wearing?" Bessie prodded.

And then it happened. The flash on the dog's bow caught her eye. She gasped.

"Oh my God, it's a diamond ring!"

Her fingers trembled as she tried to loosen the bow and remove the ring. Johnny helped her. When she finally got it off, Johnny took it, got down on one knee, and said, "Ellen Gordon, I love you, will you marry me?"

Shaking, Ellen answered, "Yes."

Everyone clapped, including the people at the surrounding tables. They had seen what was going on and couldn't help but observe the momentous occasion.

Johnny kissed Ellen. As the family crowded around the happy couple, kissing, hugging, and congratulating, they created quite a scene, but nobody cared. In fact, the other party-goers were tickled that something interesting and unexpected had happened. It would give them all something to gossip about tomorrow.

The band had been alerted about the event. Once the hubbub subsided, the bandleader announced that the band would play the happy couple's favorite song. As they played "Tenderly," Johnny said to Ellen, "May I have the pleasure of the first dance with my fiancé?"

"Yes," she said and melted into Johnny's arms.

"Are you happy?" he whispered into her ear. "I am. In fact, I'm the happiest man in the world. I was really scared you wouldn't say yes."

"Then I'll say yes and yes again. I'm happier than I've ever been in my whole life. We will be happy, won't we, Johnny?"

"The happiest," he murmured.

For Ellen and Johnny, it was truly the best New Year's Eve.

~

BEFORE ELLEN WENT TO bed, she prayed. *Danny, I hope your New Year's Eve was as perfect as mine. I hope you have a loving family and that you are as happy as I am tonight.* The tears welled up in her eyes. *How I wish I really knew that he's safe and okay.*

Is everything going to be all right now? Is what happened in my past finally behind me?

THIRTY

ABE, BESSIE, NATE, AND Pearl sat at the kitchen table making wedding plans. Amused, Johnny and Ellen listened. Finally, Ellen interjected, "Do we have anything to say about this wedding?"

"Of course, darlings. We're just talking. You can have whatever you want. You know parents, we like to think we know it all."

"Funny, I thought you did know it all," Ellen quipped.

"Okay, so what do you children have in mind?" Pearl asked. The four parents turned to Ellen and Johnny.

Ellen replied, "We'd like to get married in June after graduation. That would give us time for a honeymoon and a chance to get settled before we begin our graduate programs. And actually, we really would like you to put a plan together, so we can just say yes or no along the way, since we'll both be so busy with our final semester."

Both moms agreed they would be thrilled to make plans on the kids' behalf, subject to Ellen's approval. Ellen excused herself and exited to call her friends with the news. She called Myra first.

"You sneaky little dog," Myra squealed. "Who would have ever thought you'd be the first to get a ring? The quiet one, the studious one, the serious one. Who knew? Congratulations, I love both of you. You're perfect together. Of course, you know I expect to be the maid of honor."

"I wouldn't have anyone else, you know that, Myra." They chatted for a few more minutes, then Ellen said, "Listen, Myra, I still have to call the other girls. I'll see you back at school."

She hung up and proceeded to call the rest of her friends. By the time she finished, Ellen discovered she was famished. She went in search of Johnny and found him in the family room snoozing in front of the TV.

"Wake up, you lazy bum." She ran her fingers down his nose.

"Huh?" he snorted. "Was I sleeping? I thought I was watching the game."

"From under your eyelids. I'm starving, how about you? I'm going to make some sandwiches. Do you want something?"

"Gosh, I'm starving too. I'll help." They found the four parents still gabbing in the kitchen and having a bite themselves.

Bessie got up from the table. "I bet you kids are hungry. Sit, sit, I'll make you a little something."

"I'll help you," Pearl volunteered as she pushed back her chair. "I need to move around a bit. I'm getting glued to this chair."

After Ellen and Johnny finished eating, it was time to get packed, in preparation for departing the following morning. They all gathered together again at dinner for one last group meal.

Ellen reflected. *It's such a cozy feeling being with both of our families.* She marveled at how well they all got along. *I thank my lucky stars I've found a family that's so much like my own.*

The entire family went to bed early, since they were all still exhausted from the previous night's revelries. In the morning,

Nate and Johnny packed up their cars. Johnny kissed Ellen goodbye, as he planned to drive straight back to school, and she planned to go home with her parents and then back to school from there.

On the way home, she dreamed about her future. *Life will be wonderful from now on, won't it? Nothing else bad can possibly happen.*

THIRTY-ONE

EVERYONE HAD BEEN BACK at school for three weeks. Since Myra had no classes in the morning, she was alone at the house when the call came from the State Police. It was swift, and it was final. Nate and Pearl had been hit head-on by a drunk driver as they drove home from Titillations and had been killed instantly.

With her thoughts in turmoil, she called Bob. He told her to stay at the house while he found Johnny, and then they would go together to find Ellen. It didn't take long for the two of them to get to the house. In the meantime, Myra had checked Ellen's schedule so they would know where to find her.

Tears ran down Johnny's face. "Pull yourself together, man," Bob counseled Johnny. "You have to be strong for Ellen. This is going to devastate her."

Without a sound, the three of them got into the car. Myra informed them that Ellen could be found on her way to her lit class. They spotted her right away by the campus center. Johnny leaped out of the car and caught up with her. The instant she saw his face, she knew something was wrong. She felt the blood drain from her own face.

"What is it, Johnny, what's wrong?"

Myra and Bob joined them. "Let's go sit down," Bob said.

Myra held Ellen, and Johnny took her hands. For a second, he couldn't speak.

"Ellen, I don't know how to say this. Your mom and dad were killed this morning in a car accident."

His voice broke, and he couldn't say anything else. He held on to her as tightly as he could. She heard their voices, but they sounded far away. She could hardly hear the words. Mom and Pop? Killed instantly? As numbness overcame her, she felt her legs give way, and she passed out.

Frantic, Johnny rubbed her hands. "Get some water," he shouted.

Bob ran to get water from the campus center. By the time he returned, Johnny had revived her. "Here, Ellen, take a drink."

She felt awful, woozy, but most of all she experienced a terrible cold in her veins. That terrible cold that comes when one knows the worst has happened. The tears streamed down her face. "It can't be true, Johnny, can it?" she cried.

"I'm so sorry, I'm so sorry."

ABE AND BESSIE TOOK over. Abe gently questioned Ellen to find out who Nate's lawyer was. He called and obtained a copy of their wills so they could make funeral arrangements. He wanted to make sure their wishes were followed.

Tom and Ginny came to the funeral. Pearl's sister, Sarah, her husband, Si, and their daughter, Elaine, came from Denver. Pop's only living brother lived in a nursing home in Chicago and was unable to travel. They all wept together. The members of The Club and other friends were also in attendance.

As Ellen sat in the synagogue waiting for the funeral to commence, she looked around and was surprised at the number of people there. Several people whom she didn't know expressed their condolences. She clutched Johnny's hand as the service began. She tried hard to concentrate on what the Rabbi said.

"As evidenced by the number of people here today," he began, "you can see that for the short time Nate and Pearl were in our community, they made many friends. Both were active in the Temple and volunteered often in the community. Pearl served on the board of the symphony and the Red Cross and was an active and loyal member of the Temple Sisterhood. Nate acted as a sponsor for many organizations."

As the Rabbi went on, his voice began to sound far away, and Ellen trembled. *Mom, Pop, what will become of me? You always stood by me, even during those times when I caused you so much pain. Is this my punishment for being bad? You were too young to die. Mom, you were only fifty-three and Pop fifty-five. I still need you.* Memories flooded her mind.

Johnny nudged her. "Come, Ellen," he whispered. "It's time to go to the cemetery."

During the service at the cemetery, Ellen wept uncontrollably. Johnny had to support her as she put the first shovel of dirt over the coffins. In some ways it seemed as if her own life had ended, and it was only Johnny's firm grasp on her that kept her from falling over.

At the house after the funeral, the family and her friends all pitched in to help. Bessie, Ruthie, and Sylvia managed the food. CeCe, Joanie, and Patty kept the kitchen clean. Johnny and Myra stayed by Ellen's side. Josh and Ted set up tables and chairs and took out the trash.

Each night, Myra slept with Ellen so she wouldn't be alone. After the three-day mourning period, the girls prepared to go back to school. Myra promised to talk to Ellen's professors. "And I'll call every night."

"Thank you all for your help. I couldn't have gotten through it without all of you."

Johnny held Ellen close. Reluctantly, he said, "I have to go back to school, but I'll come back every night after class. Mom will stay here with you until all the details are worked out. Ruthie and Sylvia will stay another couple of days to help out too."

She didn't want to let him go, but she knew she must. She gave him a hug as she walked him to the door. She couldn't speak. It was all she could do to wave goodbye.

With almost all the people gone, the house felt vacant. *How can I stay here with Mom and Pop gone? It's so lonely. I can't bear it.*

Bessie called her into the kitchen where she and Sylvia and Ruthie were having a cup of coffee. Bessie, hoping to provide some closure for Ellen, said, "Here, sit and have some coffee with us. Proceeding carefully, she spoke quietly, "I know how extremely difficult this is for you," she said gently, "but we should go through the house and decide what you want to do with your parents' things. I hope I can guide you. There are things you'll want to keep. For those items, I suggest we have them moved to LA and put in storage until you're ready to use them. Then we could have a garage sale for the rest of the things. What doesn't sell can be donated to charity."

Ellen's heart thudded. *What is she saying? Is she crazy? I can't have a garage sale and sell my parents' things.*

"I'm sorry, Bessie, I just can't do that."

"I understand. It's okay … just think about it. I'll be happy to do whatever you want."

DURING THE NEXT WEEK, Ellen thought about what Bessie had said. Realizing Bessie was right, that she needed to let go so she could move forward, she decided to follow her advice. They set a date for the sale. The members of The Club came down from school to help. By the end of the day, almost everything had sold.

"I can't believe how many people came. It was like a zoo. I think I could have a career in sales. I'm sure I could sell freezers to Eskimos," Myra contemplated.

"It was sad seeing pieces of my life go like that. Poof, and all my childhood memories are sold," Ellen sniffed.

Johnny consoled her. "I know, but don't forget there is still a whole garage full of wonderful memories we will have to enjoy together."

A month had now passed, and Abe and Bessie convinced Ellen she should go back to school. Although her professors would allow her to catch up with her studies, everyone felt it was best for Ellen to get back to her routine. Reluctantly, she agreed, and on Monday she drove back to campus with Johnny. The members of The Club all worried that Ellen, in a deep depression, might do something to hurt herself. They made sure one of them stayed with Ellen at all times. Johnny was with her whenever he wasn't in class. Slowly, with the help of her friends, Johnny, and the psychologist Bessie had arranged for her to talk with, she was able to move on with her life.

In the meantime, Abe handled the financial details. Irene had long wanted to expand her jewelry business and agreed to buy Titillations. It was decided she would make installment payments for five years.

Abe contacted a realtor about selling the house. The realtor assured Abe it would sell quickly. The desirable location and condition made it ideal. Just as the realtor had predicted, on the first day the house was on the market there were three offers, and it sold for full price.

Abe also checked into Nate's other assets. He found substantial funds in various investments and decided there was no need to change those. With the money from the sale of the house, the down payment from Titillations, the monthly payments from Irene, and the money generated by the various investments, Ellen would have more than enough money to do whatever she wanted. Ellen was now a woman of means.

After Abe had completed all the arrangements, he sat down with Ellen and went through the entire financial picture with her.

"If you'd like, I'll continue to manage things for you for the present. But as soon as you think you're able, I want you to take over. I know your parents would want you to be self-sufficient. And I agree."

Ellen embraced Abe. "Thank you for taking this burden off my shoulders. Yes, please, manage everything for now. I'm really not up to it yet."

She still had the checking account Nate had opened for her when she started college. They agreed on an amount Abe would transfer to that account each month.

"If you need more money, please let me know. You don't have to worry. A millionaire you're not, but comfortable, yes."

This brought fond memories back to Ellen. She remembered Pop and his friends discussing their businesses. They asked each other, "So, how's business?" The reply varied. "I make a living." This meant one was doing okay, but nothing special. Sometimes someone bragged a little. "I'm comfortable." This meant he was doing better than making a living. Comfortable was good. Pop was always comfortable. *He always took good care of us. Thanks, Pop, for continuing to take care of me.*

For some reason this tickled Ellen. She loved the thought of being comfortable. "I'll remember, Pop."

THIRTY-TWO

AS THEY STOOD UNDER the *Chupah* on a beautiful day in June in the backyard of the Friedmans' home, Ellen felt the presence of her parents and knew they were as happy as she was as she heard Rabbi Cohen say, "Jonathan and Ellen, I now pronounce you husband and wife. You may kiss the bride."

The guests all clapped as Johnny kissed Ellen enthusiastically. Then she kissed Tom and thanked him for giving her away and hugged Ginny. She kissed both Abe and Bessie.

She felt a brief moment of sadness that Nate and Pearl weren't physically there to share this happy time with her. Yet, as she looked around, she decided Bessie had done an exceptional job in the planning of the wedding. Because of the recent death of her parents, Bessie had decided the wedding should be a small gathering of family and close friends. From the exquisite white roses and pink peonies gracing the *Chupah* to the white lace tablecloths, pink napkins, and centerpieces of pink and white roses, the yard had been transformed into an elegant setting for their wedding. It was tasteful in every way.

During dinner, toasts were made to the happy couple. The children stayed busy eating the little candies and sweet cakes and kissing everyone with their sticky little lips. Linda, looking adorable in her flower girl dress, stood and gave her toast. "Auntie Ellen, you sure do have good weddings. Can we do it again next week?"

Embarrassed, Ruthie grabbed Linda as the crowd laughed. Her toast gave the guests a lift, and the wedding turned out to be a warm and joyous occasion, despite the sadness that still lingered.

Johnny and Ellen had a wonderful time participating in the day's festivities and mingling with their guests. Finally, Myra convinced Ellen it was time to change clothes and leave for their honeymoon. Ellen and Johnny planned to spend the night at a hotel in town and leave the following afternoon for Hawaii. After they changed, they spent a few minutes with each of the relatives and friends, thanking them and saying goodbye. Lastly, they came to Abe and Bessie.

"Mom, Dad, thank you for making this day so extraordinary for us." Ellen held onto Bessie tightly and kissed her as tears welled up in her eyes.

"Mom and Pop would have loved every minute. It was perfect. I love you both." To Abe she said, "Thanks, Dad, for everything."

Abe, touched, said, "You know that we love you too. Jonathan is a lucky man, and don't forget to remind him in case he forgets. Now, it's time for you to begin your life together. Go, go."

"Thanks, Dad. I know I'm lucky. I won't need reminding. Thank you both for everything." Johnny hugged his parents, and then the bride and groom headed for the door.

The guests waited outside with rice. The happy couple ran to their car amid the rice shower. Johnny started the car and drove off.

AS ELLEN AND JOHNNY checked into the hotel, a path of rice trailed after them. The hotel clerk couldn't help but chuckle. It was obvious they were newlyweds.

The happy couple was impressed with the honeymoon suite. It was like a room out of a fairytale. A small balcony overlooked the pool and the grounds. The scene below looked lovely with the lights reflecting around the pool and twinkling around the gardens.

Ever since the night of their first party at the house, the desires Ellen had suppressed for so long had continued to resurface. Even a hasty kiss between classes could send a tremor of yearning to every part of her body. That first time had frightened her, but now, as Johnny's wife, she could hardly wait for him to make love to her.

And although she knew she wanted him, she realized she was feeling a bit timid and uncertain. Would it be magic like it had been with Kenny? Or would she freeze when Johnny touched her because of what had happened with Kenny? Her stomach knotted at the thought. *Damn it, Ellen, stop it. You love Johnny so much. How could it be anything but magic?* She sighed and told herself it would be fine.

As soon as she settled that in her mind, she had another doubt. *I've been so busy thinking about myself, I haven't thought about Johnny. Will I be the woman he's imagined me to be? Can I satisfy him as he needs to be satisfied? Damn it, Ellen, stop it, stop it. Just let it happen.*

JOHNNY HAD ANTICIPATED THIS moment for a very long time. He thought about the first time he had seen Ellen in class.

He gazed at her now and concluded that she was even more beautiful today.

He slowly pulled her to him and undressed her as she undressed him. The maid had turned down the bed, and they slid into the cool sheets. As he kissed her, Ellen could feel her hunger build. It had been building in her for so many months, she only needed Johnny's touch to set her on fire.

It was the same for him. They had both been waiting for so long, they could barely restrain their passion. She felt his erection pressing on her, and she opened herself to receive him. Almost as soon as he entered her, they climaxed together.

She looked into his eyes and giggled. "I think that's what they call a quickie."

For the moment, the mood was broken. He moved off of her, and they lay snuggled together peacefully. Then Johnny did what he had wanted to do ever since he first met Ellen—to explore and experience her body. He began at the top of her head and kissed her forehead softly. Then he kissed her eyes, her nose, and her cheeks. He nuzzled her and softly stuck his tongue in her ears, which caused Ellen to shiver. She completely surrendered herself to him as the heat in her body rose, her pulse quickened, her heart raced, and her whole being trembled with passion.

By the time he finished tasting each of her fingers, Ellen was a volcano about to erupt. Then he caressed one of her legs. He kissed, he nipped, and he licked. Oh, God, she tasted so delicious! He marveled at the silkiness of her skin and her delicate little body. She was perfect. He kissed each one of her toes, first on one foot and then the other. Then he caressed her other leg. By the time he reached her core, she was a fountain of liquid fire.

The most intimate thing a woman can do is to let a man inside her body, to be joined inside her as one. When Johnny entered her this time, the sensation was so intense that it filled her with immense joy. They moved together. She hungered and craved every inch of his body. She couldn't get enough of him, nor could he get enough of her. Then she couldn't hold on any longer.

"Now!" she cried.

They peaked and, ever so slowly, they came down together, whispering tender words of love to each other as their heartbeats and breathing slowed.

God, I adore this man, Ellen thought. *How could I have ever doubted the passion between us?* Feeling satiated, she kissed him. Together, they fell into a blissful and content sleep.

The following morning, they woke refreshed and excited about their honeymoon. They enjoyed a leisurely breakfast, checked out, and went to the airport to catch their flight to Hawaii. They discovered they once again left a trail of rice. Bob and Myra had managed to pour rice into their suitcases, leaving rice in every nook and cranny of their clothes.

"I guess we'll just have to empty our suitcases to get all the rice out," Johnny chuckled.

Ellen fumed. "Just wait till I get my hands on Myra. I'm going to kill her."

THIRTY-THREE

ELLEN AND JOHNNY RECEIVED the traditional lei greeting when they deplaned in Oahu. As they drove to the hotel, an excited Ellen told Johnny, "I can't wait to get out on the streets."

After they checked in, showered, and changed their clothes, they ventured out. They spied an outdoor market and wandered around, admiring the various goods until they realized how famished they were. They discovered a nearby restaurant and ate heavenly mahi mahi, which was coated with pistachio nuts and different from anything they had ever eaten.

"This has been a fantastic dinner, but let's go back to the market and walk around for a while," Ellen remarked. "There's still so much to see."

After a time, they realized they were pooped and headed back to the hotel. They were so tired they barely managed to make love before falling asleep.

The next day they went to the bird park, where they took pictures with the posing birds. Ellen wouldn't let the birds on her shoulder, but they seemed perfectly happy to perch on her arm.

Johnny took his picture with a bird on his head. Ellen laughed until she had tears in her eyes.

"Oh, Johnny, that is definitely you."

"Thanks a lot."

He couldn't help laughing himself. As he watched Ellen, he felt a sense of amazement at how transformed she appeared. She seemed so happy and carefree. He had never seen her this relaxed.

The days slipped away, and then it was time to head to Maui. They departed for the airport and were surprised as they looked around, noticing it appeared to be nearly empty.

"You're early," the reservation clerk told them. "People don't arrive until maybe fifteen minutes before flight time."

Johnny and Ellen sat down and studied the information about Maui. When it was close to flight time, Johnny decided he had better go to the men's room before they left.

As Ellen sat there, the flight attendant announced that the plane was ready to depart. Frantically, she tried to find Johnny. By the time he returned, the plane had taken off.

Visibly upset, Ellen screamed at him, "Now what are we going to do? How could you let this happen?"

"Calm down, Ellen. Let's go talk to the reservation clerk and see what we can do."

The clerk explained to them that when the flight was ready to leave, everyone just got up and boarded the plane.

"Was somebody supposed to meet you at the airport?" she asked.

"Yes, and our luggage was also on the plane."

"Don't worry," the clerk said, "I'll call ahead, and your tour guide will get your luggage. We'll get you out on the next flight, which leaves in an hour."

Frustrated, Ellen sat down. "Now we'll lose almost a whole

day. I just don't understand how you let this happen."

"Please, Ellen, it's a minor inconvenience. I'm sorry we missed our original flight, but we will be able to get on the next one. As the clerk told us, it'll all work out."

She sat there pouting, until they boarded the next flight. As they were ready to deplane, she finally turned to him and said, "I apologize for flying off the handle. But I hope you're right and it works out okay."

Johnny was relieved that Ellen seemed to have calmed down, yet he couldn't help but wonder. Was she always going to get this upset over the unexpected? Knowing she was still grieving the sudden loss of her parents, he hoped not.

~

THEY HAD RESERVATIONS AT a hotel on Kannapali Beach. When they arrived, the hotel staff recognized they were newlyweds. The reception clerk offered, "Instead of staying here in the main hotel, I think you might enjoy one of our beach houses. They're on the hotel grounds but quite private. And you can walk to the beach from your front door."

"That sounds delightful, thank you," said Johnny.

Johnny and Ellen loved the beach house. It had windows all around, as well as a small sitting area with a couple of bamboo love seats covered in a bright floral pattern of palm leaves, hibiscus, and hydrangeas. The drapes and bedspread were made out of the same cheery pattern. In the front there was a lanai with a couple of lounge chairs and a table. Tall palm trees outside the door helped conceal the other beach houses scattered around. They could see the beach from their door.

The hotel had activities scheduled throughout the day, which they decided to participate in. They went on sightseeing trips, and both of them took a class to learn how to play the ukelele. Ellen proved to be a complete dud, but Johnny learned to play pretty well. He knew how to play the piano, so he had some musical talent.

"I'm glad someone in this family has some talent," Ellen said. It didn't matter. Everyone in the class laughed a lot.

They also learned how to make leis and took hula lessons. It was Johnny's turn to display his ineptitude. No matter how hard he tried, he just couldn't pusha da peanut. Ellen, however, was soon undulating to "Tiny Bubbles."

"Some of us have it, and some of us don't." She smirked as she wiggled her hips at Johnny.

Johnny suppressed a giggle as he commented, "I say, if you've got it, flaunt it."

Johnny and Ellen lazed on the beach and went snorkeling. When they went shopping, Johnny happened upon a jewelry store with creaky wooden floors and ceiling fans that provided a pleasant breeze. When they entered, they discovered that the store featured an excellent display of jade jewelry. Ellen fell in love with the lavender jade, so Johnny bought a ring and pendant for her.

Then Ellen found shoes at a small boutique shoe store. There were so many shoes that she couldn't decide which one to purchase, so she bought six pairs. Johnny couldn't believe it.

"What do you need with six pairs of shoes? You can only wear one pair at a time."

She raised herself up to be as tall as possible, lifted her right eyebrow, and gave him her most haughty look. "Don't concern yourself," she responded in a voice that matched her look. "Remember, I'm a woman of means. I can buy six pairs of shoes if I want."

"Yes, your highness, of course, your woman-ness of means."

Then they both burst out laughing. "If you want six pairs of shoes, then you shall have six pairs of shoes."

My, isn't she the impish one today. Look at how far she has come. And I'm so relieved to see that she is beginning to relax and truly enjoy herself. He felt pleased he had played a part in coaxing this flower to bloom.

They ended up each evening at the Foxy Lady Lounge, which was the after-hours nightclub at the resort. After their first night, they had become well-known at the club. On that first night, they had come in wearing new clothes, and despite their best efforts to get rid of the rice, they had unfortunately left a trail of it on the dance floor. It made the floor slippery, and after people started tripping, management had to clear the floor and clean it up. Ellen and Johnny were mortified. The rest of the partiers thought it was funny and started calling them the Rices. Pretty soon, the hotel staff was calling them the Rices, too, as if it were their last name.

"Hey Rices," someone shouted, "how's it going?"

Finally, they became victims of that delightful Hawaiian disease, Polynesian Paralysis. They became totally relaxed and in tune with the rhythm of the islands. They could make love and then sit on the lanai for hours, sipping Chi Chis and staring into the distance without moving a muscle.

"Do you know what tomorrow is?" Ellen asked with a frowny face.

"I do know. It's our last day. Time to go home. What do you want to do tomorrow?"

"I think I want to spend the day revisiting all the places we've been and take one last look. Then I want to see the sunset from Napili one last time and have a wonderful dinner at the restaurant there with wine and the works."

"Sounds like a perfect day. What time do we have to catch the flight back to Oahu?"

"The flight leaves at 9:00 p.m. That will get us to Oahu in plenty of time for our return flight to the mainland."

At the end of that last day, they checked out of the hotel and thanked the staff for a memorable visit. Hand-in-hand, they viewed the sunset over Napili Bay and entered the restaurant in a somber mood. The waiters rapidly cheered them up by telling jokes and promising them they would return one day soon. Johnny and Ellen ate a fabulous dinner of rice and tiger shrimp cooked in a pineapple sauce. They finished off their dinner with a fruit tart, danced one last time, and then headed out.

When they landed on Oahu, they saw that their flight back to the mainland was on time. But when they reached the counter for the flight home, they discovered a huge line waiting to check in. They were near the end.

"Oh, dear, I hope this isn't bad news for us," Ellen said to Johnny. Turning to the man in front of her, she asked, "Do you think the flight is overbooked?"

"I have no idea, ma'am. I just got here myself."

At last, they reached the check-in counter. The clerk appeared exhausted. "It's been a zoo tonight," she said. "Um, let's see. The flight is full, so I'm going to have to put you in first class, if that's okay with you?" Ellen smiled, knowing it was more than okay.

"Thanks, I think we can manage that," Johnny added, as he grinned back at her.

Once the flight got underway, they were served a lovely late night snack, and then the stewardess gave them each a billowy soft pillow and a downy blanket. Feeling quite cozy, they fell asleep within minutes.

~

ABE AND BESSIE WERE at the gate when they got off the plane. Bessie was pleased to see the happy glow around each of them. She also saw that Ellen had that secret smile, which meant she was happy and satisfied.

"Welcome home," she said. "By the looks of you two, I'd say you had a good trip."

"Aloha. We had a fantastic time. Hawaii is gorgeous. I hope we can return soon," Ellen replied.

~

ELLEN HAD HAD A period of regret and felt guilty on the way home. *I really didn't think about Danny on the trip. Am I a bad person? Am I forgetting an important part of my life? I hope not.*

PART THREE

THIRTY-FOUR

JOHNNY AND ELLEN HUNTED for an apartment in Los Angeles almost as soon as they unpacked from their trip. They found a two-bedroom apartment not far from the University of Los Angeles campus. With the money Ellen received from Irene and the other investments her dad had made, and with Abe's prudent management, they were able to live quite well. They got out of storage the things they had saved from Ellen's family home and spent the next several days unpacking. Even with everything Ellen had kept, they still needed to buy a bedroom set and a kitchen set. Bessie insisted every couple needed their own brand new bedroom set.

Johnny proved to be a kick to shop with for furniture. He had a comment for everything they looked at. After viewing some particularly ugly bedroom lamps, pink with too many bows and ruffles, he said, "So, if we put those with art deco, then we could call it art drecko."

Ellen collapsed laughing. "Or maybe we could put them with traditional and call it traditional *dreck*. Now cut it out, Johnny.

Just because you think they're garbage, someone else might think they're a real treasure."

After an exhausting round of shopping, they found a bedroom set, a kitchen set, and some lamps, pictures, and a lounge chair for Johnny.

Now settled into their new home, the time had come to begin work at their summer jobs. As he had done for the past four summers, Johnny once again worked in Abe's office.

Ellen had a volunteer job at Children's Services managing files for the caseworkers. For each case file, she organized the notes and recorded the last visit made and next visit due. The mess the files were in appalled her. Too many clients, too little staff. She found many foster homes way past due for their visits. In some cases, there weren't even any notes on the child or children assigned to be in the home.

Every day, at least one caseworker thanked her for doing such a fine job. The supervisor expressed her gratitude to Ellen, saying, "Just promise me, Ellen, that when you graduate you'll give us a chance to hire you."

Ellen loved her job, and she determined she would do whatever it took to make the caseworkers' jobs easier. She also worried about the children mentioned in the files. They were real people to her, and she wanted to make sure they were with loving people who cared for them.

It didn't take long for her to realize that many people took in children for the cheap labor or the money. It made her sick. She prayed, as she always did, that loving parents had adopted Danny. *Please don't let him be in one of those terrible foster homes.*

~⁓~

THE SUMMER PASSED. JOHNNY and Ellen entered into their

master degree programs. They both found their weekly schedules full. Law school required many hours of study. And, because Ellen's program in social work wasn't quite as demanding, she continued to volunteer.

They managed to catch time for themselves on weekends, when Ellen experimented with new recipes. They joked about some of her gourmet efforts, like her fruit soup and Jell-O farmer's salad. To Ellen, the salad tasted like it had some kind of dead animal in it. She glanced at Johnny to see what he thought. She could see that he valiantly tried to choke it down. Trying to keep a serious face, she queried, "So what do you think?"

He avoided looking at her as he replied, "Quite unusual, don't you think?"

"Like it has a dead animal in it?"

"You rat, you were just baiting me. You know it tastes just gawd awful. But, it's okay, I love you anyway."

She did manage to have some successes, so in November they decided to invite Bob and Myra to come to Los Angeles from San Francisco. Ellen prepared some of her better gourmet dishes for the evening's meal. The four of them enjoyed being together, after not seeing each other since the wedding.

"So, Myra, how are your wedding plans coming?" Ellen inquired. "It's been, what, three months that you've been engaged?"

"They're a pain in the butt. Long distance planning is aggravating. Every time I hear from my mother, the plans become more grandiose. You know it's bad when even I think she's going over the top. I'm beginning to think I'm having a state affair instead of just a Jewish pogrom."

Only Myra could describe a Jewish wedding as a pogrom. Although it was true that sometimes a Jewish wedding could result in carnage between the in-laws.

"I am excited, though, about having us all together again. I'm hoping everyone can come in a day or two earlier so we can all spend some time catching up."

"I certainly am looking forward to it," exclaimed Ellen. "Have you picked your dress yet? How about our bridesmaid dresses?"

"Still haven't made any final decisions. I'll call you the minute I decide."

They drank wine and talked until the wee hours of the morning. Then Ellen and Johnny went to bed and Bob curled up in Johnny's lounge chair. Myra slept on the couch.

The next morning after they finished brunch, Bob and Myra got ready to return to San Francisco. "We'll keep in touch, kiddo. Thanks for a cool weekend. We had a ball. Next time you're free, let us know, and you guys can come and visit us," Myra added.

On Monday when she awoke, Ellen felt nauseated. "I hope there was nothing wrong with my food," she gasped as she threw up.

"I'm sure it's nothing, just a little stomach upset. I'm feeling fine. Just something that didn't agree with you."

Within a few days, Ellen realized it was more than a little stomach upset. She was probably pregnant. *I'm not ready for this. How can I have a baby now? We've only been married such a short time, and I'm still adjusting to married life.*

Ellen decided not to say anything to Johnny just yet. She checked the yellow pages for obstetricians in the neighborhood. She didn't want to alert Bessie either, so she made an appointment for the following Tuesday with Dr. Joseph Berger, a local physician. She wanted to make sure she was pregnant before she said anything to anyone.

However, by the time Johnny came home that evening, she was so scared that she had changed her mind. The thought of going through being pregnant again made her quake. When Johnny walked in the door, he noticed that Ellen seemed frightened. Sensing that something was amiss, he hugged her, gave her a kiss, and asked, "What's wrong, honey? You seem a bit upset."

That did it. She burst into tears. "Oh, Johnny, I think I'm pregnant, and I'm sooo scared."

It took him a few minutes to digest the news. When he realized what she had said, he whooped. "Really, Ellen, do you really think you're pregnant? I hope so."

He picked her up and cavorted around the room with her until he recognized she was not quite as elated as he was. Quickly, he sobered up. "I think the news is wonderful. This time it's going to be different. I'm here for you. Now tell me all about it."

Relief flooded through Ellen's body as she realized that Johnny seemed genuinely excited at the thought of becoming a father. "Well, once I began having morning sickness, I checked on the calendar and realized I missed my last period. That's it."

Johnny promised to go with her on Tuesday to the doctor. All week he did his best to calm her fears. They decided not to tell Abe and Bessie until they were sure.

On the day of the appointment, they arrived a few minutes early. As they filled out the forms, Ellen felt the old dread wash over her body. She felt cold even though the office was quite warm. Johnny put his arm around her and whispered in her ear, "It's going to be okay, honey. I'm here with you."

She did her best to compose herself. Shortly, a nurse stuck her head out of the door and called, "Ellen Friedman."

Johnny guided Ellen toward the door as the nurse greeted them. "Hello, I'm Dr. Berger's nurse."

"I'm John Friedman, and this is my wife Ellen. Is it all right if I come with Ellen?" he asked.

Peggy flashed him a smile. "It's most unusual to see a husband at all, let alone on a first visit, but I'm sure it will be okay."

Johnny took Ellen's cold hand into his as the nurse led them into Dr. Berger's office. The doctor came in and introduced himself.

"You must be Ellen," he said. He acknowledged Johnny. "I'm guessing you're Ellen's husband John." He shook hands with both of them and sat down in his chair. "It feels good to sit down for a few minutes. I've been rushing all day. Not that I'm complaining, mind you, but it's been busy."

His relaxed and informal way comforted Ellen. She did her best to smile. She noticed his boyish grin, crinkly blue eyes, and sandy colored hair. He seemed to be quite young.

"I'm guessing you're here because you suspect you're pregnant, Ellen."

"Yes."

Ellen described her symptoms and responded to Dr. Berger's questions. When Dr. Berger finished with his initial questions, he turned to Johnny, "I'm going to examine Ellen now. You can wait in here, and we'll come back and join you when we're finished." He buzzed for his nurse.

Johnny squeezed Ellen's hand and gave her a kiss as the nurse stuck her head in the door. "I'm ready for Ellen," she said as she smiled at the two of them.

Dr. Berger assured Ellen, "I'll be with you as soon as Peggy finishes getting you ready."

Once Ellen left the room, Dr. Berger turned to Johnny. "I sense there's something else I should know."

Johnny filled him in on Ellen's first pregnancy and the trauma it had caused her.

"Thanks, John. I'll do my best to make it easy for Ellen." Dr. Berger rose from his chair and went to examine Ellen. After half an hour, Ellen came back into the office.

"How'd it go, honey?" Johnny asked as he took her hand, noticing it was now warm. She appeared more relaxed.

"It was okay."

She had nothing more to say, so Johnny left it at that. In a few minutes, Dr. Berger came back. "I'm happy to tell you that you are pregnant and in good health. The lab tests will confirm my diagnosis in a couple of days. I expect the baby will arrive sometime around the end of August."

Johnny grabbed Ellen. "Congratulations, honey, we're going to have a baby. Me, a dad, whoa, I can hardly wait."

Now that the pregnancy was confirmed, Ellen couldn't help but feel some of his excitement. She grinned.

"We'll see you once a month for now. Please make an appointment with the receptionist on your way out."

They decided to stop and tell Bessie before Ellen took Johnny back to work. She was outside when they drove up. Bessie rushed over to the car and peered in. "What are you kids doing here at this time of day? Is something wrong?"

Johnny leaped out of the car and hugged Bessie. "Not wrong. Right! We're going to have a baby."

Bessie chuckled. "Did you notice how he said we. Some we. You get to do all the work, Ellen, and he gets all the pleasure. And Abe and I, we get to do all the *kvelling*."

By this time Ellen had gotten out of the car, and she and Bessie embraced.

"Darlings, I'm thrilled for you. When can we expect the baby to arrive?"

"Sometime around the end of August."

"Wonderful, you get to go through the nice, hot summer. I guess we'll be giving you an air conditioner for Chanukah."

"Great idea, Mom. We can discuss it later, though, because right now I have to get back to work and tell Dad."

When Ellen got home, she suddenly realized she wouldn't be able to go to Myra and Bob's wedding, as it would be too close to the time the baby was due. Immediately, she went to the phone and called Myra. When Myra heard Ellen's voice, she asked, "Hey kiddo, what's up?"

Ellen blubbered. "Oh, Myra, I'm pregnant. I won't be able to be in your wedding, and we won't be able to attend either. I'm due in late August, so it'll be too close to my due date."

"What? You're preggers?" Myra squealed. "That's wonderful news, Ellen. I'm so happy for you."

"Thank you," Ellen said, as the tears continued. "We just found out and I still can't believe it. It happened so fast. I'm so sorry I won't be able to be one of your bridesmaids."

"Well, I'm sorry you can't attend, Ellen. I'll definitely miss you. But, heck, you're pregnant!" Myra exclaimed. "Having a baby is a heck of a lot more important than my wedding. Make sure you keep me updated, or I'll kill you. Just kidding. Now stop crying and be happy. And please keep in touch."

THIRTY-FIVE

THAT NIGHT ELLEN FRETTED. "I'll be able to finish this year okay, but what about next year? I want to finish my degree, you know."

"Don't worry about it, honey. We'll have time. First things first. We have to call Tom and Ginny, Myra, and the rest of the gang. They'll kill you if you don't let them know right away.

Ellen interrupted. "I already called Myra when we got home. I had to let her know we won't be able to attend their wedding and I can't be a bridesmaid."

"Oh, I hadn't thought about that. No, that wouldn't be a good idea since it'll be too close to when the baby is due. Well, that's one less call to make," he reflected. "Once we've taken care of letting everyone know, we need to sit back and enjoy this time. You'll be a princess, because I'm going to wait on you hand and foot from now until the baby is born."

Ellen snorted. "Ya, I'd like to see that. Between school and work, maybe I'll get a little princessing from midnight to one a.m."

ELLEN'S PREGNANCY PROGRESSED UNEVENTFULLY. Johnny did most of the cooking, since kitchen smells continued to nauseate Ellen. Now, they got to joke about Johnny's cooking, especially his mac and cheese casserole. The vanilla wafers he put on top to replace the bread crumbs he thought were necessary to create a crust provided some fun conversation. Surprisingly, though, it tasted quite good.

They both finished the school year with good grades, but were exhausted. Ellen complained about looking like a cow.

"Yes, you do resemble a bovine," Johnny teased her, "but a beautiful one. And, because you're such a gorgeous cow, I've planned a week in Monterey."

Ellen squealed. "You're definitely the best husband in the world." She gave him a big smack on the lips. "Of course, I expect the princess treatment for the entire week, or did you forget about that?"

"No, I didn't forget. And I'm duly remorseful that I haven't lived up to your expectations, but I promise princess treatment for the whole week."

They enjoyed a fabulous week at the ocean and came back refreshed. Johnny went back to work for Abe, and Ellen resumed her job at Children's Services. They had been using their second bedroom as their study, so they re-organized the room to convert it to the baby's room and made space for their desks in the living room. Once they'd finished, Ellen announced her plans for decorating.

Johnny groaned. Ellen's plans meant more work for him. Paint, wallpaper, and assemble baby furniture.

"Having a baby is a lot of work," he grumbled.

"Don't complain. I'm the one doing the work. Believe me, I'd be happy to change places with you. You carry, I'll paint."

"Okay, sorry. I'll get right on it."

254 | ROCHELLE PADZENSKY

BESSIE, RUTHIE, AND SYLVIA planned a baby shower for Ellen in the middle of July. All the guests had a great time, and Ellen got almost everything she could possibly need.

With everything now in place for the baby's arrival, the final days of Ellen's pregnancy dragged on. She often rubbed her stomach, saying, "Puhleeze, baby, come already. Mommy is tired."

At last, he decided to arrive on August 27, 1962. The family declared him a beautiful baby. They named him Nat, after Ellen's father. As Ellen looked at her baby, she couldn't help but feel sad that she didn't have a picture of Danny to compare to Nat. At the same time, she said a prayer for Danny and felt grateful that things had turned out well this time. After all, what would have happened if Johnny hadn't wanted this child or had deserted her? She shuddered to think of any such possibilities.

Ellen wrote to Kathleen O'Connor, her former teacher, and sent a picture of Nat. In her letter, she told Kathleen how blessed she felt and that she still prayed Danny had a good home and still thought about him often. She hoped wherever he was, he was a happy child.

Within a few days of Nat's birth, Johnny and Ellen called Tom and Ginny with the news and told them that pictures were on their way. Tom and Ginny were overjoyed. "Now don't you forget to keep in touch with us," Tom said. "And pictures, and more pictures please," chimed in Ginny.

ELLEN AND JOHNNY SOON realized that taking care of a baby was a nightmare. And a daymare. Nat seemed to need something every minute of every day and every night. Thank

God for Bessie. She came over each morning and helped Ellen get organized. Finally, they all settled into a routine.

Nat had a sunny disposition and proved to be a delightful baby. Ellen loved taking care of him, but she was ready to resume her schoolwork. One day, about three months after Nat was born, she told Bessie, "I want to go back to school next semester, but I don't see how I can do it."

"Not to worry," Bessie said soothingly. "I have a solution for you. Abe talked to his cleaning lady. You remember her, don't you?"

"Yes, Maria, isn't it? Isn't she the one whose husband died at a very young age and she had to bring up her four children alone?"

"Yes, that's right. Well now that her children are grown, she would like to quit her night job and take things a little easier. She told Abe she'd be thrilled to take care of Nat so you can finish school. She's a wonderful woman, and you can feel secure that Nat will be in good hands."

Maria Elena Gonzales was not what Ellen envisioned. A slight, five-foot-tall dynamo, she had long black hair that she wore in a braid coiled on top of her head. She had a twinkle in her black eyes and still looked like a young woman. After only a short time, it was obvious to all—by the way Maria talked to Nat and the way he cooed at her in response—that they loved each other. Ellen was amazed at the energy of this slight woman. She could cook, clean, and take care of Nat all at the same time. Johnny compared her to the ultimate corporate wife.

Ellen resumed her studies. She had classes three mornings a week, and she worked at Children's Services the other two mornings. This gave her ample time to spend with Nat and yet satisfy her needs.

Johnny graduated in June and procured a job with a prestigious Los Angeles law firm, Benton, Berger & Fine. Judd

Benton, who hired Johnny, expressed surprise that Johnny wasn't going into Abe's firm; although he told Johnny he was delighted to have him join them.

"I enjoyed working for my dad's firm, but now I'm ready to experience a different area of the law," Johnny assured him.

The experience and knowledge gained from working for Abe all those years were of immense benefit to Johnny. After only a period of six months, he brilliantly handled a particularly difficult case, and the partners warmly commended him. No longer was he Johnny Friedman, he was now Jonathan Friedman, Esquire, a well-respected lawyer with a bright future.

THIRTY-SIX

ELLEN GRADUATED WITH HONORS the following December in 1963, and went to work as a regular employee of Children's Services. Because of the many things she'd learned as a volunteer, she gradually introduced minor changes into their system.

One of the ideas she proposed was a savings program. She would provide the seed money of $10,000 from her investments. Her ever-present concern for Danny always prompted her to think about the welfare and future of adopted children. She explained to John how she wanted him to set up a foundation.

"When a child comes into our system, a savings account is started for him. If he gets adopted, the money goes with him and can't be used by the adoptive parents. It's money that just belongs to him. If the child doesn't get adopted, but stays in our system, then he gets the money when he leaves as an adult. Do you think I'm nuts or do you think this can work?"

"What a splendid idea," John told her. He went to his law library and pulled out some books. "I'm sure we can work it out. Give me some time," he assured her. Then he gave Ellen a hug. "You're definitely a special person, Ellen Friedman."

THE YEAR FLEW BY. Nat had just celebrated his second birthday when Ellen realized she was pregnant again. The family expressed its delight. Bessie suggested it was time for them to buy a house. They couldn't possibly squeeze another child into their apartment.

And so they began the great house hunting adventure. They saw big houses, small houses, ugly houses, fabulous houses, outrageous houses, but none of them were their house.

"Will we ever find a house we like?" Ellen moaned.

"There is a house out there for you, I promise," answered Susan, their real estate agent. "I think I know now what you want, and I will do everything I can to find it for you." She put her hand over her heart to signify her intent to keep this promise.

After not hearing from Susan for two weeks, Ellen became discouraged. She was about ready to give up, when Susan called and told her she believed she'd found the house they wanted.

Susan was right. It was the right house for them—a three-bedroom ranch with a double garage. The owner had added another room plus a double garage to the existing house. The piece de resistance proved to be the original garage. A separate building several yards behind the new addition, the owner had converted it into a work area for making furniture. John and Ellen envisioned remodeling it into a house for Maria, so she could be close and still have her own life.

Maria cried when she heard Ellen and John's plan for the garage. "This couldn't be more perfect. I've wanted to give my house to my youngest daughter and her husband. It'll be just right for their little family and give them a chance to save money to start their own business."

When all the details of the sale had been completed, Ellen and

John hired Maria's son-in-law, Tony, to do the remodeling work. He would do the kitchen first and then the garage for Maria.

"The trick will be to get the kitchen done before this baby is born," Ellen told Tony as they reviewed the plans.

"Don't worry, I promise it'll be done in time."

Ellen and Bessie then took on the task of shopping for drapery materials, carpeting, and accessories.

"Gosh, I thought we had enough accessories," John groaned. "Don't we have enough stuff already?"

Patiently, Ellen explained that a big house requires more stuff. Plus, they needed to make a big-boy room for Nat.

"Yes, dear." John had learned that if his wife was happy, he was happy. Besides, he really did trust her judgment.

Nat was talking now and had lots to say about everything. John and Ellen called Maria "Mama Maria." Nat changed it to mamaria. "Mamaria, milk, cookie."

Maria looked at him and said, "Milk and cookies, what?"

"Peez, tank you." The family cracked up over Maria and Nat.

But Ellen noticed there were times when she didn't share in their merriment. *What's wrong with me? Why do I feel these pangs of jealousy? Should I be staying home with Nat? Am I giving up another baby like I gave up Danny? This is stupid. I know Nat loves me, and I know Maria would never let Nat think that she's his mother. I should discuss this with John sometime and make sure I'm doing the right thing. I can't fail another child.*

And then she thought about the child she carried now. *Should I stay home with this new baby? I love this child already. I'm so happy Nat will have a sibling. I always felt bad that I didn't have a brother or sister to share with.*

As Ellen continued to experience pangs of uncertainty, Tony finished the kitchen and they moved into their new home the month before the new baby was due.

"I'm now ready to have this baby," Ellen announced to the family. "The house is ready, and I'm ready." But the baby wasn't ready. The new baby was two weeks late. In the meantime, Ellen just kept working. "Better to be working than home worrying and complaining."

Finally, she was born on May 12, 1965. A beautiful little girl they named Pamela. Her Jewish name was Pearl after Ellen's mother. Pammy, as they called her, inherited the job as the new princess in the family. It had been such a long time since there had been a girl in the family that they all were eager to spoil her. Even the boys loved holding her and making faces for her to smile at them. Everyone in the family adored Pammy. She was such a sweet baby.

Ellen sent pictures of Pammy to Tom and Ginny and Kathleen and Greg O'Connor with her next letters and expressed her joy with her growing family.

Secretly, though, even after all this time, Ellen, who was now twenty-eight, was still driven by guilt for giving up her illegitimate child. She loved her job, but more than that, she felt bound to help as many children in foster care as possible. So, despite some misgivings, Ellen went back to work in the mornings when Pammy was six weeks old. She knew she could trust Maria to take excellent care of her. *I hope I'm making the right decision. I hope I'm not making a big mistake.*

THIRTY-SEVEN

JOHN SET UP A foundation, helping Ellen achieve her dream of providing a savings account for foster children in the Family Service system. As Ellen sat in her office going through the statements for the accounts, someone knocked on the door.

"Come in." It was Barbara Barnes, one of the foster mothers who loved the plan. "Barbara, hi, come sit and have a cup."

Barbara and her husband, Don, had been part of the foster parent program for several years. They had three children of their own and usually two foster children at any given time. For years, Barb had tried to save some money from each state check she received for each child. She had opened savings accounts with this money, to then be given to the children when they left foster care.

Ellen and Barbara were kindred spirits. They both had the same feelings about the children who found themselves under state care, and both worked tirelessly to make things better.

At the end of each month, Barb came into the office and gave Ellen whatever was left from that month's check. Ellen always looked forward to Barb's visits. Barb delighted in telling Ellen of her children's triumphs. They exchanged stories of the funny things each of their children had said or done.

On this particular day, everyone in the office noticed that Barbara Barnes was agitated. When Barb entered Ellen's office, Ellen saw how drawn Barb appeared. She invited Barb to sit down and went to get the coffee. When she returned, she closed the door, handed Barb her coffee, and sat down.

"Barb, I can tell something's wrong," Ellen said. "Please let me help. Tell me what's going on."

Barb peered at Ellen. "Other than Don, I've never told anyone about this before, and you're probably the only other person I can tell. I know I can trust you to keep this confidence." The tears flowed, as Ellen handed Barb a Kleenex.

Barb dabbed at her eyes. "I got pregnant when I was fifteen. I was just a kid and really didn't know much. My parents sent me off to some relatives in another town. When the baby was born, it was taken away from me and put up for adoption. I never had any say in the matter. I never had a choice. That's the way it was. My parents were mortified and never spoke a word to me about it. I was a bad girl in their eyes, and it was best not spoken about. I never saw the boy who got me pregnant again, and I never found out what happened to him." She took a sip of coffee.

Ellen could feel her body grow cold. Barb's story was too close to her own. *I mustn't let on anything.* Ellen tried to arrange her face to be neutral as she said, "I'm so sorry, Barb."

Barb sniffed and blew her nose. "When I was old enough, I left home and went to California, where I met Don, and we fell in love. I told him what had happened, and he was okay with it. We got married, had children, and we've been happy and blessed. But I never really forgot or got over what happened."

She paused for a moment and wiped away the tears. Then she pulled an envelope out of her purse.

"This came in the mail the day before yesterday. It's a letter from the daughter I gave up, saying she found out I am her biological mother and she would like to meet me. She wants me to come to Kansas City at the end of the month."

Barb's hand trembled as she handed the envelope to Ellen.

"I've been crying ever since, and I don't know what to do. Don thinks I should go, but I don't know."

Ellen swallowed hard. She trembled herself. This could be her. Someday it might be. She fought for control.

"I can't tell you what decision to make Barb, but I know that whatever you decide will be right."

"I somehow think I should go. If my daughter took the time to find me, then she deserves to meet me. Yes, I think I should go."

"Then by all means, go. You know whatever happens, Don and I are here for you."

She clasped Barbara's hands in hers. "Call me at any time if you need me. Come in when you get back and tell me all about how it went."

Barbara got up and gathered her belongings together. "Thanks, I needed you just now. I needed someone who could understand and help me make my decision." She put down her coffee cup and departed.

Ellen closed the door after her and sat down, shaking. The staff wanted to know what had happened. "Just one of those things," Ellen told them.

~

ELLEN COULD HARDLY WAIT to get home and tell John about Barb's visit. Unfortunately, he called and said he would be working late on an important case. By the time he came home, she had already fallen asleep.

In the morning, after Maria left with the children and they

sat at the breakfast table, she confided in John. "What if Danny finds me," she cried. "What will I do?"

Again? Is Ellen ever going to be able to deal with this like an adult? It's time for her to let it go. John exploded. "For God's sake, Ellen, grow up. It was a long time ago. You're married now with a family of your own. It's time to move on. If Danny finds you, so be it. We'll handle it." He shoved his chair away from the table and exited the room. Ellen heard the door slam.

Ellen sat at the table, stunned. *What just happened? Why is John so angry with me? My God, he left without kissing me goodbye. He's never done that before. What have I done? Maybe he's right. Maybe I'm just being a big baby.* The egg she had been eating suddenly seemed greasy and unappetizing, and the coffee smelled rancid. Then anger boiled up inside of her. *I have every right to be worried, so damn you, John Friedman. You can just go to hell.*

She could hardly get anything done at work that day. She relived the scene over and over and couldn't make any sense of it.

That night at dinner, she and John didn't speak to one another, only to the children. Maria sensed something was wrong and took the children to her house to play games after dinner. After Maria left, John glared at her, got up from the table, went into his office, and slammed the door.

Ellen went to the bedroom, undressed, and crawled into bed trembling. She curled up into a fetal position, rocking back and forth, and wept until she finally fell into a restless sleep, tossing and turning and reaching for John. The next morning when she got up, John was already gone. His side of the bed had not been slept in. Somehow she managed to get dressed and get to the office, where she spent the morning shivering and aching.

When her supervisor, Natalie, saw Ellen, she said, "My God, Ellen, you look just awful. Whatever is the matter? You'd better get yourself home, before you give whatever you have to everyone in the office."

"Thanks, Natalie, you're right." Relieved, Ellen rapidly cleaned off her desk and went home. Maria had the day off, since the children were spending the day with Gram and Papa, so when Ellen got home she was able to undress and fall into bed. She spent the rest of the afternoon worrying about what might happen if they didn't resolve their argument.

WHEN JOHN CAME HOME that evening, he took one look at Ellen, and his heart lurched. She had dark circles under her eyes and looked pale. *What have I done? She seems so fragile, as though she will break in the slightest breeze.* He dropped his briefcase, ran to her, and gathered her up in his arms.

"I'm so sorry, Ellen, I don't know what came over me. You know how much I love you. I never meant to hurt you."

"Goddamn you, John Friedman," she shrieked, beating him on the chest with her hands. "Why? How could you be so mean? What did I say that was so terrible?"

"It's just that I keep hoping you'll learn to deal with this without falling apart every single time something reminds you of your past."

Ellen bawled and shook so hard that she could no longer beat on him. She would have collapsed if John hadn't caught her. He held her, murmuring his love to her until she stopped crying. After a while, she admitted she might be wrong.

"You're right, John. I've been thinking about it and I know it's time for me to face it like the adult I'm supposed to be."

John, relieved, once again begged her forgiveness. "You know I will always support you, no matter what. We'll talk about it later, I promise. Right now, I'm famished, how about you? I'll make us some dinner."

Ellen gave him her little crooked smile. "Yes, I'm starving too, so let's eat."

~~~

WHEN BARB CAME IN at the end of the month, Ellen couldn't tell whether or not things had gone well. "Hi, Barb, when you're finished, come into my office." Barbara nodded.

Within minutes, Barb entered Ellen's office and plopped down on the couch. "You went to Kansas City?" Ellen asked.

"Yes."

"And how did it go?"

Barb grunted. "Not good, not bad. My daughter is full of anger. She confronted me almost immediately and wanted to know why I didn't keep her, why I didn't love her. I tried to explain how it was in those days in a small town. That I had no choice. That's just how it was. Afterwards, we did spend some time talking about her family, and I told her a little bit about mine."

"So then what happened?" Ellen wanted to know more.

Barb took a drink of water. "When I was getting ready to leave, I asked her if she wanted to see me again and meet my family. She said she didn't know right now. And I honestly don't know if I want to see her again, either. It makes things so complicated. As it is, the pain of what happened never leaves me. I pay for that indiscretion every day of my life. The worst part is, as I told my daughter, I had no choice in the matter. My parents never talked to me about my pregnancy, let alone the topic of sex. Hell, I didn't even really know how you got pregnant. That's just how it was in small towns in those days. Nowadays, they teach sex education in schools."

Ellen handed Barb the Kleenex box. Barb blew her nose. "I was glad to see her, though, and know that she has a good home and a good life. It answered a lot of questions for me. I don't have to be haunted on that score. We decided to keep in touch once a year, just so we can exchange any information that might be important. When I was ready to leave, she did give me a hug. It was all very awkward."

"I think," Ellen said, "that as time passes, there will probably be some softening by both of you. But if not, you may have to accept that you'll never see each other again, and that may be just as well."

"You're right, I'm sure, Ellen. Right now I'm just kinda depressed over the whole thing. It wasn't what I thought or hoped it would be. My hope was that she would be happy to know me and understand why I gave her up."

Ellen got up and patted Barbara. "No matter what, I'm still your friend, and don't you forget it."

Barbara smiled. "Thanks, I know I'm lucky to have a friend like you. Oh gosh, look at the time! I have to fly. The kids will be home from school soon."

THE THINGS BARBARA HAD said weighed heavily on Ellen. Thoughts she had kept buried all these years, since the time she and John had talked about it in college, floated to the surface. *I wonder what my life would be like if I'd had a choice about what to do. Like Barb, I was too young and immature to have a baby and take care of it. And now, if my son finds me, will it be as heartbreaking as it seemed to be for Barb? How will my children and family feel if they find out about Danny? On one hand, I want him to find me, so that, like Barb, I can know he's been well taken care of and is happy. And yet, everything in my life is so good now, and I'm so blessed, I'd hate to have it change. I've often thought about abortion as a choice, ever since Myra talked so much about women's rights. Am I wrong to think about it, maybe even to wonder what I would have done if it had been a viable option? It doesn't feel wrong to consider it as a choice for women, but I feel guilty. No, it feels wicked thinking such thoughts. And now that I've heard Barb's story, do I even want to meet my son? What will I do if he finds me?*

~

THAT EVENING AFTER THE children were in bed, she told John about Barb's visit that day and what had happened when she went to meet her daughter. Then Ellen told him about her own reaction.

He sat without speaking for a few minutes, and then he said, "As far as the abortion issue, I've always believed a woman should be in charge of her own life and her own body. I don't believe another person can decide something of such a personal nature. In my opinion, it's a decision between a woman and her own God. So no, I don't think it's wicked to think about it. And I don't think we should try to foresee the future and decide what we'll do if Danny finds you. Things change all the time. Let's deal with it when and if it happens."

She digested what he said. "I agree. The other thing that has me concerned is what should we tell Nat and Pammy? Do we tell them anything, or do we keep silent? What if Danny finds me and I decide to meet him? Do we tell Nat and Pammy then?"

"I can't answer those questions right now. I'd have to see what the situation looks like when it happens. Rest assured that whatever happens, we'll handle the decisions together, as always."

She seemed comforted by his words. "You always know the right thing to say. No wonder you're such a good lawyer. Enough of this talk. Now, take me to your bed and say the right things to me there."

John chuckled as he picked her up and took her off to bed. Even after six years, he still enjoyed making love to her. When he married Ellen, she was still a girl with a girl's body, but now she was a woman—ripe, full, and delicious. It made him hunger for her body even more.

He loved her favorite ways of making love to him. She kissed the hollow in his neck and worked her way down with her tongue to the inside of his elbow and then down to his fingers. She put each finger in her mouth and gently kissed and licked them. It drove John wild.

They made love until their passion was spent. Ellen snuggled into his arms and thanked him in her most proper manner. John smiled to himself. *That's why I love this woman. She makes love like a wild thing and then thanks me like a prim and proper schoolteacher.*

He kissed her lightly on the nose. "And thank you, madam, for a job well done."

~

A FEW DAYS LATER, John said to Ellen, "I've thought about our conversation, and I believe that when Nat and Pammy are old enough to understand, we should tell them about their half-brother. Siblings have close connections with each other, and someday they may want to find him for one reason or another."

Ellen nodded as she listened to his words. *I'm not sure I even want him to find me, let alone have my kids try to find him. I need to resolve that issue myself.*

"Having thought about it, I don't think I want to tell Nat and Pammy unless Danny finds me. What will it say to them about their mother? I think we should let sleeping dogs lie for the moment."

THIRTY-EIGHT

JOHN RUSHED IN THE door, grabbed Ellen, and kissed and hugged her.

"You're home early. Something is up, I can tell," she said.

"You are looking at the newest partner of Benton, Berger & Fine. As such, I'll be responsible for opening and managing a new office in San Diego. What do you think of that, Mrs. Friedman?"

Ellen gasped. "A partner already! I can't believe it. It's wonderful." She put her hand over her mouth. "Oh, my God, that means we're going to have to move to San Diego, doesn't it?"

John frowned. "Yes we will. This could be wonderful, don't you think?"

"I don't know. I need time to think about it," Ellen replied and then paused, as if in deep contemplation. "I don't think I'll have a problem finding a job. I'll have a problem leaving this one, though; you know how much I love my job. What about Maria? I think she'd come with us, don't you? We're family. I'm sure she wouldn't leave the children. And the kids, well kids are flexible, but it'll still be hard on them. Oh, the house, we'll have to leave our beautiful house and Papa and Gram. Oh, and all your family." She sat down, breathless.

John tried to calm her. "One step at a time. I know it's a shock, but we'll work it out."

His heart sank. They had settled into a good life here surrounded by family and friends. In spite of the fact that Ellen was doing so well, he knew she was fragile, especially now that she'd begun to worry about the possibility of her son trying to find her one day. She needed the stability the family provided. But it couldn't always be about her. This move was about him, and he knew it had to be made. He *had* to make it happen. This was the opportunity he'd been working toward. And opportunities like this didn't come around every day.

He saw Ellen put on a determined façade. "I'm okay. I know we'll work it out."

Although he didn't say anything, John was certain she had another inner battle to fight. They hadn't been back to San Diego since the funeral. It could be difficult for her to move back to where her parents had last lived. For the moment, though, there was no need to continue to discuss the matter or think about it. The children were spending the week with Papa and Gram, and Maria was spending the week with her grandchildren, so they'd made plans of their own to go to the theater with friends. "Look at the time," he said. "We'd better get rolling."

They had an enjoyable evening at the theater, and even though Ellen appeared a bit reserved, she seemed to be okay. Relieved, John felt confident that things would work out.

~

JOHN KNEW ELLEN SPENT a sleepless night worrying about the impending move. He woke up several times and could tell by her tossing and turning that she was concerned about it.

272 | ROCHELLE PADZENSKY

The next morning at breakfast, Ellen revealed what she'd wrestled with all night. "Do we really have to make this move, John? We've been so happy here. Is this the only chance you'll have to make partner? Is there some way we can stay here and still have it work for you?"

John sighed. "I'm sorry, Ellen, but it can't always be about what you want. This is an important step for me and for the firm. The decision has been made. And as far as the partners are concerned, the sooner I can relocate and get the new office up and going, the better. They have chosen a location already, and it'll be ready within the next two months. We probably need to start shopping for a home as soon as possible."

Ellen bit her tongue but remained silent.

John checked the time. "I guess the newest partner better get his ass on the road. It wouldn't look good for me to be late on my first day as partner."

He came around the table to kiss her, but she turned her head. He left without either of them saying goodbye.

John's stomach knotted, but he knew he couldn't give in on this to Ellen. It was too important. This was necessary for his career growth, and she needed to accept that and support him for once.

~

THEIR RELATIONSHIP REMAINED STRAINED for the next few days. Ellen had never realized John might have another side to his personality that she really didn't know or understand. He'd always been so patient and supportive. *What's going on?* she wondered, as she felt his distance. She began to panic. What would she do if John decided to leave her? What if he thought his job was more important than his family? Thoughts related to the loss of her parents and old fears of being abandoned returned. As she continued to think it over, though, she realized John had always done what was best for her. *Isn't it time I think about what is best for him? I guess I really have been acting selfishly.*

A few days later, as she thought more about the move, she realized she was beginning to feel some excitement about living in San Diego. She had never really thought LA was the best place to bring up a family. A smaller city could be pleasant. It would be difficult, because they had settled in so well here, but not impossible.

When John came home that evening, she told him she thought relocating could work out okay.

"I'm sorry I ruined your wonderful news," she offered. "It was selfish of me. I'll do what I have to, to make it work."

John held her close, and she knew he was relieved. Ellen could tell he didn't know how to mend this rift any better than she did. She guessed he felt thankful that she'd taken the initiative.

He kissed her lovingly and said, "First we need to find a house. Any ideas on where you might like to live?"

"I'm not sure yet. Let me think about it. I loved living near Balboa Park, but then I've been thinking about La Jolla or maybe Pacific Beach. We'll just have to see what's available and what we can get for our house."

"Money won't be a problem. The firm will handle the down payment and will help negotiate a mortgage. Just one of those perks of being a partner. I'll also have an expense account for entertainment purposes."

Ellen raised her eyebrows. "Well, aren't we becoming la de da. Excuse me folks, the Friedmans will be entertaining this evening, and Mrs. Friedman will pour. Whoa. I think I'll like that part. You know how I like to entertain." She giggled. "It sounds like we'll be busy. I hope it won't spoil our time with the children and your time with me. I wouldn't like that, you know."

"Doesn't Dad always have time for Mom and the kids and the grandkids? He taught me a long time ago that family always comes first, and I've made my priorities plain to the other partners. Fortunately, they agree. That doesn't mean it will always be nine to five. You already know that some cases can require late hours for several days. It's one of the realities of life."

"Okay, Jonathan Friedman, Esquire. I'll contact the agent who sold my parents' house, and we'll make plans to house shop next weekend."

A disagreement resolved. A relief, thought Ellen.

"Sounds good to me," John said. They decided it would be best to let the children spend the weekend with Papa and Gram.

"I'll make a hotel reservation for just the two of us." John gave Ellen his best sexy pose, flexing his muscles. "Any place special you'd like to stay?"

"You decide, as long as it's romantic," she murmured with that crooked smile of hers.

"Aha." John winked at her as he waved and sauntered out to the garage. It would be a good end to a bad argument.

THEY HAD A GLORIOUS weekend. It was fun looking at houses again. On Sunday they found a house they loved. Two stories, four bedrooms, a playroom, a living room, and a formal dining room that could seat twenty. The kitchen was outdated but large, with ample eating space. A nice-sized laundry room, office, and guest room completed the main floor. Outside it had a lovely patio, roomy yard, and a small but beautiful swimming pool. Nearby were a small greenhouse and a carriage house. With some remodeling, the carriage house would make a good home for Maria.

Toward the back of the property was a gazebo, and beyond the gazebo, a wooded area with a pond and a bridge. On the other side of the bridge was a summerhouse where the children could play, camp, and sleep in the summer. That sold them on the house.

Ellen beamed. "What a wonderful home for the children. I know they'll love it here."

John agreed. The owners of the home had died, and John knew their children were anxious to settle the estate.

"I'm sure the sellers know a lot of remodeling is necessary to bring the house up to date," John told Nancy, their real estate agent. "I anticipate that they will be amenable to negotiating. Let's find a quiet place to sit down and come up with a proposal."

They found a restaurant and ordered tea and sandwiches. Nancy then took out a yellow pad, the brochure from the house, and her book with mortgage information in it. After some discussion, they settled on the offer they wished to make. Nancy promised to get it written up and signed by them before they left. She would then get it to the sellers' realtor the next day.

"When do you think we'll know?" Ellen inquired.

"We'll put the usual three-day timeframe," Nancy promised them. "I'll call as soon as I know."

"Thanks for your hard work, Nancy." John turned to Ellen. "Anything else, dear?"

"I think that's it."

They shook hands and walked to their cars. Ellen and John went back to the hotel to pack and check out. On the way home, they stopped at a charming restaurant for dinner. Ellen was full of remodeling and decorating ideas. Over dinner, John, amused, listened to her as she chattered away.

"You do realize we don't have the house yet and you've already remodeled and redecorated the entire place," John said.

She flipped her hair at him. "It's ours, I know it. Your job is to pay the bills and smile." Sassily, she stuck her tongue out at him.

He guffawed. "You're right, I know it."

Two days later, Nancy called to tell them the owners of the house had made a counter offer. Ellen's heart fell. Could she have been wrong?

John commented, "Ellen, don't worry. It's normal. We'll ask Nancy what our counter offer should be."

After some discussion, they came up with a new figure. Ellen sweated out the next two days, and on the third morning, Nancy called to say their offer had been accepted. John's family was both happy and sad. Happy about the new house and John's new job, but devastated that John, Ellen, Maria, and the children would be moving.

They moaned, groaned, and planned farewell parties. John and Ellen extracted promises from the siblings and Papa and Gram that they would make frequent family visits.

Ellen gave her two weeks' notice, and, as expected, complaints abounded. "How can you do this to us? You can't just leave us." It almost killed Ellen. Her heart pounded as she contemplated leaving her job. She had worked so hard to make things better for abandoned and abused children. How could she leave them? She comforted herself and the staff at Family Services as best she could and promised she would keep in touch.

She had already contacted friends in the Social Services department in San Diego. As she predicted, before they even arrived in San Diego, she was offered a job. With a sigh and her fingers crossed, she prayed this would be a good move for all of them.

THIRTY-NINE

PLANS FOR REMODELING THE house were underway in earnest. They had found an architect who was in tune with the ideas they had for the house. He intended to work with the basic structure and update and refine it. John and Ellen, excited with his suggestions, hired him with instructions to begin at once.

As they had done previously, Ellen and Bessie began the shopping marathon. Even with Bessie's help, it didn't take long for Ellen to admit she felt overwhelmed by the project. One day as they browsed some of the local shops, she told Bessie, "This is a much bigger job than I thought it would be. Help!"

As usual, Bessie had the answer. "I know a fabulous interior decorator, Bett Sanders. If you'd like, I'll call her."

"Sounds good to me. Please call her and set up a meeting."

Bett and Ellen hit it off right away. Soon they were knee deep in sketches, fabrics, paint samples, and pictures of furniture. As far as John was concerned it was total chaos, and he doubted anything good could come of it.

"Really, Ellen, is all this necessary?" he whined. "I can't believe you can tell what anything is going to look like from all these bits and pieces."

She chuckled. "You're kidding. Remember, I lived with Myra. This is a piece of cake. With Bett I actually have a good idea what things will look like. With Myra you just had to go on good faith. Oh, I've been so occupied with the house that I almost forgot to tell you. Myra called. Bob got a fantastic job with the State Department in Singapore, and Myra got a job with the diplomatic service. Unfortunately, they have to leave immediately, so we won't have a chance to get together before they leave. I'm both happy and sad. It's a great opportunity for the two of them, but I sure will miss them."

"Wow," John responded. "I didn't expect things would happen so soon for them. I'm truly happy, though. This is what they've been hoping for."

~

AS PROMISED, THE HOUSE turned out to be magnificent. The architect did an outstanding job, and between Bett and Ellen, the decorating brought it all together, a seamless blending of the old and the new. The relocation was accomplished, and John, Ellen, Maria, and the kids settled into a pleasant rhythm.

John and Ellen renewed old acquaintances. They joined the synagogue and became active in numerous organizations. They entertained often, so they could enlarge their circle of friends.

Life was good. Ellen rarely thought about Danny anymore. She had put him on a back shelf in her mind, and once in a while she thought about him and prayed he was well and happy.

The new office did well, and Ellen loved her job. The children grew and brought pleasure to their parents, and Maria seemed forever young. Almost four years just seemed to fly by. *This all seems too good to be true. Can it last?*

PART FOUR

FORTY

SEVENTEEN-YEAR-OLD MARK WISEMAN HAD always known he was adopted. From the time he was old enough to understand, his parents, Steve and Vicky Wiseman, told him stories of how lucky they were to get him. They told him how much they loved him and that they couldn't love him more if he were their own flesh and blood.

He knew it was true. They were wonderful parents, and he loved them with all his heart and soul. And, yet, in the back of his mind, he always had this niggling thought. Who was his real mother, the mother who gave birth to him? Why did she abandon him? Didn't she love him? Did something terrible happen at his birth that caused her to give him up? He wanted to know. No ... he *needed* to know.

His parents knew how Mark felt. His dad had promised he would do everything in his power to get the information. As a prominent Denver lawyer, Steven Wiseman was able to call in some favors, and now Mark sat in a small windowless room in the City and County Building in front of a large oak table on which sat a manila envelope. As he stared at the envelope, the hair on the back of his neck and his arms stood at attention like soldiers in formation. He wished his dad could have been with him, but he understood the impropriety of the favor Dad had called in. His father had to maintain distance, so no questions could be asked.

Mark picked up the envelope and slowly removed the documents it contained. There it was.

Mother: Ellen Gordon

Age: 17

Father: Unknown

My God, Mark thought. *She was a teenager, just like me. The same age I am now. I wonder how she felt when she saw me.* Now that he knew her name, he was certain he had to find her. He *had to* talk to her.

Mark focused on the document in front of him. The birth had taken place in Colorado Springs at Penrose Hospital. His parents had adopted him through the Jewish Family Service in Denver when he was about six weeks old.

Shit, from the looks of this, I was illegitimate. No father listed. Was my birth mother raped? Not enough information. His stomach churned and his hands tensed. *I need to know more.*

He checked his watch. *It's past four. How did it get to be so late?* Carefully, he put the papers back into the envelope and left them on the table as instructed. He got up, pushed the chair back under the table, shut off the light, and exited.

～

HE WENT TO THE parking lot and got into his car. As he drove up Sixth Avenue, he tried to organize his thoughts. *What is the best way to find her?* He knew there were people who could help find biological parents, but he also knew it could be a time-consuming search that might lead nowhere. *Will she even want to be found?* As he pulled into the driveway of his home, he saw his mom waving to him from upstairs. She was in the kitchen when he went in. She handed him a glass of milk and some cookies and said, "Is everything okay?"

"It was pretty scary, Mom, to open an envelope and see a piece of paper with my birth mother's name on it. I'm not sure how I feel yet, but I know I must keep searching for her. I hope we can all talk it over tonight."

Not wanting to probe him any further, she replied, "Um, I really don't know your dad's plans for this evening. We'll see when he comes home. In the meantime, keep me company while I get dinner ready."

Victoria Wiseman was a trim five foot four, with golden brown hair, slightly myopic brown eyes, and an athletic grace to her precise movements. Mark loved to sit with her in the kitchen and watch her as she effortlessly went about her tasks.

Mark heard his dad drive into the garage. Bursting with the need to discuss the day's findings, he began talking as his father walked in the door.

"Are you busy tonight, Dad? I want to talk with you and Mom about today."

Steve stopped to kiss Vicky before he answered, "I'm never too busy for you, Mark. I'd like to hear about what happened today, and I also have some things to discuss with you as well."

As they ate dinner, Mark told his parents about the contents of the envelope. Lastly, he said, "It isn't enough. I need to find her and talk to her."

"I knew that would be the case," Steve replied. "Do you remember Jim Messenger? He's the private investigator I sometimes use. Well, Jim has been involved in finding biological parents for the last couple of years. He's had some successes. I spoke with him today and asked if he thought he could help. He's agreed to give it a go as soon as we get the information to him."

Mark could hardly contain his excitement. "You're the greatest, Dad. I knew I could count on you. And you too, Mom. You're both great."

"Just don't get your hopes too high, Mark," his father cautioned. "Nothing may come of it. It could turn out to be a cold trail. Sometimes you get lucky, and sometimes you don't."

FORTY-ONE

FRUSTRATED, MARK CHEWED ON his pencil. He had so many things to think about as he sat at his desk in his room. *Don't feel like doing my homework. I need to be doing something else.* Like his unknown birth father, Kenny, Mark played football. Now that the season was over, he had an excess of pent-up physical energy.

First, his love life was going nowhere right now. As with most boys his age, he wanted to have sex with his steady, but so far she had refused to go all the way. *Probably for the best. Crap, what if she got pregnant? What would my parents do?* Even though he knew they loved him as their own son, still ... he was adopted after all. Would they want to give up on him? It was foolish, he knew, but in the back of his mind there lurked a small doubt that they might discard him, just as his birth mother had done.

Then there was the pot thing and the group of guys he knew that smoked weed. He and his friends wanted to experiment with it. They talked a lot about it, but again there existed the problem of what would happen if they got caught. Scholarships and acceptance to the right schools could be jeopardized, not to mention what their parents might do.

And most of all, he was antsy because they hadn't heard anything from Jim Messenger in what seemed like forever. He wanted answers. *Shit, life stinks right now.* At the moment, he felt like a cranky teenager. And he wanted action. So far, Jim had searched records from Arizona, New Mexico, and southern Colorado towns. He planned to change his search to the north and include Denver, Boulder, Fort Collins, Greeley, and Wyoming. Mark wanted to find out if Jim had discovered anything since his last report.

Vicky was waiting for Steve when he entered the house. "Mark is fussing," she told him. "He's wanting to talk to you about Jim Messenger. He's anxious for some information."

Steve kissed her. "And hello to you too. Let me change my clothes, get organized, and then I'll talk to Mark."

Vicky gave him a squeeze. "Didn't mean to pounce on you, honey, but Mark's been like a caged animal today. I'll let him know you're home."

She went to Mark's room and knocked. "Mark, your dad is home. As soon as he changes, he'll be ready to talk with you."

"Thanks, Mom, I'll wait for him in the den."

When he went into the den, he flopped down into his favorite chair, fidgeted, and finally switched on the TV.

"Hi, son," Steve said as he entered the room. "Your mom tells me you're really antsy today."

"She's right. It's seems like we've been waiting for a really long time. Shouldn't Jim have found something out by now?"

"As Jim explained, this isn't his full-time job. Stop and think about it. He's already eliminated several places where Ellen could have come from. Be patient. He's a good researcher. If there's information to be found, he'll find it. I'll give him a call, though, and get a progress report."

"Thanks, Dad. I feel like he should be getting close. When do you think you can call him?"

"You don't give up, do you?" he chuckled. "Tomorrow, I promise I'll reach out to him."

~

AS PROMISED, STEVE CALLED Jim the next morning and explained that Mark was itching for an update.

"Steve, glad to hear from you. I was just working on a progress report. I've finished with the northern towns. Couldn't find any trace or clue. I'll try Denver next. I doubt Ellen Gordon came from Denver, but you never know. I'm working on a case in Nebraska for the next couple of weeks, so I'll be checking some of the likely towns there too. I don't have much hope, but it's worth a shot."

Steve blew smoke from his cigarette into the air. "I know you're doing your best. It's just that Mark is getting anxious. What do you suggest I tell him?"

"I know, believe me, I understand his angst," Jim grunted. "Tell him that sooner or later we'll find a clue. Nobody disappears into thin air. We just haven't found the right starting place yet. But I will. It just takes perspiration and persistence, both of which I have in abundance."

Steve chortled. "I'll tell him just that. In the meantime, send your report so he'll have something tangible to see. Thanks again, Jim."

Steve called Vicky and reported the conversation with Jim.

Vicky sighed. "I'll give Mark the message. I hope Jim finds her. It's certainly distracting him. I'll see you when you get home."

She hung up the phone and went back into the kitchen to get dinner ready to put in the oven. That night at dinner Mark expressed his disappointment, but seemed to understand there was nothing more anyone could do at the moment.

Several weeks passed with no news. Mark seemed to have calmed down and resigned himself to being patient.

⁓

ON A SUNNY MONDAY morning, Steve went into the office late. His secretary handed him a message from Jim. *Please call as soon as possible. Have news.*

Excited, Steve put down his briefcase, cleared his desk except for a yellow legal pad and a pencil, and called Jim.

"Jim, Steve Wiseman. Got your message. What do you have for me?"

"I believe I've found out where Ellen Gordon came from. It's amazing, sometimes you don't have to look any further than your own nose."

"What are you telling me?" Steve asked.

"It appears Ellen Gordon came from Denver. Her dad owned Gordon's in downtown Denver in the forties and early fifties. He had a daughter named Ellen who went to East High School. She left during her junior year. I don't know yet what happened to her after that. Mr. Gordon had a serious heart attack, sold his business, and moved out of the state. I'm still working on getting more details, but I knew you'd want to know right away what I found out."

Steve's heart thumped. Suddenly he was filled with mixed emotions. He wanted Mark to find his birth mother, and he'd always promised to help his son in any way he could, but on the other hand, he was filled with trepidation. Would Mark's feelings for his adopted parents change? This could alter all their lives. He took a deep breath.

"That's wonderful news, Jim. I can't believe she actually lived in Denver. Do you think you can come to dinner tonight? I know we'll all want to know the information as soon as possible."

"Give me a couple more days. I'd like to see what else I can learn, then I'll be happy to take you up on a dinner invitation. The good lord knows I don't get many home-cooked dinners. Why don't we say Thursday night?"

"Thursday night it is. I don't think I'll even tell Mark until Wednesday. Otherwise, he'll be camping on your doorstep. Thanks, Jim. We'll look forward to seeing you on Thursday."

As he cut the connection, Steve wondered how to tell Vicky. He realized his hands were shaking as he contemplated how this news would affect all of them. *Damn, life can be so difficult sometimes.*

He dialed home. When Vicky answered, he still wasn't quite sure how to begin. Finally he said, "Hi, hon, how would you like to have some company for dinner Thursday night?"

"What did you have in mind?"

"I just talked to Jim Messenger. He has news about Ellen Gordon. I believe he's found out where she came from, and I thought we should all hear the news together."

Vicky gasped. "Oh. My. God. Oh, my God! Are you sure?"

"Jim seemed certain. He wants a couple more days to check out his information and to see if he can get more details, but he wanted me to know he'd had a breakthrough. So I invited him to dinner."

"What are you going to tell Mark?"

"I think I won't tell him anything until Wednesday."

"Good idea," Vicky commented. "But will we be able to contain ourselves and not spill the beans for three days? I'm so hyper right now that if he walked in the door I'd probably shout it out loud."

"I know. We'll just have to try and be ourselves. This is

important for all of us. How we handle it will make a difference in how Mark handles it."

Vicky took a deep breath. "You're right, of course. I just want you to know that now that the time has come, I'm scared to death. For myself, for you, and mostly for Mark. As much as he wants to know, I'm not sure he's ready."

Steve felt his chest heave again. He whispered, "I know. I'm scared too. But it's important to Mark, so whatever happens, we'll accept it."

Vicky's voice cracked. "Yes, I know you're right."

Reluctantly, Steve added, "I've got to get to work now. Try to compose yourself so Mark won't suspect anything. Just remember, I love you very much."

"Okay." He could hear her sobbing as she hung up.

~

THE NEXT THREE DAYS seemed like living in hell. If Mark noticed anything, he chose not to say anything.

After dinner on Wednesday, Steve casually said to Mark, "I spoke with Jim. He has some news for us. He's coming to dinner tomorrow night."

Mark paled. "Does this mean he's found Ellen Gordon?"

"I don't think he's actually found her, but he's found out who she is and where she came from. We'll just have to wait until tomorrow to find out."

As expected, Mark became nervous. He couldn't sit still. He peppered his dad with the same questions over and over. Steve tried to calm him down and urged him to be patient for one more day.

The night seemed endless. They were all sleepless, each in their own thoughts about the information they were about to receive.

"MY, AREN'T WE ALL cheery this morning," Vicky chirped. "Guess none of us got much sleep, huh?"

Tight-lipped, Mark answered, "You're right, Mom. I tossed and turned all night. I'm scared. I want to know, but I don't want to know."

She squeezed Mark. "I understand. It'll be okay, it's just that you've wondered for so long."

Steve joined them. "It's a big day for all of us, son. It's the waiting that's tough. Once we get the information, we'll all feel better."

"I've got a big day ahead of me," Vicky added. "I want to make a marvelous dinner for Jim. He deserves it."

MARK WATCHED AT THE window for Jim. As soon as he drove up, Mark shouted, "He's here." He ran to open the door.

Steve went to the door and greeted Jim. "Good to see you,"

"Steve, Mark, it's nice to see both of you again." Jim sniffed. "Mmm, something smells delicious. I've spent most of the last few weeks out of town, and I'm sick of restaurant food."

Mark interjected, "I'm anxious to hear what you have to tell us."

Steve tousled Mark's hair. "Go wash your hands, and we'll see you in the living room."

Vicky had a tray of hors d'oeuvres already set out.

"What can I get you to drink?" Steve inquired.

"Scotch and soda, please," Jim said.

Steve poured a scotch and soda for Jim and for himself. He made a screwdriver for Vicky and poured a Coke for Mark.

Mark came into the living room and sat down next to his

dad. After they all piled their plates with hors d'oeuvres, Steve turned to Jim. "Are you ready to tell us what you know, or would you prefer to tell us after dinner?"

"I can see by the expression on Mark's face that if I don't start talking now, he's either going to burst or murder me!"

Steve, Vicky, and Mark nodded. Jim proceeded to tell them about Gordon's and Nate Gordon. He filled them in on what he'd learned about the family.

"They lived not far from here actually, just off of 17th Avenue and Monaco. They belonged to Temple Emanuel. Nate and Pearl Gordon had one daughter named Ellen, who went to East High School. She never went back to school after Christmas vacation of her junior year. Nobody ever saw her again. It was rumored she went to Montana for a special program."

Jim paused to take a drink and have an hors d'oeuvre. He proceeded with the story. "After the first of the year, Nate Gordon had a heart attack. When he recovered, he sold his business, and they moved to California."

Steve, Vicky, and Mark sat stunned. To think Mark's mother had lived only minutes from here. If George Washington High School had not been built, Mark would have gone to the same school as Ellen had attended. It seemed unbelievable.

Jim then pulled a book out of his briefcase. "I was able to get a yearbook, and I found some pictures of Ellen. I thought we'd look at those now."

Mark could scarcely speak. Now that the time had come to actually see a picture of his biological mother, he wasn't sure how he felt. A cold chill passed through him. Feeling paralyzed, he just sat and listened as Jim spoke.

They adjourned to the den to sit on the couch. Mark sat in the middle with Steve on one side and Vicky on the other. "There's not a lot of pictures of Ellen but enough so you can get an idea of what she looked like and what she did in high school."

Mark opened the book to the first page Jim had marked. It contained photos of members of her class with a list of their activities. His hands shook as he picked out her picture. The three of them were silent as they gazed at it.

She's so pretty. Mark read the list of her activities: debate, drama club, pep club, and Spring Fling Committee.

Vicky put her hand on Mark's hand. As she looked at the picture, she could see a resemblance to him.

Steve felt a stab in his heart. How sad her parents must have been. Such a beautiful girl. If she were my daughter, I probably would have wanted to kill the boy who did this to her.

No one voiced their thoughts as they viewed the picture. Mark turned to the next marked page. Debate club. Ellen was seated in front in this photo. Another picture featured the club sponsor, and the other picture was of the officers.

Mark wondered if his father was in this picture. It was useless. He had no way of knowing if the boy who fathered him had even gone to school with Ellen.

Vicky's heart leaped when she saw the picture of the club president, Kenny Johnson. It was the eyes and the forehead. It had to be. In that moment, she knew in her heart he was Mark's father. *Oh my God*, she thought, *a Gentile. No wonder they sent Ellen away. Besides the fact that they were both too young, intermarriage between different religious groups just wasn't an option back then.* She kept her thoughts to herself, though. She didn't want Mark to know or even speculate.

The next picture was the drama club. Everyone wore costumes portraying characters they had played in various school productions. As club secretary, Ellen was also in the officers' picture.

The next set of pages was for the pep club. There were so many girls all wearing club uniforms that it was difficult to find

Ellen. Finally, Mark spotted her in the front row, but it was hard to see her clearly. There must have been a hundred girls in the picture.

The last picture was the Spring Fling Committee. Again, Ellen was seated in the front row.

"Jim, can we keep this yearbook?" Mark inquired.

"Yes, I was able to buy it. I knew you'd want it."

"So, Jim, what's next?" Steve asked.

"Generally, the Jews from Denver who relocated to California settled in the larger cities, such as Los Angeles, San Francisco, or San Diego. The most likely place is LA. So I would say, let's continue our search in California, starting in LA."

"Good," Steve said, "I know you'll find her."

During dinner, Mark's thoughts and stomach churned as he digested the information they had just learned. *Shit, this is harder than I thought it would be. It's scary. What if I find her and she doesn't want anything to do with me? How will I feel?* He squirmed as he sat patiently waiting for the evening to end.

Still too stunned to talk much, Mark barely managed to say thanks and goodnight to Jim. Then he excused himself, took the yearbook, and went to his room.

"This has been quite a stressful evening for Mark," Vicky noted.

Steve wrapped his arm around her. "For all of us, actually."

He escorted Jim to the door. "We'll look forward to hearing from you."

"As soon as I have any information, I'll be in touch." He took Vicky's hand. "Thanks again for a fabulous dinner. It helps keep me going when I get discouraged."

Vicky smiled. "You're most welcome. Anytime. I love a good audience." She waved goodbye as he made his exit.

Then she turned to Steve. "I don't know about you, but I'm

exhausted. I'll do the dishes in the morning. Let's just go to bed."

"I agree," Steve yawned. "It's been quite a strain. I just hope Mark can handle the information and take it in stride. Seeing pictures of his birth mother had to be tough. As much as he wants to know, there's got to be a part of him that's afraid to know. It's got to be hell."

Vicky nodded in agreement. Even though she felt certain she knew who Mark's father was, she also knew she must keep silent about it—even to Steve. *Yes, hell is when you know in your heart who the father is and also know you can never tell anyone. It could be hurtful in so many ways. Best to keep it quiet.*

FORTY-TWO

IT WAS FRIDAY AFTERNOON, and the staff was all sitting around in Ellen's office discussing the activities of the week.

Sherry turned to Kathy. "So, Kathy, you okay? We missed you the last few days."

"I'm okay, thanks." Kathy sat there, looking down at the floor as she twisted the tissue in her hand. Finally, she said, "I ... uh ... I, uh ... I want to tell you what happened last week."

She glanced at the group and tore the tissue into little bits. She could see their curiosity.

"I was in San Francisco." Her voice trembled as she went on, "I ... uh ... well, I had an abortion."

Ellen coughed. *Well now that's what you call a showstopper. My God, I had no idea.*

The members of the staff eyed her with open mouths. Kathy viewed their shocked faces. "About three months ago I was out with a friend at a bar. I met a guy, and we hit it off. As the song says, it was just one of those things. Anyway, I had a bit too much to drink, and I ended up going home with him. He wanted to have sex. I said no."

She swallowed, took a deep breath, and said in a strained voice, "He raped me. He hurt me badly. I knew right away I'd made an incomprehensible mistake. He wasn't a nice man. I got myself out of there, went home, took a shower, and scrubbed myself raw. I tried to wash him out of my mind as well as out of my body." She paused to take a drink.

"That is disgusting," Naomi said. "I don't care to hear anything more about it." She stood, turned, and briskly strode away, her heels clicking anger with her every step.

As soon as her footsteps faded into the distance, Sherry commented, "That's just Naomi, don't worry. Go on, for God sakes."

Kathy looked down, her face now red, and said, "Unfortunately, a few weeks later I realized I was pregnant. I was frantic. I broke down after a few days and told my friend about it. I told her I wanted an abortion, but I didn't know what to do, since there's really no way to get one." Tears ran down Kathy's face. The tissue she'd been holding now lay shredded on the floor.

Ellen handed her the box of tissues and said, "It's okay, take your time."

Kathy blew her nose and sniffed. "After she calmed me down, she told me about an underground group of Protestant ministers and rabbis. She promised she would try to get an appointment for me. A few days later she called and told me to meet her at her church after work."

Kathy took another drink of water. "I was shaking when I got there. My friend sat down with me and told me how she had faced the same problem and how her minister had helped her. She said he would understand. 'He is here to help when help is needed. He won't blame you or think you're evil. I promise,' she told me.

"She then took me by the hand and led me into the minister's office. After she introduced us, she quietly left. The minister asked me to tell him the circumstances of the pregnancy. We must have talked for two hours.

"First, he wanted to know why I didn't report it to the police. I explained that I had gone to his place willingly. If it came to light, the system and the public would say I asked for it. He said he agreed and feared for my health and welfare if I was forced to carry this baby.

"He explained that he belonged to a group of clergymen who had concerns for women with, as they put it, problem pregnancies. A group of doctors in the San Francisco area help them. It's relatively safe, as doctors who perform abortions are rarely prosecuted there. Or, if I had the money, he told me I could go to London where abortion is legal."

She paused for a moment. Everyone on the staff hung on her words. "Of course, going to London was not an option." Kathy cleared her throat. "He referred me to a doctor in San Francisco, and I had the abortion last week. I wanted you all to know, in case, God forbid, any of you should find yourself in the same unfortunate position. I can't tell you how relieved I am that I didn't have to have that awful man's baby. Everyone was so compassionate and helpful while I was there. That's it. I just wanted to share it with all of you, my best friends. You don't have to be alone."

The staff just sat there, stunned. None of them had ever heard anything like this before.

"My God, ministers and rabbis. I never heard of such a thing. I don't know what to say. I'm speechless," Sherry said.

"All I can say is how lucky you were to find this group," Rebecca remarked.

"Uh, oh, here it comes," Josie whispered to Sherry. "Becca's women's rights speech."

Sherry suppressed a giggle and said, "Shhhh, just let her get it over with."

Rebecca glared at Sherry. "Yes, Sherry. It makes me happy to know there's a group of men out there who recognize that women have a right to say what happens with their own bodies. It makes me furious that a group of men in our legislature think they can tell a woman they have jurisdiction over what happens to her. I say, when men start having babies, then maybe, maybe, I might let them open their mouths, but until then, let them keep their damn mouths shut! So there."

Ellen sensed the tension break. Familiar ground now. They all talked at once and questioned Kathy about the experience.

Finally, the group broke up. Many of the women in the group congratulated Kathy on her courage—the courage to do it and the courage to talk about it. They would be buzzing for weeks— each one happy to have the knowledge that there was help out there, even if they could never, or would never, avail themselves of it.

As Sherry often said, "It's one thing to say what you'd do when you haven't walked in someone else's shoes. Once you're in them, they may pinch, and you might find yourself changin' your mind."

After everyone left, Ellen thought about what Kathy had said. *My, how things are changing. I certainly admire her courage.* Ellen couldn't help but think how different things might have been if she had had that option. *Could I ever do what Kathy did if I were in her shoes? I don't know.*

Then she thought about what Judaism said about abortion being permissible if the life of the woman is at risk, either physically or mentally. Certainly Kathy's situation fit this description. Ellen could see that Kathy had suffered extreme trauma, but what about the long-term? It seemed to Ellen that over time Kathy would probably recover from the trauma she suffered now, but the harm done to her in the long-term would have been irreparable if she'd been forced to have a baby as a result of an abusive and repugnant one-time event with such a man. *But, then, who am I to judge? What do I know?*

Eager to get home, she cleared her desk and left.

FORTY-THREE

ON A CLEAR, SUNNY Tuesday morning a few weeks later, Ellen observed the sun glitter on the water like a thousand diamonds. It made her eyes hurt to watch for long. The flowers flaunted their colors, and Ellen appreciated having this day off for a state holiday. She wanted to enjoy every second of another beautiful San Diego day as she walked on the beach.

When she arrived back home, she collected the mail and went into her office. Her eyes fell upon the letter. The return address was Mark Wiseman, Denver, Colorado. Her heart did flip-flops in her chest. She didn't know how she knew, but it had to be Danny. He had found her. Even though she had always known this moment might come, she was frightened. With shaking hands, she opened the letter.

Dear Mrs. Friedman,

If you are the Ellen Gordon who had a baby on July 10, 1954, at Penrose Hospital in Colorado Springs, Colorado, then I believe you are my birth mother.

I am the adopted son of Steve and Vicky Wiseman. My name is Mark.

My family is going to be in San Diego next month. My father will be attending a legal conference, and my mother and I will be joining him. I would like to take this opportunity to meet you if that is okay with you. I will understand if you don't answer this letter and do not want to meet me.

You can write to me if you want to meet.

Sincerely,

Mark Wiseman

Numb, Ellen read over the letter several times. Then she reached for the telephone and dialed John's number.

When his secretary answered, she could barely whisper, "Doris, this is Ellen. May I speak to John, please?"

"Hi, Ellen, how are you?" she asked warmly, as she was quite fond of Ellen. Ellen always treated her as a person and not just as some nondescript entity who answered the phone.

"Fine, Doris, thanks." Her lips trembled so she could hardly respond.

"I'll put you through now," Doris said.

"Hi, honey, what's up?" John asked. Ellen never called during business hours unless it was important.

"I got a letter from Danny. He found me, and he wants to meet. I'm scared, John. I don't know what to do."

John paused. Finally he said, "It's okay, honey, we'll find a way to work it out. Tell you what, my afternoon is pretty free. Let me clear off my desk, and we'll have lunch and discuss it. I can be home before one."

Relieved, she answered, "Thanks, I'll be waiting."

She hung up and sat there, unable to move. Her mind, however, filled with myriad thoughts.

What does he look like? Are his parents nice? What do they think about this? How does he feel? Oh, God, what will I tell the children? On and on her mind raced. *I'm not ready for this. Yes, you are. You've known for years this moment would come. You always knew Danny, I mean Mark, would find you. Pull yourself together, girl.*

SHE CONCENTRATED ON DOING some menial tasks to help her get through the rest of the morning. John came home as promised. Knowing Ellen as he did, he recognized the look in her eyes. He took her hand. Ice cold even on this warm day. He cuddled her.

"It's going to be okay, honey, I promise. Can I make you something to eat?"

"I'm not sure I can eat, but a cup of tea would be nice."

They sat in silence in the kitchen. John wanted to give Ellen a few minutes to collect her thoughts, then he broke the silence.

"May I see the letter?"

Without a word, she handed him the letter. It only took him a minute to read it. He gazed at Ellen. "If you think reading this letter was difficult for you, just think how tough it was for him to write it. He's probably been searching for you for a long time. He has no idea who you are or if you even care about him. Yet, he's gone out on a limb and let you know he wants to meet you. He must be a strong and courageous young man. Have you thought about what you want to do?"

"Are you kidding? Of course I want to meet him. I just don't know what I should say to him. And Nat and Pammy, how are we going to tell them? I'm really scared. I have no idea how to handle this."

"First things first. You need to compose a letter to him and let him know you want to meet him, wherever and whenever he wants. I'm guessing everything will hinge on that first meeting. There's no point in getting ahead of yourself."

"You're right. I'll write a letter this afternoon. Tonight we'll discuss how to tell the children and the rest of the family."

"Sounds like a good idea. If you're okay, I'll go back to the office for a bit."

She nodded her assent.

He stood up and leaned over to kiss her. "I'll see you when I get home."

AFTER HE DEPARTED, SHE sought out Maria. She had confided in Maria during the time when she and John were having problems related to her anguish over the possibility of this day coming. She told Maria about the letter and gave it to her to read.

After Maria read it, she looked up at Ellen. "I've prayed many times that this would happen. It's time for you to meet. This has been the missing piece in your life. I pray it will bring happiness for all of you. If not, at least you'll know."

Ellen thanked Maria for her wise words. She went into the study and drafted a letter to Mark. She wrote and erased, then wrote and scribbled over what she'd just written. Finally, she had a letter that satisfied her. She sat back and re-read it.

Dear Mark,

I've always known your letter would come one day. I've looked forward to receiving it, but now that it has come I find I am filled with fear and trepidation.

I am your birth mother, and I very much want to meet you and your parents. I want to express my gratitude to

304 | ROCHELLE PADZENSKY

them for adopting you and keeping you safe.

I have prayed for your safety and happiness all these years, and I anticipate with pleasure actually meeting you.

I will be happy to meet you at your convenience when you are in San Diego. I think it would be best for us to meet privately first. After we meet, I hope we can get together with your parents and my husband. Perhaps we could all go out to dinner and spend the evening together.

Hoping to hear from you soon.

Ellen

She copied the letter onto her stationery and put it in an envelope for John to read.

After the children were in bed, Ellen took out the letter. Wordlessly, she handed it to John. He read it through twice.

"It's a good letter, Ellen. It's warm and promising. I think it'll make him feel comfortable about meeting you. I'm also glad you suggested we meet together with his parents afterwards. I'm sure they're just as anxious and nervous as you are. They're probably wondering if you'll replace them in their son's heart. It's just so difficult for all of us. I hope we can put together a winning relationship."

Ellen couldn't help but chuckle. "You are ever the consummate lawyer, John Friedman. Always negotiating."

"That's true, and I'm proud of every successful negotiation I've ever made. Now, as to the children ... I've thought it over, and I'm against telling them anything right now. Let's wait and see what happens. Besides, they are at an age when it might be harmful for them to know. At nine, Nat might be okay, but at six, I'm not sure Pammy would understand."

Stunned, Ellen said, "I thought you said you were for telling the children. I was the one who was hesitant. What made you change your mind?"

"I'm not saying never, Ellen. I'm just saying not right now. I just don't think it's a good idea right now."

"No, John. I've been thinking about it too, and I think you're wrong. I don't get your reasoning."

"Just hold the phone a minute, Ellen, and let me explain. What if, for example, Mark just wants to tell you to your face that you're an awful person and he never wants to see you again? Would you want the kids to know about him if that's the case?"

Ellen shook her head as John went on. "Or, what if he is nice but just wants to meet you and know who you are and then never wants to see you again? Should the children know about him then?"

"I get your point, John. You're right. So by the same token, we shouldn't tell your parents and the rest of the family yet, either." *This has just become so complicated, I don't know what to think.*

"Actually, I think we do need to tell the family, and the sooner, the better. It's been an elephant in the room for a long time now, and it's time to clear the air. It's all bound to come out sooner or later. This'll give my family time to adjust to the circumstances." John looked to her for agreement.

"I guess so. We should plan to spend the weekend then. I'll call Mom tomorrow and see what I can arrange. I think the children should stay here with Maria."

John thought about it for a moment and agreed. The next morning, Ellen called Bessie to make arrangements. Ellen knew that Bessie found the whole thing strange because of the way she worded her request, but she promised to do as Ellen wanted.

After she hung up, Ellen went into the bedroom, sat down on the bed, and bawled. *How can I tell them? What will they think of me? I don't even have the words to tell them? I know I must do this, but how? Oh, God, help me.*

FORTY-FOUR

NOW, IN THE MIDDLE of the day, John's sister Ruthie sat in her living room. This was unusual because nobody ever just sat in Ruthie's living room. Both the living room and the dining room were reserved for *State Occasions*, such as entertaining important guests and for family dinners during the high holydays, Passover, and other momentous family occasions.

Agnes, Ruthie's cleaning lady, meticulously cleaned these rooms each week. She polished the silver candelabra, the silver ashtrays, and the silver Ronson lighter on the coffee table. She carefully washed the crystal centerpiece and crystal candy dishes. She polished the furniture on a regular basis, and the wood gleamed in the pale daylight. She misted and cleaned the plants weekly. She vacuumed the carpets in a swirl pattern, and unless the rooms were being used, there were never any footprints in the carpet.

As she sat there, Ruthie reviewed the events of the past weekend. *Oy vey. I always thought we were just a normal family. We don't have anyone who's really famous, and we don't have anyone who's notorious. We've never had any religious intermarriage in the family. We may have a few members who are a bit eccentric, but nothing to write home about. We've always been just your average American Jewish family ... until now. And now I find out our Ellen had an illegitimate child. And he's adopted and we're going to meet him. Oy, what is this world coming to?* Ruth put her hands over her eyes. *I must get myself together. Just let me get through this without hurting anyone, most especially Ellen. This must have been such a burden for her all these years. Mom and Dad seem to be taking it pretty well. They're probably shell shocked. I'll call Mom in a little while and make sure they're okay. Oy, oy, I never thought anything like this could happen in this family.*

She sat there until she felt strong enough to move. In time, she got up and went to her bedroom. She didn't even notice she had left footprints in the carpet.

⁓

ELLEN AND JOHN WERE emotionally exhausted. The news shook the family like an earthquake. The family was totally unprepared for such news, but by the end of the weekend, everyone seemed to come to terms with it. As John drove home, Ellen shut her eyes and reviewed in her mind the reactions of the various family members.

She turned to John and asked in a low voice, "How do you think it went?"

"I think once they all got over the initial shock, they were pretty okay with it. Listen, it's going to take some time for them to adjust. But, as you know, the sun, the moon, and the stars set on you, so in the end they'll all accept it because they love you. It'll be okay. Now it's time for you to prepare to meet your son."

At this thought, Ellen's heart leaped into her throat. She was unable to speak, her throat felt so full. After a few minutes she spoke. "Yes, you're right, God help me. John, please help me."

Gently, John massaged her neck. When they got back to San Diego, they were so spent that they didn't even bother to unpack. They went into the house and fell into bed.

FORTY-FIVE

ELLEN SAT IN HER office and fidgeted. Another fantastic San Diego day. Unfortunately, she couldn't appreciate it. Too many things going on. John had seemed strange ever since the letter from Mark arrived. Even though he said he was supportive of Ellen meeting Mark, he appeared unusually edgy. No matter what they talked about, an undercurrent signaled that something was going on, but Ellen couldn't put her finger on just what was bothering him.

And now, today, was the day when she would meet her son. She paced around her office and looked at her watch every minute or two. Time was indeed dragging. She hoped Mark hadn't decided to back out and prayed he wouldn't have an accident on the way to her office. She had one ridiculous thought after another.

The knock on the door startled her. "Come in."

The door opened slowly. As soon as she saw his face, she knew he was indeed her Danny. Those were Kenny's eyes staring at her.

An awkward moment ensued as they stared at each other. Neither of them knew what to do. Then Ellen extended her hand and said, "I'm Ellen."

He took her hand. "I'm Mark."

"Please, Mark, sit down and tell me about yourself and how you found me."

He sat on the couch, and she sat on a chair facing him. Mark stiffened, and his jaw clenched, and suddenly the room felt as though bolts of lightning were clashing all around them, as he asked the question every adopted child wants to ask his birth mother.

"Why did you abandon me? Didn't you want me?"

Ellen felt like she had been stabbed and her blood was now rushing from her body. She didn't expect this to be the first thing he wanted to know, and she wasn't sure how to answer him. She looked into his eyes and moistened her dry lips with her tongue.

"I wanted you more than anything, but I was too young and immature to take care of a baby."

She paused as she considered how to say what she wanted to say next. After a few moments, she continued. "My parents were concerned that having a baby at such a young age would ruin my life. At that time, having an illegitimate child was, well, considered shameful. Since I was still a minor, I had no choice in the matter. I had to do what my parents thought was best for me."

She noticed his face had relaxed somewhat, but he still seemed skeptical.

She went on, "Don't get me wrong. My parents, your grandparents, were wonderful, loving people. I'm sorry you'll never know them. They were both killed in an automobile accident several years ago."

She paused. Silence. Like an expectant mother, he waited. "While I waited for you to be born, I made a quilt for you, made up of squares with animals and other items on them. Each square had one of my favorite things in it. When the nurse brought you to me before I had to surrender you, I swaddled you in the quilt. I named you Daniel, by the way, because I felt like I was throwing you to the lions. You looked at me, and I knew you would be strong."

Ellen's voice faltered. She grabbed a tissue and dabbed at her eyes.

Mark made a choking noise, and his face reddened. "I used to call that my bankie. It's still in my closet somewhere. Of course, it's just a rag now. I especially loved those animals ... the bear, the monkey, the Scottie dog, and the cat. My favorite was the tiger with the green eyes. I knew I'd been wrapped in the quilt, but I didn't know you made it."

Again silence. He waited. Ellen, heartened by his comments about the blanket, felt slightly better now. She reached for an envelope on her desk.

"I have two other children now, your half brother and sister, Nat who is nine and Pammy who is six. I've put some pictures together for you." She handed the envelope to Mark. "Now, please tell me about yourself and your family."

They talked for the next two hours. He told her about school and his friends, about his home and his jobs. He told her he planned to attend the University of Colorado in the fall and hoped to become a lawyer like his dad. He talked about his parents and how they helped find her.

"Mom and Dad are so super. They knew how important it was for me to find you. Dad called in favors from lawyers and judges he knew in order to get the records. It was actually kind of weird. I went down to the courthouse into this empty room. Just an envelope on the table with the documents inside. That's all. Dad hired a private detective, who works in his free time to find birth parents. Also, since he travels for his job, it gave him a chance to check phone books and people in other cities for clues. It took him a long time to find you. He found the East High yearbook and gave it to me, so we could see what you looked like."

Ellen shook her head in surprise. She had forgotten about the annual. It was such a long time ago, and she hadn't even saved hers. Too much pain attached to that yearbook. Mark's face had a question on it. *More questions?* She nodded. He took a deep breath, and with his eyes down, asked, "Could you tell me about my father and who he is?"

Ellen was definitely not ready for this request. It hadn't dawned on her he might be interested in finding out about his father too. She had been so consumed by her own guilt and absorbed by her own needs that she never even thought about Mark's needs. She wondered what she might say that wouldn't destroy Mark.

"When I told my parents I was pregnant, they arranged for me to stay with friends in Colorado Springs until I had you. Your father knew I was pregnant, but I left school and never saw him again. Afterwards, I went to San Diego to live with my parents. He never knew anything about you. I feel I must keep his identity confidential, at least right now. Let's leave it at that. Is there anything else you'd like to know immediately?"

Mark, still with his eyes down, clutched his hands together, as though in prayer, and said in a wavering voice, "I guess I still want some proof that you really did want me, other than what you said."

Ellen sagged as sadness overcame her whole body. "I wish I had something, but I don't. I know how hard this must be for you."

He frowned but didn't comment on her answer. "It's late. I promised Mom I'd pick her up by three thirty. I have to go now. I guess we'll see you at dinner tonight."

The stab of pain Ellen felt when he spoke of his mom

surprised her. She tried to keep her voice light as she responded. "We're eager to meet your parents. John, my husband, may have already met your dad today. He's also at the conference. Anyway, we'll meet you at the restaurant at six thirty."

Mark got up to leave. Another awkward moment.

"Thanks for seeing me."

Ellen didn't know whether to shake his hand or give him a hug. She gave his arm a squeeze and grasped his hands. "I'm so happy we were able to meet."

~

ELLEN SAT AT HER desk for the rest of the afternoon, unable to do any office work. She kept going over her meeting with Mark. One minute she felt happy, thinking it went well. The next minute she felt despondent, thinking he didn't like her, didn't believe her, and didn't ever want to see her again.

As the shadows fell over her desk, she realized it was time to go home and get ready for dinner. She had mixed emotions about that too. Was it really the right decision to meet Mark's parents? *Well, it's a done deal, so I might as well get on with it.*

She had arranged for the children to have dinner with their friends. John was home when she arrived. He met her at the door with a questioning look. "How did it go?"

"One minute I think it went well and the next ... I don't know. What I do know is that he's a wonderful boy. His parents did a fantastic job. He's smart, polite, and well spoken. Just a super kid. I'm happy he has such a good home."

"I think I know what you mean. I met his father today at the conference. Seems like an amiable guy. Eager for Mark to be fulfilled and satisfied. Hey, we'd better get going. Time is running short."

"I need to shower. I'll be ready in a jiffy."

Ellen took a shower, put on her make-up, and combed her hair. Then she slipped into a soft flower print dress in shades of magenta, blue, and green.

John looked her over. "You are beautiful."

"Thank you. Now stop gawking, and let's get going. We don't want to be late."

~

THE WISEMANS STOOD OUTSIDE the restaurant when Ellen and John drove up. After parking their car, they made their way to the entrance, where the Friedmans and Wisemans introduced themselves. John then suggested they go into the restaurant.

It was the same restaurant where Ellen had first confided in John about "Danny." Where their romance began to blossom. Where John had first kissed Ellen. It had become their favorite restaurant on Coronado.

The host led them to a quiet corner where they could talk. John ordered cocktails for the adults and a Coke for Mark. During dinner, Steve and Vicky told stories about Mark. It was really quite pleasant.

Mark gazed at Ellen and John and said, "I looked at the pictures of Nat and Pammy. Now that I know I have a half brother and sister, I'd like to meet them. It's hard to believe and also exciting."

He looked at his parents. They nodded. "I talked it over with Mom and Dad, and I was kinda hoping maybe you could come to Denver during the holiday break, and we could all spend some time together."

Ellen felt simultaneously overwhelmed and overjoyed. *He doesn't hate me. Thank God. Perhaps we can have a relationship.*

Quickly, John responded, "Thanks for the invitation. We'll think it over and see if we can work out our schedules. We'll be sure to let you know."

John couldn't know how angry and upset Ellen was at that moment. She tried to give him a gesture that would let him know this, but he avoided looking at her.

"We'll be glad to hear from you," Vicky said graciously.

The Wisemans had planned for their departure the next day right after the conference, so they said their goodbyes after dinner.

The Wisemans thanked the Friedmans for dinner, and the five of them awkwardly hugged. Both Ellen and Mark had been more relaxed tonight, so the hug Mark gave Ellen seemed genuine.

"We'll keep in touch," Ellen promised.

Ellen waved as they drove away. *A good beginning. The whole day went better than I thought it would, except for John's response to their invitation. What the hell was that about? I need to talk to him.*

NEITHER OF THEM SPOKE on the way home. When they got into the house, John took Ellen's hand, led her into the den, and sat down with her on the couch.

"I don't know what got into me tonight," John said. "As long as Mark was just someone we talked about, I was fine with him. But after his letter arrived, and especially tonight, when I saw him and he became a reality, I guess I got jealous. I was afraid that after meeting him you'd think more about him than about the children and me. But I realize how foolish that is. He has his family, and you have yours." He glanced at Ellen to see if she might be ready to forgive him.

316 | ROCHELLE PADZENSKY

When Ellen didn't respond, he went on.

"I'm so sorry about how I've behaved. Of course we'll tell the children, and of course we'll go to Denver, that is if you'll ever forgive me for my recent behavior, most especially for how I acted tonight."

"I'm glad you finally told me what's been going on with you. I've been concerned and angry and debating about how to discuss it with you. Shit, you've given me a bad few weeks, and you made me especially angry tonight. So thank you for letting me know."

Repentant, John continued, "I know, my behavior was deplorable. How many ways can I say I'm sorry? How about I'll call tomorrow and accept their invitation?"

Wordlessly, Ellen kissed him. That was all the answer he needed.

The next evening they told the children. An older brother? How exciting! They wanted to meet him right now. When they found out they would meet Mark over the holidays, they began to make an assortment of plans. Ellen suggested they each make a booklet, showing things about themselves. She encouraged them to include pictures of themselves as well. Then, she said she would immediately mail the booklets to Mark.

Both John and Ellen were relieved when the children finally went to bed. They had worried about the children's reaction to the news that they had an older brother. Fortunately, it had gone well, beyond their expectations.

FORTY-SIX

KATHLEEN O'CONNOR, ELLEN'S FORMER teacher, mentor, and long-time friend, died the day after Thanksgiving. After Ellen received the call from Kathleen's daughter, she sobbed.

"Oh, John, I'll miss her so. Without her during that awful time, I'd never have made it. She forced me to be strong. And, for all these years, she's been my refuge. When I had to give up Mark, when my parents died, she's always been there for me."

Ellen called and apologized to Greg, Kathleen's husband, for not being able to attend the funeral. "We've already planned a trip to Denver during the holidays, so it's impossible for me to come so close to our trip. But I promise we'll see you then."

"Ellen, don't worry. I understand, and I'll be happy to see all of you and spend time together whenever you can make it."

"I'll let you know when we'll be there," she assured him. Then, she hung up and bawled. John just let her cry, understanding she had to grieve for the loss of her friend.

"Kathleen would have loved meeting Mark. After all the years we spent talking and speculating about him and his fate, it would have made her happy to know it had a happy ending."

John did his best to console her, but he knew only time would help ease the pain of her loss.

In the meantime, John and Ellen made plans for their trip to Denver. Ellen had not been back since she had left all those years earlier at this very same time of year. She wanted to take the children past her childhood home, downtown to the store that had once been Gordon's, by the Temple, and past her old schools. She wanted to tell the children stories of her childhood in Denver.

Steve and Vicky had planned a couple of events for the two families as well, giving them all a chance to get better acquainted with each other and for Mark to meet his siblings.

The Friedmans decided to go to Colorado Springs on their first full day in Colorado, so it wouldn't interfere with Greg's or the Wisemans' plans. Greg, Kathleen's husband, planned to spend the holiday in Kansas with his family and would be leaving the Springs two days after they arrived, so John, Ellen, and the children would leave Denver after breakfast and spend their morning with him.

The children were excited at the prospect of their first airplane trip and also at the opportunity to meet their brother. John looked forward to seeing Denver and learning more about Ellen and her childhood. It would fill in some gaps about Ellen, the girl.

They arrived at dusk to a light snow. Nat and Pammy had never seen snow before, and they were ecstatic. Even though they had seen pictures, they could hardly believe it really existed, and they were anxious to touch it. Steve, Vicky, and Mark were at the gate at the airport as they deplaned, since they planned to drive them to their hotel.

When Nat and Pammy saw Mark, they attacked him with

hugs and kisses and questions. As an only child, Mark was overwhelmed, and as a teenage boy, he was embarrassed by little kids hugging and kissing him. To Nat and Pammy, this was standard procedure. All the cousins in California always behaved that way and talked all at once.

Ellen smiled as she remembered her first initiation by the Friedman clan as they tackled her with hugs and questions. She knew how confused Mark must feel at this assault.

John had made reservations at the Brown Palace Hotel. On the ride there, he invited the Wisemans to dinner.

"I think Ellen is eager to eat in the Ship's Tavern. Is it still as good as she remembers?"

"Absolutely," Steve responded. "We'd love to join you; it'll be a treat for all of us."

They arrived at the hotel. To make things easier for the Friedmans, Steve handed John the car keys and parking ticket for the rental car he had picked up on their behalf earlier and parked in the hotel garage.

"It's a black Buick, license plate 7784," Steve told John. "We'll wait for you in the Ship's Tavern while you get checked in. Don't rush. We'll have a drink while we're waiting."

During dinner, they discussed plans for the week. A day to visit old haunts followed by dinner at Bauer's, another of Ellen's favorite places. Steve had tickets for them to see Liberace and tickets to the Harlem Globetrotters for the kids.

"What memories that brings back," Ellen remarked. "My friend Bev's dad always took us to see the Harlem Globetrotters and the circus and whatever else came to town. We had so much fun."

Dinner lived up to their expectations. The children peppered Mark with questions and answered his questions. By the time dinner was over, they hung adoringly on Mark and didn't want to leave. "Do we have to go, Mom? We want to stay with Mark."

"You'll have plenty of time to see him all week. Now we have to get to bed so we can go early tomorrow morning to the Springs."

"Do you still remember your old neighborhood, Ellen?" Steve asked.

Ellen chuckled. "Some things you never forget. I know exactly where your home is. I don't expect to have any problems finding it."

"All right, then have a good day tomorrow, and we'll see you tomorrow night at our house." They thanked John and Ellen, and said their goodbyes.

On the way to Colorado Springs the following morning, they stopped in Castle Rock for breakfast. As a treat, Ellen let the children have cinnamon rolls.

"Umm, these are just as good as ever," Ellen said approvingly.

They all agreed. As soon as they'd filled their stomachs, it was time to go. It didn't take long before they were on the outskirts of the Springs. As they drove to the O'Connors', the memories flooded back. Even after all these years, Ellen felt a stab of pain. John grabbed her hand and gave it a squeeze.

"Are you okay?" he said softly.

She nodded, then spotted the house. "There's the house. Just park in front."

Greg came out to greet them. "You haven't changed a bit, Ellen, even after all these years."

She gave Greg an affectionate pat and introduced him to John and the children. They went into the house. Greg had prepared some coffee and hot chocolate for the kids. After they were settled, Greg turned to Ellen.

"When I was going through Kathleen's files, I found the papers and letters you wrote to her in this folder. I know she'd want you to have them." He handed the folder to her.

Ellen thumbed through the papers, letters, and cards. "Here are the papers I wrote about my dad and mom. Hey kids, you'll enjoy reading these. It'll give you some idea of what your Grandpa Nate and Grandma Pearl were like. I'm so sad you never got to know them."

Then she saw the letter she had written to Kathleen when she first arrived in San Diego, five days after she'd given birth to Mark. She knew immediately that she had the exact proof Mark wanted. Silently, she blessed Kathleen for keeping all her letters and cards.

"Greg, I can't thank you enough for this. You'll never know how much this means to me, and you'll never know how much Kathleen meant to me. She was a wonderful person, and I'll miss her always."

Greg snuffled as he patted her hand. "I know, I miss her too."

They spent the next couple of hours catching up. Finally, John interrupted. "It's time to have some lunch. I understand Michelle's is the place to go for a super duper treat. Everybody get your coats and let's go. I'm treating."

"You beat me to it, John. I was just about to suggest lunch myself."

The Friedmans followed Greg to the restaurant. After having lunch and specialty treats, they said their goodbyes to Greg and promised to keep in touch. After hugging Ellen, Greg shook hands with John and handed each of the children an envelope he took out of his coat pocket.

"Happy Holidays, kids. Enjoy!" he told them.

They thanked him and got back into the car. Then they each opened their envelope. "Mom, Dad, it's Chanukah gelt," they shouted excitedly. "Can we go shopping?"

"That was very nice of Greg," John said. He pulled a piece of paper out of his pocket, read it, and drove in the wrong direction.

"John, you're going the wrong way."

"Not really. That is, not if I'm going to stop at Tom and Ginny's."

Ellen's heart just about stopped. "You found Tom and Ginny?"

"I did, and they are anxious to see us. That's why I wanted to leave after we ate."

"John Friedman, you're the best."

The kids wanted to know who Tom and Ginny were.

"Very old friends of Mommy's."

Tom and Ginny had moved and now lived in a different house. When the Friedmans rang the bell, Ginny came to the door.

Ellen's heart dropped. Ginny had gotten old over the years since she'd last seen her. Then Ellen saw Tom in the background. If she hadn't known it was Tom sitting in his wheelchair, she probably wouldn't have recognized him.

"Come in, come in," Ginny greeted them. Ginny and Ellen embraced. Then she shook hands with John. "And this must be Nat and Pammy. Let me look at you two. Well, aren't you just the best children?" She hugged them too.

"Now, you don't have to hog them, Ginny. Ellen, come give old Tom a hug."

Ellen embraced Tom. Both children got hugs as well.

"Come here and sit down, and bring us up to date," Tom said. "I was tickled when John found us and let us know you were going to be in the Springs for the day. What a wonderful surprise."

They had lost touch after Pammy was born, so they had a lot of catching up to do. Ginny brought out her red velvet chocolate cake and some coffee. The smell of the coffee and the aroma of the cake made Ellen shiver, as she remembered the day her parents had brought her to Tom and Ginny's to stay during her

NO OTHER OPTION | 323

pregnancy. Ginny had made her cake that day, too, and Ellen remembered it had tasted like a lump of coal and stuck in her throat. She also remembered the evenings she had spent quilting with Ginny as they all listened to the radio. She shivered again as she recalled how they all felt when the call came that Pop had had a heart attack. *Stop it. That was another time and another place. Forget it, things are different now. You're not that girl now. Let it go.*

As they sipped their coffee and ate Ginny's cake, they reminisced. Then it was time to go. Again promises were made to keep in touch.

The children fell asleep as soon as they got into the car. Ellen told John about the letter she had found in Kathleen's files.

"I'm happy for both of you. I'm sure this will resolve a lot of issues. If it's okay with you, I'd like to read the letter when we get back to the hotel."

"Absolutely, I want you to read it."

They were quiet during the rest of the drive, each lost in their own thoughts. John experienced a sense of pleasure with what he had learned about Ellen today. He was glad she'd had a happy life before the pregnancy. How sad that one mistake had changed the course of her life forever. He hoped meeting Mark would finally heal some of the wounds of the past. He would certainly do his best to help.

Ellen couldn't keep her mind off the letter. *I hope this will prove to Mark that I truly did want to keep him. Perhaps this will help him realize I had to do what I thought was best for him. I hope this will set his mind at ease, so he can get on with his life.*

When they returned to the hotel, they had some time to rest before they got ready for the evening's activities. Nat and Pammy set out to explore the hotel. After they were gone, Ellen took the letter out of the folder and gave it to John to read.

Ellen observed John as he read and noticed it brought a tear to his eye. When he finished, he told her, "I feel certain this will make Mark believe you truly did love him."

~

THEY RELAXED FOR THE next hour, and then Ellen took a shower while John went to find the kids. They finished getting ready and prepared to leave for dinner at the Wisemans'.

When they got to their home, Mark answered the door and the children flung themselves into his arms once again. Now that he knew Nat and Pammy, their attack tickled him. Ellen got a kick out of observing her younger children with her older son.

While they ate appetizers and conversed, Ellen gestured to Mark. Quietly she said to him, "Greg gave Kathleen's file to me today when we visited. I found this letter in it. I think and hope it will answer the questions you have concerning my feelings for you." She took the letter out of her purse and gave it to Mark. "Can we go somewhere private for a few minutes?"

They excused themselves and went into Steve's office. While Mark read the letter written just days after his birth, Ellen tried to sit quietly, but she couldn't help but fidget with her skirt, watching for a change in his expressions as he read.

When he finished, Mark smiled. Ellen's heart rejoiced.

"Thank you," he said, as his eyes became moist. "I think I'm beginning to understand now. I can see from this letter how hard it was for you. Thank you for this."

I believe I have accomplished my mission. She put his hand in hers and said, "I'm glad I could do this for you. I hope it puts your mind at ease to know you were loved. Now you can get on with the rest of your life."

They went back to the dining room, and somehow the

atmosphere had changed. It seemed more relaxed and genuinely friendly now, and everyone had a pleasant evening.

~

THE DAYS FLEW BY. By the end of the week, the Wisemans and the Friedmans knew each other pretty well, and they all relaxed. Ellen knew how tough it must have been for Steve and Vicky, and she was grateful for their gracious ways. Nat and Pammy had become quite attached to Mark and he to them. They decided to write and keep in touch, with hopes of getting the children together again soon.

The Wisemans went to the airport to see John, Ellen, and the kids off. Mark grasped Ellen, kissed her cheek, and said, "Thanks."

The tears that had been building up all week finally escaped from her eyes. A flood. Ellen was embarrassed, but she couldn't help it.

"Mommy, don't cry. It's okay, we'll see Mark again," Pammy said in an attempt to comfort her mother.

John coughed. "C'mon, everyone, it's time to board."

He handed Ellen a tissue and hustled the children and her toward the gate. John tried to get them settled in their seats as Ellen wept.

Once the faucet was turned on, she couldn't seem to make it stop. She blubbered until John became exasperated. He tried to console her, but the tears kept flowing. Finally, after what seemed an eternity, she regained her composure. Everyone expressed relief.

"I feel so stupid," she said. "But I just couldn't help myself."

"I know," John told her gently. "It's definitely been an emotional week," he added, as he massaged her head and her neck. Exhausted, she fell asleep.

LATER THAT EVENING, AFTER they got home and were getting ready for bed, Ellen remarked to John, "I learned something important today. I realized I'm not Mark's mother, and he's not my son. Yes, I'm his biological parent, but Vicky is his mother. She's the one who fed and nurtured him. She's the one who stayed up nights with him when he was sick. She's the one who witnessed his firsts: his first smile, the first time he rolled over, crawled, took his first step. She's the one who took him to his first day at school. She's the one who brought him up to be the young man he is today. Not me. I've had that pleasure with our children. It's time for me to let go of the thought that he's my son."

John gazed into her eyes. "I'm so proud of you, Ellen. And to everything you just said, I say, amen."

THE TIME HAD COME to get back into the swing of things. John and Ellen spent New Year's Eve with Abe and Bessie and the rest of the family.

"It's been a good year, John, an excellent year. I think this next year will be even better. Happy New Year, darling. I love you so much," she murmured as she kissed him.

She felt content. Finally, she felt at peace.

"Um, you taste so good. I love you too, my darling. Now let's go home and really celebrate."

"Yes, lets."

FORTY-SEVEN

THE HOLIDAYS WERE OVER, but instead of the usual January doldrums, there existed a high level of excitement in Ellen's office. The Supreme Court would soon be handing down its decision in the Roe v. Wade case.

The staff discussed the possibilities every day at lunch. As was her wont, Rebecca gave her standard speech.

"No man should be telling me what I can or cannot do with my body. It should be my choice, not some yahoo's who can't even get pregnant. If men could get pregnant, this wouldn't even be an issue. Abortion would absolutely be legal. So, as far as I'm concerned, men should have no say at all concerning this question. When they can have babies, I might consider letting them have a word. Until then, men, butt out!"

Many of the girls cheered, as this represented the thoughts of most of the women in the office.

"I fully support choice," Toni said. "To me that means the choice to have an abortion or not to have an abortion. I don't think someone else, especially the government, should be making that choice for me." She stared at the other women. "I believe I would choose not to have an abortion. But I haven't been faced with that choice. There are too many *what ifs* that could influence me. I want to be able to do that, if God forbid, I find myself in that situation. I also want all women to have that choice, not just me."

Most of the women applauded.

"Yes," Sherry said. "Freedom of choice for all."

"I'm sorry," said Jill. "Abortion is morally wrong. In my mind, it's murder."

Rebecca interrupted her. "Exactly, Jill. In your mind it's murder. It's not murder in my mind. But you shouldn't be imposing your religion or morality on me. I have my own moral standards. I'm a big girl. I can decide what's right for me. I don't need you to make that determination for me."

"Just hold on a minute," Ellen intervened. "You know, Becca, many women feel the same way as Jill. Aren't they entitled to their opinion too?"

"Damn, Ellen. You're right. I'm sorry, Jill. I shouldn't have pounced on you. I apologize." She got out of her chair and gave Jill a conciliatory pat on the arm.

"It's also a question of control, isn't it?" suggested Carol to the group in the room. "Aren't there a lot of men out there who still want to control women? And certainly, this is one area they want to control."

Barbara chimed in. "I also think that for many who are against legalized abortion, the issue hasn't been personal. I think if they were in the position of having an unwanted pregnancy, the gears would shift pretty quickly."

Ellen spoke. "I think we all know abortions are going to continue to take place regardless of whether they're legal or not. What I want is to keep women safe from back alley abortions that could kill them or prevent them from ever having another pregnancy. I want rape and incest victims to be able to have an abortion without the additional stigma of it not being legal. I want women to have a safe environment and qualified personnel to help them. And if it's determined a child has little chance of survival, its mother should be able to make the decision that works best for her. In my mind, *that* would be a moral decision."

And so it went, on and on, day in and day out. Even now, after eighteen years, Ellen wasn't sure what her choice would have been, if *choice* had been an option.

I know I was too young to have a baby. I was just a child myself, and no child should be expected to go through childbirth. It's too traumatic for a young girl.

I look back and see how many lives were affected by my actions. How it changed my parents' lives. I can see now that without Myra and my beloved John, I might have remained in that depression and never recovered.

And, my son. I see how it colored his life all these years. Wondering who his mother was, why she had abandoned him. I hope now that we've met, he'll be able to move on. And his parents. I can see how they've bled over the years, trying to help him find his mother, even if it meant destroying their relationship with him.

I know once they found out, it affected John's family too. And our children. I'm sure it's had some effect on them that I'm not even aware of at this point. Especially now that they know they have a half-brother. They're still young. The full impact hasn't hit them yet, but as they grow older, I'm sure they'll have their own doubts and questions.

For me, if it had been an available option, abortion probably would have been my choice. Especially before I felt any life. It may have been a black moment in my life, but certainly not the hell it's been all these years. I'm a different person now, thank God. I know I'm a good person whose life has value. I know now that one mistake does not make a person bad or evil or immoral. I think John would say I've finally grown up.

~

THE DAY ARRIVED, JANUARY 22, 1973. The office buzzed with excitement as the women waited for news of the decision. The atmosphere was electric. The announcement came. The Supreme Court had voted to legalize abortion.

The women screamed. They laughed and they cried. They hugged one another and danced around the room. Ellen also cheered. Not just for the freedom of choice, but because she had finally found freedom from guilt.

"We're free, we're free, choice at last," shouted Rebecca.

"Yes, choice at last!" shouted the women, who were both relieved and elated about this long-awaited decision.

~

LITTLE DID THEY KNOW that although they'd won the battle, the war had only just begun.

Glossary of Yiddish Words

Balaboosta – a terrific housekeeper
Bashert – fate
Chupah – marriage canopy
Dreck – cheap, worthless, trash
Haimish – down to earth, a real person
Kibbitz – to have a friendly conversation
Kvell – glow with pleasure, usually over grandchildren
Mensch – honorable, decent person
Nafka – prostitute
Nosh – snack
Nu – So, what's new, many other meanings
Oy/Oy vey – Oh, my God, woe, don't tell me.
Plotz – bust, burst, frustrated to an extreme
Punim/Ponem – face
Shegetz – Gentile boy
Shlep – drag, move or perform slowly
Shlepper – a gopher, low man on the totem pole
Shmattas – rags, cheap, junk
Shmeltz – glow with pleasure, usually over grandchildren
Shmoozer – friendly aimless talker

Author's Note

Since *Roe v. Wade*, much has happened. Several acts of Congress have sought to make abortions more difficult or to completely abolish abortions, including the Helms Amendment (1973), the Hyde Amendment (1976), and Ronald Reagan's Global Gag Rule (1984).

Planned Parenthood continues to fight for women's rights in court and in the public forum, and they also continue to expand their programs to support women's health in a variety of ways. Planned Parenthood is the largest national provider of sex education. They also provide cancer screenings and other health programs for women.

The rate of death from abortion has substantially decreased since *Roe v. Wade*, an important factor to consider when we look back at what happened to women as a result of being forced to seek illegal, back-alley abortions. The threat that women will once again be forced to make such choices is difficult to fathom.

Although Planned Parenthood and NARAL Pro-Choice America have repeatedly won in court, in one Supreme Court decision the ruling provided that states have the right to ban, restrict, or apply restrictive requirements. This has opened the door for states to pass laws that ban or severely restrict abortions, even criminalizing it.

In 2007, the U.S. Supreme Court placed further restrictions

on a woman's ability to make personal medical decisions about her pregnancy. Despite having struck down a similar law just seven years earlier, on April 18, 2017, in *Gonzales v. Carhart* and *Gonzales v. Planned Parenthood Federal of American, Inc.,* the court, in a 5-4 decision, upheld the first federal legislation to criminalize abortion. This decision makes it a federal crime to take certain steps when performing a second-trimester abortion, and, in effect, overruled a key component of *Roe v. Wade* that it had previously affirmed over and over again—that women's health must be the paramount concern in laws that restrict abortion access.

Going even beyond this ruling, one state has now passed a law that will make it illegal for a woman to seek an abortion under any circumstance, once there is a heartbeat, which occurs even before a woman usually knows she is pregnant. The governor signed it into law as soon as it reached her desk.

It seems, from the times in which we are living, that there is a movement toward state interests to justify abortion restrictions and even convict women who seek abortion under any circumstances, without any thought of punishing the male who impregnated her. Additionally, some religions have their own laws regarding abortion. For those people, their religious rights are also being challenged.

It appears that women no longer have the right to privacy and the right to make their own decisions about their reproductive health. We have once again gone back to the past and are faced with fighting the battle to restore our rights. Planned Parenthood and NARAL are fighting every day to preserve the right of women to make their own decision.

~ Rochelle Padzensky
June 2018

About the Author

Author Rochelle Padzensky worked in several areas of the financial field where she had considerable public contact. She soon realized that everyone had a story and every story had a life-changing moment. Fictionalizing and telling these stories has become her passion.

Rochelle has lived in Denver most of her life. Married with two children and four grandchildren, she is now retired. She enjoys writing and is a member of Rocky Mountain Fiction Writers. She loves to travel, cook and spend time with her friends while enjoying all Colorado has to offer.

Acknowledgments

To my husband, Herb, my number one supporter and cheerleader. To my consultant, Susie, who held my hand from start to finish. To my editor, Donna, who gently urged me on to make my story be the best it could be. To my cover designer, Pam, who let me know when my ideas were not on track.

And to all the other people who made this book possible, from the beginning to the end, my most grateful thanks. I never knew how many people it takes to turn a story into a published book.

www.ingramcontent.com/pod-product-compliance
Lightning Source LLC
Chambersburg PA
CBHW030017180626
46810CB00001B/84